I0539005

The World Outside: Order Out of Chaos

Matthew J. Coleman

Published by Plexus Publications LLC

www.plexuspublications.com

Cover Design: Zachary L. Ward

ISBN: 978-0-9976690-0-8

For my parents,
who always encouraged me
to keep writing.

CONTENTS

ACKNOWLEDGMENTS

It is difficult to limit the list of people I would like to acknowledge. Writing a book is a process, and there were many contributors along the way. From my father giving me a book about writing to my mother being my first fan, it's hard to know where to begin. But I'll make a gallant effort nonetheless. Thanks to Mike N., for allowing me to learn how to tell stories at his expense; Jon B., for being my first muse; Sarah B., for being my first unrelated fan; Emily S., for being a patient editor; and Zach W., for allowing me to see my writing for the first time; and to everyone else I didn't name: Thanks!

Prologue

The world was changed. Only the great cities remained. It was never intended to be what it became: a place to send those you did not wish to see any more. But when the force fields came on, the age of the World Outside began.

The migration started slowly, a trickle at first, but as the wars grew intolerable, the people came with ever-increasing numbers to the cities. They came for refuge; for only there could one truly escape the horrors of the wars.

It started between the nations – petty quarrels over bits of land. Ironically, it was this same land that became the final victim of the wars. The destruction and desolation was vast and complete. Few places where one wished to live remained.

The reasons for the wars, like so many things that turn out to be unwarranted, were forgotten and have faded into vague memories. When the aliens arrived from the blackness of space, cooperation became a necessity. There was little choice, after all.

When they came, no one knew why. When they began to take people, no one knew why. When they began attacking and destroying Earth's cities with impunity, no one knew why. Silence was all that they shared with the residents of Earth. A strong defense was imperative.

Their ships brought fear and terror wherever they went. Monstrous, merciless behemoths. Only after the development of the shields did things began to change. Soon, the great cities were incased in the shields: cocoons for those living within and barriers for those without. Not everyone made it in before they closed permanently.

Following the development of the shield systems came a flurry of technological wonders. Tunnels for automated vehicles were excavated deep within the earth for travel between the great cities. Deep enough to avoid contact with the alien ships, and deep enough to ensure that those residing in the World Outside stayed there.

Food production was an understandable concern. Greenhouses, built at the tops of the cities for maximum sunlight, provided all that was required. It was a delicate-balancing act to feed so many.

The miracles of technology seemed almost endless when the manipulation of the human genome became possible. Diseases thought incurable became extinct. Genetic engineering emerged. Surgeons learned how to cause mutations of almost any kind. Body customizing, as it came to be known, was outlawed. Creatures so mutated were called humants, for human-mutants.

The legal system did not escape the pull of progress. Police monitoring devices were installed on every street corner and in every room of every building in every city. It was simple: if you were caught committing an illegal act, you paid the fine and went free. If you couldn't pay the fine, you were thrown out of the city into the World Outside. If you had enough money to pay the fine, you could commit murder.

One political leader proclaimed, "Nothing could possibly go wrong with our system. Everyone is covered, and the system is impenetrable."

He was wrong.

Chapter 1

"Progress is defined by those
who benefit from it."
Stephen Blake

I have been a reporter for as far back as I care to remember. It's been so long that I've lost track of the number of people I've interviewed and I've interviewed them all: from criminals awaiting ejectment to powerful businessmen to slick politicians. Each had a story to tell, but they were all the same to me; just the subject of my next news report. None of them had ever given me pause. That was, until I received the assignment that was to be my final story.

For two weeks I contemplated my assignment, a time that seemed to drag on for forever. Two weeks to worry and fret. Two weeks to wonder what questions I could possibly ask that might be significant. I had never had such trouble preparing for an interview.

My name is Paithar Ranston and the job that had troubled me so was the interview of Stephen Blake, a man who stood accused of murder – again. He was not the first, or even the second, or third person suspected of murder I had interviewed. That was not what my thoughts dwelt upon. What made him different was that he had just returned from the World Outside; the first person in history to do so. No one comes back from that place, no one. And yet he *had* returned, and now stood accused of the same crime for which he had been expelled from the cities in the first place. It was all very intriguing to an old reporter like me. I could hardly wait for the interview.

It seemed that the authorities were gathering evidence to present at an upcoming trial against Mr. Blake, a trial meant to return him to the World Outside. Only the national press coverage of his celebrated return had even made a trial possible, most people are simply sentenced and sent away. A persistent rumor had made the rounds among the reporters with whom I worked that neither the public nor the press were even supposed to have known about his return. It was a rumor I could never verify since my paper was not a favorite of the politicians. We were one of the last holdouts – unwilling to regurgitate what the government fed the news outlets.

Because the government has a way of getting what it wants, my superiors believed it was a simple matter of time until Mr. Blake was expelled once again. They did not wish to waste any more time than absolutely necessary in getting an interview. It made my wait all that much harder.

Interviewed criminals always seem to say the same things: "I didn't do it." or "I'm innocent, I tell ya." They are always concerned about themselves but Mr. Blake was different, and his story spoke for itself.

When at last the time came for our interview, despite the anxiety and nervousness I felt, I had fallen asleep at my desk. I woke with a start when the alarm on my phone went off. It was 2 a.m. While trying to gather my thoughts and push the sleep from my head, I remembered, with some annoyance, why Mr. Blake had requested such an odd interview time. He tried to avoid the sounds of commotion, preferring a calm, quiet atmosphere. Only later would I be able to fully appreciate this.

In the ensuing minutes awaiting his arrival, I kept myself busy gathering my things and thoughts. I suppose most people would not have considered it wise to interview in the middle of the night a man twice accused of murder. Despite my concerns, I found that my curiosity overrode them. "After all," I had convinced myself, "if anything went wrong, the police cameras were there to protect me."

When he arrived I unlocked the door for him and we quietly proceeded to my office. When we got there, we made our formal introductions and sat down – he on the outside of my desk and me on the inside. Aside from his clothing and a small stack of papers, he had no other belongings with him. Finally feeling at least partially alert, I placed a small recorder on my desk and turned to take a closer look at him.

He was a large man, standing six-foot-one. Physically he was in good condition. He had the body of an athlete, albeit one in a rougher sport like football or boxing. He had a number of scars in visible places. He had mostly dark hair, with a few streaks of gray. He was a handsome man by most standards.

When he arrived, he was wearing a black beret, a long trench coat, and a pair of black leather gloves. His beret was made of the most exquisite black leather and had a silver dragon embroidered on its left front. The dragon straddled a wall holding a man within its arms that it guarded fearlessly. He reluctantly relinquished his beret and coat when I offered to hang them up, but he left his gloves on. I was afraid to ask him why.

His voice was quiet but firm and possessed a quality that I found hard to discern at first. Eventually I would come to recognize it as authority, a character trait that permeated his very being.

It did not take long to realize that Stephen was a hard man to know and earning his trust would be a monumental task. Through most of our interview he considered me with suspicion. I have never doubted that he would give his life for those he considered his friends.

With our introductory pleasantries completed, I nervously fumbled over my words.

"Okay, Mr. Blake, I don't really know what to ask first. I suppose you should just start at the beginning."

Smiling knowingly, he began. The following is not exactly what he said, but I have endeavored to maintain, with as much exactness as possible, his story. I became engrossed almost immediately and remained so throughout the entire time we spoke. It is a story I will never, can never, dare not ever, forget.

As he talked, it was almost as if he was reliving everything that he said, the good times and the bad; and it was virtually impossible not to live it with him. When he spoke, not only did you hear his words, but you felt them as well. I wondered how a man whose life had been so filled with bad times could maintain his sanity.

*   *   *

So, they want to put me back in the World Outside, do they? Well, heh, here's my story.

Ever since that fateful day when I was only twenty-four years old, my life has never been the same. It started out just like any other day, but it certainly ended differently. I had no idea that when I left my house that morning I would never return to it or even see it again. I looked for it after returning from my exile; but it was gone, replaced by one of those high-rise, cookie-cutter apartment buildings that seem to be everywhere anymore. Convenient places for the government to store its citizenry.

I had just finished my breakfast and had enjoyed it very much. It was the first eggs I had had in a long time; it's hard to grow eggs in those hydroponic farms. Just as I was finishing what would become my last meal, I heard a man's yell for help echo up through the walls of my house, followed by a loud thump, then silence.

Of course I immediately ran to see what had happened in my basement and upon my arrival and to my horror, I discovered a dead man lying in the tracks of my track car.

I quickly went to help him, but it was of no use, he was quite dead. As soon as I was close enough to see, I noticed a rather large gash in his head. It was a horrible sight indeed and try as I might, I couldn't keep my last meal down and retched fiercely. I was still sensitive to death then and felt a cold chill run up my spine.

Before I knew it, I could hear approaching police sirens in the distance. Despite the gruesome scene before me, I wanted to know what had happened; how could a dead man end up in my house? I waited with the body for them to arrive.

Upon arrival the police jumped from their car, drew their weapons, and pointed them at me! I quickly found myself in handcuffs being shoved into the back seat of the police vehicle. I made feeble attempts to proclaim my innocence, but I was so stunned that my protests were timid at best and didn't last long.

I watched through the window of the police vehicle as the body was removed from the scene. Once the police had returned to the car, I once again attempted to plead my innocence, but a frighteningly cold stare from one of the officers ended that promptly. Silently we headed off to the police station. When we arrived, I was taken inside and thrown into a holding cell to await my hearing. My wait was not long.

Within the hour the police returned, this time to take me to the court room where I stood before a very tired, or perhaps bored, sentence-giver. Naturally I pleaded innocent once again to the charge of murder. But when they produced the digital recording of me killing the man I had found in my basement I literally fell back into my seat – silent and completely dumbfounded.

In my mental torpor I was sentenced to $1,000,000 or life imprisonment in the World Outside. The sheer magnitude of what was happening only heightened my inability to react appropriately. Only after being informed that a search of my assets had revealed my inability to pay the assessed fine, and after being roughly grabbed by the guards to be returned to my holding cell, was I finally able to snap out of the stupor I was in. Shouting with vigor only then did I passionately claim innocence to the charges against me.

I was appalled and stunned, but nothing in that court room was more disgusting than the judge's enormous yawn as he handed out my sentence; I shall never forget him for it. In the midst of his yawn, he flicked his wrist as if to say, "Take him away."

After being returned to my cell, I found myself completely bewildered how such an atrocity could actually be taking place in our so-called 'perfect' system of justice. I found myself wondering if this had ever happened to anyone else besides me. At that time I didn't even have an inkling of how drastically my life was about to change. I was going to have to learn to live a completely new way, unlike my former existence, in every possible way.

I was used to grocery stores and restaurants – not wondering what or when my next meal would be, if ever. I was used to a comfortable bed in a room with a temperature kept somewhere in the comfortable seventies – not sweating or freezing and sleeping on whatever kept me off the damp ground and away from the rodents, comfortable or not. I was used to meeting people for the first time and not wondering if they would try to kill me for the half-loaf of bread that I had. Many times I spent a sleepless night hoping that my cuts wouldn't become infected or the colds I got wouldn't kill me. I was literally starting my life over from scratch. But I was too lost in my thoughts to ponder the fact that my old life was quickly passing away.

Needless to say, I did not have the sum of money required of me, and so I was sent to a jail in the city for processing and to await my departure into the World Outside.

That jail was a filthy, dirty, dark place. I had never been to a worse place in my life before then; the government was good at hiding these ugly places from society. I felt really sorry for myself during my short stay there, but had I known what was awaiting me, I would have appreciated my time there much more than I did.

The three days I spent there was not pleasant in any sense of the word. The guards mistreated me, the other inmates mistreated me, and it felt like even the walls were laughing at me. I slept fitfully, always waking in a cold sweat. I was living a nightmare; many times I would wake up only to discover that what I had been dreaming about was my reality.

It amazed me then, and has since, the speed with which they processed prisoners out of society. It didn't seem to matter how much of an upstanding citizen you might have been before getting there, you were no longer a part of civilized society with the simple push of a button.

Physical torture accompanied the mental torment and even the small hope of being in decent health when I was sent outside was being beaten from my mind along with the health of my body. The prison guards changed me; they tried to steal my self-identity. By the time we left the prison I could do little else but grovel for mercy. And to think, I was only one of many.

It didn't matter how big any of the prisoners were, the guards beat and kicked them the same as everyone else. I'm sure they never figured that anyone would ever come back from the World Outside to take revenge on them.

For a long time I dreamt up ways that I might exact my revenge. I could think of little that would provide such pleasure as returning from exile to take it with the same lack of mercy that was afforded me. The hope of revenge was all that some of the condemned had left to live for, but revenge cankers the soul.

It took many years to arrive at the realization that revenge serves only itself. Once revenge is achieved, he who sought it is no better than he on whom it was taken. No, at some point I realized that my greatest revenge would be to survive my condemnation to a world that by all accounts was un-survivable. The best revenge I could have ever hoped for was coming back from there.

Since my return I have had the opportunity to see of the faces of some of those who sent me out of this *civilized* world, and many of them had great disdain for me; many were just plain shocked. I am not the broken man I'm sure they thought I would have become."

*　　*　　*

It was all that Stephen could do to say the word 'civilized,' I knew that his attitude about the world I still considered civilized, my home, was vastly different than my own. Initially I stiffened at the indictment that he made against it, but loosened as I continued listening.

*　　*　　*

Above all the tortures inflicted on me by that jail, was the fact that they didn't allow me to contact my only living relative until the third day, not long before my time to leave.

My parents died a long time ago, when I was only eight; they died in a track car accident. That left only me and my little brother Pauly, er, I mean Paul. Paul is two years younger than me, he was only five at the time. If we have any other relatives I don't know them.

After their death, we were separated and sent away to different foster homes, but we made a dedicated effort to stay in touch. We wrote letters almost every week and even managed to call and see each other once in a while. We were as close as we could have been even though we no longer lived in the same city. It seems like our lives have been filled with separations.

When my brother left his foster home, I was already half-way through college. I had decided to major in hydrological engineering. Of course I got a lot of jokes about this as I proceeded through school, but I enjoyed it just the same. With all the water handling and filtering that's necessary to maintain the huge cities, I thought it would be a good career to get into.

My brother decided not to follow in my footsteps but instead got a job with an upwardly mobile electronics company. He had acquired quite an interest in computer science and electronics in general as he had grown. We stayed close then, no longer bound by legal guardians or geographical separation.

By the time I graduated from college and had gotten myself an apartment, my brother had gotten three promotions, been sent to a technical school by his company, and was engaged to be married. I don't know what happened to his engagement because I never had a chance to ask him about it!

*   *   *

Here Stephen became silent for a few minutes, but showed no emotions other than his deep silence. Despite his silence I could tell that the demons of his past still tormented his thoughts.

*   *   *

11

How strange life can be sometimes, huh? Well, finally my last day in the jail arrived after what seemed like an eternity. I was at last given the opportunity to make that one videophone call. Of course, I called Pauly right away, uncertain what I would say.

He could tell immediately that something was wrong when he answered and saw me on the other end looking beaten and disheveled and he asked me, "What's wrong Steve? You look like death-warmed-over."

I could see no reason to beat around the bush and had a time limit so I blurted out, "Pauly, I've been sentenced to the World Outside. Somebody framed me for a murder in my track-car garage, and I don't have the money to pay the fine."

All of the color drained from his face and he looked sick. After a moment he managed to croak out, "Whad'ya mean you're going to be sent into the World Outside, Steve? People who go there never come back." His voice trembled somewhat and he was obviously shaken.

"I know, I know, Pauly. I don't know how it happened. Somehow they have a recording of me committing the crime. But you know me, and you know I couldn't hurt a fly. I've been in the transition jail for three days now, and I'm going to be leaving in about an hour," I continued.

His eyes were tearing up as he realized this would be the last time he was likely to ever see or talk to his brother again. I could see the little timer on the video screen ticking away.

"I've got to go now Pauly, I'm out of time. I love you," I finished. All I could get from Paul's response was, "No, Steve, wait! I love you t..." and then the screen went blank, and he was gone.

I didn't have much time to ponder my last conversation with my brother; instead, I was quickly herded back to my cell where I was given my last meal. It consisted of an undercooked, minuscule steak, a piece of bread that was green and fuzzy from the mold growing on it, and a glass of warm water that had a dark hue to it.

I had not yet had the opportunity to experience the pains of starvation, so I refused to eat the bread. I was sick the rest of the day because of the bad food and the butterflies in my stomach. I would have plenty of chances in the future to be sick from something I ate, but *usually* that was because it was better than starving to death like so many did in the World Outside.

When I finished my crude last meal, I was collected by the guards and taken to a semi-truck, together with the other doomed souls that I had grown to know in my short stay. To inflict one last torture on us, the guards cuffed our hands to the opposite ankle, right to left and vice-versa, just before being literally thrown onto the truck.

We bumped into each other and the side of the trailer as the truck drove. Many of us got some nasty bumps and scrapes on the way, but because of the way we were bound, what could we do to protect ourselves?

After the jostling trek to our destination, the back of the truck was flung open and we were thrown out as if we were nothing more than bags of rubbish. That's probably precisely the way they viewed us. Still bound, we had no way to block or break our falls. I was lucky enough to land on my side, merely knocking the breath out of me. Others among us suffered broken bones while still others were not quite so lucky.

After we had all been thrown from the truck, those of us that could still stand had our hand-to-ankle cuffing released only to have our hands re-cuffed behind our backs. We were forced forward by the guards, trying not to trip over our fallen comrades.

I looked up to see where we were being herded and could see a high-rise building that was located on the edge of town, right where the huge force field was. I had never seen the field so close before and found it to be a most impressive sight.

It glowed red and pulsed slightly. I could hear a powerful low hum coming from it. An even more impressive sight was one I would come to know later: seeing the whole field viewed from the outside. It is a bright beacon in the night. It lights up the sky like the full moon – only red. You can see one from miles away.

Looking up I could see the top of the building some thirty floors up. Since the force field curves inwards as it ascends, the building nearly touched it at its top. Extending perpendicularly from the uppermost floor was a short walkway leading to a room that went right up to and through the force field. Where they met, the field appeared to cut the room in half; half on the city side and half in the World Outside.

Upon entering the front door of the building, we were stuffed liberally into an awaiting elevator. It was hot and hard to breath on the elevator, and the ride seemed to take an extremely long time. We were unable to move about and as the doors finally opened, we literally fell out.

Entering the room at the end of the elevator ride, I could see that one whole side of the room was the force field. Its bright red glare so close was nearly blinding and gave the whole room an ironic rose-colored look. Nothing could have been further from the truth.

We were lined up against the wall opposite the force field while an officer stepped up before us where he addressed us.

"As you all know, you have been sentenced to life imprisonment in the World Outside for whatever assorted crimes you have committed. There are no other alternatives aside from execution here and now by a fatal gunshot. There is no dishonor in this choice. Therefore, all those who wish to participate in this alternate punishment, step forward now."

I laughed in my mind, thinking how strange it was that the officer had chosen to use the word 'honor' in his offer, for there was certainly very little honor in the way we were handled or the situation we were in. Even though I knew that all of the other prisoners desired to escape their fate somehow, none of them stepped immediately forward.

"Okay then. For your information, we are now in perimeter building number six. Here this building joins with the city's force field allowing us to open a small gate to the World Outside. Soon the timed field will fade, and you will begin the second leg of your journey," he finished apathetically.

At that point two of the prisoners slumped to the floor in a faint. One of them looked quite ill, and it was obvious that he needed medical attention. The calloused guards only pointed and laughed and did nothing to help him.

After the officer's speech, there was a short five minute wait, then there was a loud creaking and groaning sound within the building as the force field began to fade.

The noise grew steadily more intense and increased in volume until it had reached the point of deafening, but it stopped abruptly as the field finally faded out of existence within the room.

Soon after, we were led into the area of the room located on the other side of the force field, stepping across the broad metallic strip which allowed the forcefield to flow around the building. On the wall just opposite where the field had been there was a row of holes just large enough for a crouching man to crawl through.

The officer began again, "You have now come to the second and final leg of your journey. Have any of you changed your mind about the execution?"

Feeling the full pressure of the situation at last, two people broke away from our line and stepped forward. Such precision is rarely glimpsed. For the two men stepping forward were bound to a chair, blindfolded, and shot dead all within the space of sixty seconds. And with what we had just seen freshly imprinted into our memories, no one else stepped forward when the officer asked, "Anyone else?"

Gaining no response to his inquiry, he went on, "Okay then. These holes will lead you to the pods that will take you to the outside world, after which you will be on your own. Any last questions? No? Then buckle your seat belts for your own safety, but what's one germ more or less?" he finished while holding his belly and laughing hard.

After that he left and one of his junior officers stepped up and said, "Okay, you, in there; and you, in there." On down the line he went to the very last of us indicating which tunnel was to be ours. Even the prisoners requiring medical attention were loaded into their pods with such indifference for their survival that it made me sick.

I felt sorry for those prisoners because I knew that there was no way they would be able to vacate their pod on their own, and I have often wondered if the guards even bothered to buckle their seat belts. I can't say that I believe they did. They were, in all reality, being loaded into their coffins.

I crawled through the tunnel that I had been assigned and discovered the opening to my pod in the floor. I looked down at what resembled nothing more than a deep bathtub with a rim that went over my head when I sat down in it. The only difference between the two was a couple of buttons, a lightly padded seat, and a glass top.

After climbing down into my pod, I noticed a metal wall that slid down to cover the entrance to my tunnel, which then moved slowly down the tunnel towards me. This I assumed was for those prisoners unwilling to get into their pods on their own. When the wall reached my pod's opening, it began to pivot on its base until it had reached a horizontal position over my pod's entrance. Once the metal wall had reached this point, a clear top slid into place, and I felt a wrenching in my gut as I heard it lock. There would be no turning back now.

Finding and moving a cloth on the floor in my investigation of the pod, a cloth supposedly meant to serve as a blanket, I discovered a small porthole. It was dirty, and I rubbed it in my effort to see through it. Far below me was the base of the city, and between it and my pod was a vast red field.

As I continued investigating my small craft, I found a compartment labeled: FOOD SUPPLY. Naturally it was empty, no doubt through the thoughtfulness of whomever prepared the pods. Also, during my search I found a small speaker on the dash where the two buttons were located.

I waited intently for the next instructions. Instructions from the speaker commenced in a smooth recorded voice. The voice told me to buckle my seat belt for my own safety and that my pod would be departing in two minutes. I buckled my seat belt.

I have never wanted two minutes to last so long as I did then, but it was over altogether too quickly. When the last second ticked away, my pod fell from its perch high in the city while the little engine ignited and blew me towards my destination.

I looked back at the building through the opening on the top of my pod as it quickly faded from my view, and as I looked back for the final time, I glimpsed a prisoner as he fell to his death from his pod's bay. Evidently, he had tried to wedge himself into the space between the metal plate and the top of his pod. But, with insufficient arm length to span the width of the bay, he had simply fallen when the pod fell away.

As I watched him fall, I turned toward the bleak and depressed world for which I was heading. With this as the last memory of the real world, I leaned back in my seat and watched my future approach. Oh, and how wretched it looked.

Chapter 2

Despite my circumstances, I enjoyed the pod ride. The little engine didn't make much noise, and there wasn't much turbulence. Floating through the air, surrounded by the warm glow of the force field, I felt good for the first time in three days.

Before that day I had never had the opportunity to see a sunset with my own eyes. Brilliant color literally filled the sky before me as beams of light poked through a thin layer of clouds. It's amazing some of the things that mankind has given up to live within the safety of the red glow of the force fields; beautiful sunsets is just one of them. I watched as the sun sank below the horizon. I thrived on those last few moments for I knew what lay ahead – at least I thought I knew.

At last my pod began to decelerate and descend towards the bleak, scorched ground below me. I was quickly approaching a city that had crumbled in upon itself from some prior terrible destruction.

Suddenly, I felt sick. The butterflies in my stomach were working overtime. I clenched my hands tightly while gritting my teeth in an attempt to prepare for landing. The realization that I was about to enter the World Outside, and that I would never see my home or the beautiful clean streets of a city again, hit me with the force of a bullet.

Instinctively I knew that if I did not maintain control of my emotions, I would not survive the ordeal ahead. I was petrified and wanted to find a dark, hidden place in which to hide.

Survival in the World Outside requires clear thinking. Emotional reactions often lead to poor choices. Unfortunately, they were about all I had left, and they were threatening to eat me alive.

My stomach contorted from the fear that swept over my entire being when at last the ground came into clear view. The entire surface was covered with debris. So many buildings, cars, and other objects had been destroyed or simply abandoned and left to rot it was impossible for me to tell what any of them were as I flew quickly overhead. I looked around, trying to discern the place that I would land, some clearing where I could do so safely, but there was none. I am certain that pods are shot out randomly to land where they will. Why should anyone in the city be concerned where the pod of a condemned individual lands?

I was low enough and slow enough then that I could tell I would be landing in the city I had reached. I wondered if landing in a city would be better than landing in the middle of nowhere. The only thing I was relatively sure about was that my landing would not be pleasant.

I didn't have much time to think about landing since it happened very suddenly. With a brief flash a small retrorocket on my pod fired, causing my craft to come to a complete stop in mid-air. I was thrown violently forward straining the shoulder harnesses. The pod fell to the ground with a loud thud, I have no idea how far I fell. The light padding didn't provide much cushion and it was a painful landing. Amazingly, besides a few bruises and a bump on my forehead from being thrown forward into the glass, I was fine.

Of course, I could complain about the comfort of the pods and the fact that the harnesses didn't prevent me from hitting the glass. But, like everything else that is associated with transporting convicts to the World Outside, the designers didn't seem overly concerned about disgruntled customers ever being around to make a complaint.

The pod rocked back and forth for a few seconds before falling silent. My heart nearly stopped when, all of a sudden, the glass on top blew away to allow me to vacate. Quickly the outside air rushed in. It is hard to describe the stench that belongs to the World Outside. So much can be told from scents that linger in the air: death, decay, rotting garbage, and smoke. I had never smelled anything but the perfect, filtered, climate-controlled air of the city. It was decidedly unpleasant and I crinkled my nose in disgust.

I laid there for a moment feeling the cool upon my face. The temperature within the city's force field had never been allowed to fall below a comfortable seventy-two degrees Fahrenheit, but the air that began to fill the pod was nearly twenty degrees colder. I shivered. Then, before any course of action was possible, they were upon me.

A group of people dressed in rags, covered in grime, with snarls on their lips grabbed me forcefully, cut my harness and pulled me from the pod. If I thought the smell of the air had been bad, their smell made me gag as they flung me to the ground. I landed with a thud, knocking the breath from me. They demanded all that I had.

The only possessions I had been allowed to keep throughout my processing were the clothes on my back. My assailants stripped me of them as they searched me very thoroughly for any other valuables. I can only imagine what kinds of things that they were looking for, but I did not have to imagine where they might find them. I felt violated and pleaded with them to stop through the tears that filled my eyes. Throughout my time in the World Outside I have never ceased to be amazed at what condemned convicts manage to get past the guards.

When they found nothing more than the clothes on my back they became astonishingly enraged. It is not difficult to describe the beating I received then. I can describe it with a single word: savage. I have no idea how many there were but they surrounded me while they took turns with me. I could overhear those that were awaiting their turn discussing the possibility of selling me to make up for their perceived loss. All I could do was put up my arms in a feeble attempt to defend myself. I have no idea just how long this went on; I lost all track of time.

Meanwhile, back in the *civilized* world, my brother had boarded a track transport and was on his way to Chicago. I can only guess what his thoughts were as he traveled. I've no doubt that he wondered how this could have happened to his brother. I understand that, once he arrived at the police station, they were less then helpful. Of course they were all certain that they had 'gotten their man.'

Undaunted by the resistance that he found and unwilling to give up, my brother's efforts were tenacious. Somehow be managed to get a copy of the recording that allegedly showed me committing murder. I don't know how he got it but I suspect that there are at least a few individuals in the justice system that probably ought to be in the World Outside themselves.

I have seen the recording that convicted me and it does indeed look suspicious. Since I wasn't actually in it, I wonder if it was an imposter in a real recording or if it was completely fabricated. I can only imagine what Paul thought as he watched someone, that looked very much like his brither, bludgeon another human being until they were dead.

Immediately following the grisly killing the recording showed the figure that was supposed to be me leaving the garage only to return a few brief moments later and lean over the body. Unlike the grim determination on the face of the man that left the garage, this figure had a terribly confused look on his as he leaned over and tried to help the unfortunate victim. That is the only part of the recording that matches what actually happened that day: me trying in vain to save him.

Once Pauly had a copy of the recording he took it back to his home in Minneapolis. The police recordings of his house showed him watching it again and again and again, looking for something - anything. I don't know what he was looking for, I doubt even he knew in the beginning. But watching it became something of a ritual in his life as he did it every day. I'm sure as the days dragged into months he must have faced mounting frustration. But, as I said before, his tenacious efforts would eventually pay off. I'm sure every detail of the recording of that killing etched itself into his memory. It must have been the source of more than a few troubled dreams. I just wish it was not the last vision he had of me.

*   *   *

At this point in our interview, Stephen became silent, momentarily overcome by his memories. I can only guess what thoughts tormented him. He stared blankly into space and wrapped his bottom lip under his front teeth. It was apparent that his emotions wanted to emerge but he controlled them and did nothing more. It was approaching 3 a.m. and we broke for a short time and each had a drink. As we sipped our drinks I said nothing, letting Stephen decide when it was time to continue.

*   *   *

Back in my miserable existence, things were going from bad to worse. I was experiencing new pains like I had never before. Grabbing a handful of my hair, my largest attacker began to drag me. I grabbed at his wrist in an attempt to break free but all I could manage was to lessen the pain as he dragged me along. My naked legs left streaks of red behind me as he pulled me over whatever jagged obstacles found their way into our path.

All of my captors enjoyed my writhing and taunted me. I found myself wanting to be dead. How could it be any worse than where I imagined I was headed?

Eventually I could smell and see smoke filling the air. All but a few of my tormentors left at that point. Making an effort to see where we were going I managed to twist my neck enough to make out a few fires burning in old barrels. Then, as suddenly as it had all began, it was over. My captor dropped me without warning and disappeared into the surrounding buildings.

As grateful as I was that he had set me free, I was afraid to move, afraid to draw any further attention to myself. Besides, I thought, where would I go if I did move? Instead, I curled into a ball and breathed as shallow as I could. I really didn't think I would survive another attack. Even if I had wanted to move, I didn't have the strength to get up. I simply laid there hoping to die.

After a few moments, a large man dressed in camouflage emerged from the surrounding haze and approached me. If it had been physically possible I would have curled into an even tighter ball. All I could do was squeeze my eyes closed as tightly as I could as I prepared for the worst. I flinched as he leaned over me but instead of hitting me he quietly picked me off of the ground and placed me over his broad shoulders. He didn't speak a word as he stood. I looked back at my pod as we moved away from the area. It was far off in the distance and I could only make out a corner of it. I kept my eyes squarely upon it until it disappeared from my view. It was the last connection I had with all that I had ever known.

Something told me that I had nothing to fear from this man and I relaxed, closed my eyes, and said nothing. Even if I had been concerned about his intentions, I would not have had the strength to do anything about it.

He followed a winding path through the streets. Even in my poor condition I could tell that he was doubling back on his own tracks. Then he quickly turned and entered a partially standing building.

The large front door had been pushed aside and hung from only one hinge. Inside I noticed large holes in all the walls. No doubt, I thought, from the fighting that this building had been a witness to. Dust and other debris blew about the room from the wind that entered through the open door, windows, and the holes.

We continued through the first room further into the building. I wondered where he was headed when he stopped short and then, looking about, stamped his foot loudly on the floor. Having done so, he backed up and a section of the floor lifted with a slight creak.

A man with a large menacing gun emerged from the hole, pointing his weapon at us and asked, "What be the password?" He had a thick English accent. It was strange to hear his accent and realize that he must be from another part of the world. It was my first experience with another nationality, but I quickly came to know that the World Outside consists of the entire world outside of the cities; a whole world of exiles.

As I considered the man's accent, the one carrying me answered the challenge with, "Eagle's Nest."

After receiving the password, the man in the hole responded by stepping aside and allowing us to enter. The man carrying me then handed me down to the man in the hole. Then he entered himself, closing and locking the door above him as he did.

Beyond the sentry's perch a tunnel descended some twenty feet. It had rusty metal rungs attached to its side.

The man who had rescued me once again took me over his shoulders and descended the rungs until we emerged into the basement of the building. When we reached the bottom he set me down into a comfortable chair and I at last had a chance to get a good look at him.

He was over six feet tall and very muscular. He wore the same camouflage type uniform as members of the military and his sleeves were rolled up straining against his biceps. He had a face that looked like it had been chiseled out of stone with a firm chin and wore a black leather beret on his head.

After setting me on the chair he took his beret off and spoke to the others assembled in the room, instructing them to provide assistance to me.

With his beret off I noticed that he had blonde hair that was cropped on his head in a flat top. He had the beginnings of a mustache and goatee. He looked at me with concern and I could see that he had crystal blue eyes.

Quickly the room sprang to life. Some of the people there had been in the middle of a game, some only half-dressed, but they all rushed to bring me some clothing and food and to attend to my wounds. I must admit, I was seriously confused at this point. Within my first hour I had received two very different welcomes into the World Outside. As grateful as I was, I found myself worried that it would all change suddenly and I would once again find myself fighting for my life.

Looking about the large room cautiously, I could see that it was split into sections by piles of various items: boxes, crates, and even shelves. Later, I would learn that these sections served as a kitchen, sleeping room, and conference room.

My nakedness overcame my suspicion and I dressed in the clothing I was given: camouflage pants, a t-shirt, and a pair of sturdy boots with socks. None of the clothes fit just-right but I was glad to have them just the same. One of the people then came to help me to the table, while another set a half-loaf of bread and glass of water in front of me, pushing an unfinished game out of the way.

It wasn't much of a meal, but the feelings that I found arising within me while I ate were better than any I had had in days. Could it be that I had stumbled upon a group in the World Outside that would not beat me, but actually seemed concerned about my wellbeing? Only then did I dare to wonder if life in the World Outside might not only be survivable, but bearable. As I ate my small meal the man who had saved me pulled out a chair, sat on it backwards, and asked me my name.

After my answer he stood, extended a hand and introduced himself by saying, "My name is Captain Derik James Baxter and I am the leader of this rag-tag bunch that you see here." He motioned to the others as he spoke.

I counted ten souls, including Captain Baxter and the man that guarded the door, as I looked about the room. They were all dressed in various clothing, some in old military uniform pieces, some in brightly colored shirts but nearly all of them had one thing in common: they all had a black beret either on their head or stuck in their belt.

Captain Baxter started to ask me another question but was roughly cut short. Before he could finish his sentence, there was a loud thud as a gigantic axe head came crashing through the ceiling. It pierced directly above the opposite end of the table at which I sat, sending pieces of splintered wood and plaster in all directions. The sound startled and terrified me all at once. I had only just escaped one brutal beating and was not yet ready for another.

The wood-splintering crash was followed soon after by another and another as the axe continued chopping. When the axe head was withdrawn from its final chop there was a sizable hole in the place. An enormous unnatural looking head, one that had to belong to a humant, came through the hole. Surveying our group, it laughed disconcertingly.

I had never seen a real humant before then in person, only in pictures in newspapers and textbooks. I had always been curious about them. What kind of person is willing to subject another to the process of becoming a humant, and why were there people willing to undergo this process? Under any other circumstance, I might have tried to talk to this humant, but all I wanted to do then was run and hide.

This humant's head had leathery wrinkled skin with a light covering of gnarled and tangled fur, all a muddy brown color. It had a large forehead and its mouth was filled with unhumanly sharp teeth that made up its evil, toothy grin. Two large tusk-like teeth extruded from its bottom lip. With a guttural laugh, the humant's head retreated and was replaced by a pair of leathery, furry hands which began to rip at the hole to make it bigger. This was an amazing feat considering the wood that it easily tore through consisted of half-inch plywood laid on top of two by twelve floor joists.

I sat mesmerized in a stupor of terror as pieces of wood flew in all directions. Before that I never believed that someone could actually become petrified by fear. Some of the wood even fluttered down and hit me. I was simply unable to believe that such a creature could actually exist. My mind was clear of all but my terror. So there I sat, jaw agape, fixed to my chair.

While the humant had been chopping and clawing at the hole, the Englishman had emerged from the entrance tunnel and was getting extra ammunition for his weapon. The others were also grabbing weapons and ammunition and were taking cover behind various items scattered about the room in preparation for whatever was coming.

In the ensuing scramble for cover, a large pistol was accidentally placed in front of me on the table. I had never seen, much less used, a gun in my life and looked blankly at it. But it was to be a fortuitous event.

The first shot of our impending battle was fired as a new humant, different than the one that had made the hole, was lowered on a rope through the opening. This humant looked like nothing more than a normal human albino. Still I sat paralyzed as I watched him come closer and closer, not knowing what to do.

The albino humant slid quickly down the rope to come within a few feet of me. Adrenaline at last filled my veins and I began to move away from the table. But before I got more than a couple of feet, someone shot the humant square in the chest.

Immediately the humant let go of the rope and fell landing squarely on the table directly in front of me. My heart raced and I found that I could barely breath through my clenched throat as I took in the gruesome scene before me. I couldn't help but vomit the first fresh food I'd had in days.

Recovering slightly and looking up, I fearfully watched the hole for more humants to emerge. New sounds from the entrance tunnel drew my attention as a cry arose from within the group that we had been ambushed. We were flanked by humants coming through both entrances.

The first humant through the tunnel was, and still is, the biggest creature I have ever had the misfortune of seeing. He, it, was a true monster and I recognized it immediately as the same humant that had made the hole in the ceiling.

This humant was an incredible eight and a half feet tall and four and a half feet wide. He looked like one big muscle. He was so big, in fact, that I am surprised he fit through the tunnel. He smiled as he emerged, showing his inhumanly sharp teeth once again. I could see that he still carried the huge axe that he had chopped the hole in the ceiling with. As he emerged he happened upon Captain Baxter's hiding place behind a crate near the tunnel's opening.

The surprise gave Derik little chance to react and we all got a second chance to see the strength of this humant as he lifted Derik by the neck with one hand and threw him half-way across the room where he landed in the bedroom section. He grimaced in pain as he hit a cot, causing it to skirt across the floor and clang into the wall loudly.

Everyone in our small group watched Derik with grave concern and had it not been for the distraction provided by the monster-with-the-axe, the humant then standing on the table in front of me would not have been able to get there. Finally able to move I retreated quickly from the table. I don't know what caused me to do it, Lord knows I had trouble using it later, but as I left the table I grabbed the pistol that was lying there and dove behind a pile of boxes located nearby.

Without a second to spare, the monster that had attacked Derik growled inhumanly and rushed towards him, lifting his axe high. As it moved away from the entrance tunnel three new humants came into the room. Hefting the axe, the monster stopped in front of Derik. One of the group that had been hiding behind an upturned cot stood, ran towards the creature, jumped into the air, and delivered a flying kick to the side of its head.

The man was small but solidly built. The raw power of the kick was obvious, despite what happened next. As his foot met the creature's head, it flinched only slightly. Even though he had caused no damage it did get the creature's attention and made it very angry.

Growling and with surprising speed the monster lashed out grabbing the karate-man by his throat. As with Derik it threw him into the nearest wall with a thud. He hit the wall upside down and slid quickly to the floor, knocking him unconscious. He fell forward to lay flat on his front.

During the commotion the remainder of our group had managed to shoot and kill all but two of the humants that had entered the room. The two that remained had taken cover and were now returning fire. I will say this, one of the humants that had survived is one of the strangest creatures that I have yet to see.

It had four arms, two on each side. They extended from the mid-point of its chest, and were set in some sort of strange bone socket configuration that allowed it to turn its arms completely over so that the bottom arm would then be on top and vice-versa. This setup gave the humant quite a bit of mobility as it did a series of complex somersaults to land behind a pile of crates. This may not sound like a particularly frightening humant, but it could spin its arms rather quickly and could deliver blows with fists, or worse bladed weapons, in quick succession. It held four sharp swords.

By contrast, the other humant, had gotten his cover quite by accident. The table where I had once been sitting had been accidentally knocked onto its side by the weight of the four-armed creature as it had launched itself from it. Unlike its companion, it looked nearly human, with only a slightly oversized head with one large eye set in the middle of its forehead. This eye was completely black. As he was descending the rope a bullet sheared through the rope and he had fallen behind the table.

After reaching the floor the four-armed humant was making his way towards the unconscious karate-man. Grasping a sword in each of its hands, it spun its arms in a blur of motion. Firing at it seemed to be useless as the bullets actually ricocheted off of the whirling blades.

The blades tore through some crates and a mattress that lay in their path. As I watched, the Englishman launched himself from a set of shelves nearby. Flying over the humant's head he fired a single shot downward, into the top of the humant's skull. Falling forward, blades flew in all directions. One nearly hit me on its way to the opposite wall. Unfortunately, one of them injured the Englishman and he fell to the floor. It was a miracle that no one else was hurt.

Angered by the irritation and distraction that the karate-man had caused, the monster-with-the-axe turned his attention back to Derik and raised his axe high above his head once again. As I watched the axe go up, I put my head down so that I would not have to witness yet another gruesome scene. Looking down, I saw the gun in my hand that I had completely forgotten about.

Immediately, thoughts of Derik helping me and rescuing me from certain death flooded my mind followed quickly with a desire to destroy the beast. How could I watch this thing end the life of my new friend? How could I cower in fear when I had the chance to repay what he had done for me? Looking up I gritted my teeth, aimed the gun, and squeezed the trigger.

The monster made such a large target that even I couldn't miss the first shot I had ever taken. But even though the shot that landed should have killed it, all it did was throw me to the ground. My shot hit him square in the chest, but where a heart should have been and where it should have ceased beating, there was only mutated flesh that festered and twitched after being hit. Although my shot wasn't enough to kill this obscenity, it was sufficient to cause it to stumble backwards a short way and drop its axe.

When I saw that my bullet had not killed the beast, my courage wavered and as I watched the bullet wound close before my very eyes I could feel the blood drain from my face. Looking at me with a snarl on its face, it began to lumber towards me. What I did next was purely reflexive. Had I had to raise the gun or aim again I doubt that I would be here today. Without thought, with blind terror filling every fiber of my being, I squeezed the trigger a second time.

This shot landed in the creature's bicep and turned it sideways. From my position on the floor I fired every bullet in the gun, slowly pushing the beast away from me. Even after I had depleted my ammunition, I continued to pull the trigger until the battle was over.

It didn't take long for the rest of the group to follow

my lead and we were all firing upon the thing in a vain attempt to kill it. Rounds were flying everywhere, all aimed at the monster. It amazed me that it still stood after taking so many shots, but it was no ordinary beast. Slowly, the impact of all the bullets drove it back to a second rope that had been lowered through the hole. This rope, unlike the other, was made of metal and could not be shot in two.

Slowly, it began to ascend the rope! It swung back and forth precariously as we continued firing. Its ascent was slow, but it finally cleared the hole and was gone. Our motley group continued firing for a few seconds after it was gone, as if doing so might somehow finish it off. None of us could believe what we had just seen.

The rest of the battle was short work for the most dangerous part had gotten away. Until my experiences in the World Outside I had always believed that humants were without emotion, however the humant with one eye did have one emotion - fear. It was backing slowly towards the kitchen trying to put as much distance between itself and the battle raging around it as possible. It grew closer to a man that was cornered in the kitchen section who screamed in abject terror. Quickly, one of the other members stood and, with a single shot, ended the battle.

Standing on my weak and wobbly legs, I could see the look of terror in the man's eyes as he continued to scoot away from the dead humant. When at last he reached the cabinets behind him and could go no further, he covered his face with his hands and sobbed. If I had not felt like doing similarly, I might have thought it a strange reaction for a member of this group. But, as I would grow to know him, I came to understand why.

It took a minute or two for us to begin venturing out of our hiding places, and then only after we were confident that the attack was over. The first to move was Derik and he was quickly at the side of the man in the kitchen.

After ascertaining that everyone would be alright the group began shuffling about the room, picking up broken objects, spent shell casings, and humant bodies. Derik stepped towards me with a hand outstretched and said, clasping my hand firmly, "My thanks to you, I owe you my life." Then, turning to the others, asked them all to introduce themselves.

As each member of the group approached I found it difficult to concentrate on what any of them said. I caught a name here and a name there, but my mind was solidly upon the awful scene that had just played out. Never, not even in my nightmares, had I ever imagined that I would be involved in such a thing. And yet there I stood, gun in hand, splattered with blood, being patted on the back for what I had done.

Derik must have seen it in my eyes. "It's always the very hardest when you have to kill for the first time," he explained. "We've all been through it, and killing in defense only numbs the horror a little. Whether you feel the need to be alone or to talk about what you're feeling right now, we will respect your wishes."

Somehow Derik's words began to break through the fog of disbelief that surrounded me and I shook my head slightly as if to remove it. Then, realizing that I owed my life to this group I spoke to them.

Introducing myself I tried as best I could to thank them for what they had done for me. I could not have understood then just how fortunate I had been to have been found by Derik when I was.

Slowly they all approached me one-by-one introducing themselves again. The first one was the man that I had seen attack the humant with his bare hands, or I guess I should say, his feet. His name was Bill Owens, but I came to know him simply as the karate-man.

Following Bill I met Miguel Sanchez, Phillip Lawrence, Max Harrd, Clay Linley and the others. I was also introduced to the only woman of the group, Dr. Gene Taylor. The last person I met was the man that had cowered in the kitchen area during the battle. He approached with great trepidation and only after Derik's encouragement, finally introducing himself as Keith Olson.

Right away I noticed a distinct resemblance between Clay and my brother Paul. If I had been anyone other than Paul's brother I would not have been able to tell them apart. Over time I would come to know each member of the group individually, some better than others, but they would all become my family in the World Outside.

"What is this place?" I asked Derik.

"This is our home, our hide-out, our everything. We haven't always lived here, but we have lived here longer than anyplace else so far. You are in what used to be Bloomington, Illinois. But, when you're in the World Outside, one place pretty much looks like all of the others – destroyed.

"We don't have much but you're welcome to what meager things we do have." Then, giving me a smile, he patted me on my shoulder, "But now it's time for some well-deserved and sorely-needed rest. We have some important things to talk about tomorrow." He then showed me to my new 'bed'.

Our beds consisted of well-used cots. I would miss my comfortable bed many times, but honestly, I was simply too exhausted then to give it any thought. I would have the next morning to ask the many questions that filled my mind.

Chapter 3

"Only by opening a book can you truly know what's inside."
Derik Baxter,
During a NeMEx

Whatever feelings of safety and security I may have thought I had found, it all dissipated the very next morning. Awaking from a restful sleep that I no longer believed was possible, I was surprised to find that a guard had been posted to my cot.

He did not try to restrain me from rising but simply followed me as I went about the morning. To say I was confused by this turn of events was something of an understatement. So when I finally saw Derik, I immediately assailed him with my thoughts.

Derik greeted my inquiries with a smile and simply said, "Come on Stephen, let's go get breakfast."

Despite my insistent questioning, Derik remained distantly quiet throughout our meal. He did break his silence a single time to ask me if I had slept well. When we finished our meal Derik stood up, loudly shoving his chair back from the table. Then, looking directly at me, he spoke, "Well Mr. Blake, now that you've had a good breakfast and a good night's sleep I want you to come with me. There's something I want to show you."

The odd events of the morning did not encourage me to follow him. But I knew all-to-well what the alternatives could be. So, standing myself I simply nodded and followed. We were joined near some lockers by Max Harrd, where we all dressed and gathered some gear. It looked very much like we were leaving the safety of the hide-out and I once again found the sick feelings of anxiety gripping me.

Derik and Max didn't talk much during their preparations but I did overhear mention of something that they referred to as a NeMEx. With rising concern I wondered what they were talking about but by that point I figured it was a waste of time to ask them about it.

Departing the safety of the group's compound, I found myself reliving all of the terrible feelings I'd had just before my pod landed and the terrible events that had occurred just after. Only then did I realize how much relief being with this group had provided me.

In an attempt to assuage my fears, I tried once again to talk to Derik. It did little in this regard as his answers were brief and lacked emotion.

When I asked him what a NeMEx was he simply responded that we were going on a mission of exploration. That answer just about drove me mad with angry confusion. What we could possibly hope to find in the hell that was the World Outside was beyond me. Trying to mask my annoyance I asked him what we were looking for. To this I got a cryptic response.

"We never know until we find it."

Needless to say, this line of questioning left me more confused than when I had begun. I decided it best to stop talking and so I simply followed them. I stayed as close as I comfortably could. Even though the morning had been filled with emotions that conflicted with the ones I had felt just the night before, I was still fairly certain that my safety was best served by the two men I was with.

The silence that seemed to be the rule of the day was torturous but I did find the courage to break it from time to time. When I thanked Derik again for saving me he answered coldly, "Your thanks are not necessary."

Bewildered by the continued reticent treatment, I rather blurted out, "Why did you save me?"

Derik pondered a moment before answering, as if deciding whether a response was warranted, but at last said, "In the World Outside, the group that any particular individual is most likely to end up belonging to depends in large part upon who finds them first. So, in order to give every person possible the opportunity to live a decent life in this wasteland we are forced to call home, we take every person that we find under our wings and hope that they choose to become a part of our world."

Again, I found myself confused. Why, then, were they treating me as they were? Hoping I would soon understand, I followed my question with another by asking how they had found me.

"We don't actually see many pods in any one place. The pod computers are programmed to shoot them off in random directions and the amount of time their engines last varies greatly. Every scheduled pod departure, we send one of our teams to a high point in the city to see if any of them are headed in our direction. Every once in a great while one puts down near us.

"Whenever a pod does head our direction we do our best to be the first ones there. Unfortunately for you, you now know firsthand what happens to those that we are unable to get to right away. Luckily for you, the group that took you shies away from conflicts they are likely to lose. They decided you weren't worth losing their life over."

Pondering the import of this, I was silent myself. What would have become of me had I not had the fortune of landing where and when I did? I was silent then until the evening.

By nightfall, having had no food to eat, I found myself wondering anew about the intentions of my hosts. Finding a suitable spot to make camp, Derik and Max dug into their packs and started to eat their dinner. I had not been offered a pack of supplies and I was not offered any food then. I had not had anything to eat since breakfast and the long trek had made me feel weak. Entirely expecting to be invited to share, I was astonished when, not only was I not included, but each of them turned away from me when I sat nearby in order to finish their food. Once again, I decided to keep my thoughts to myself, choosing to believe that all would make sense soon enough.

The next morning, my hosts again had a bite of breakfast while I was left to quietly watch them eat. The entirety of the next day was the same. We wound through the countryside, every now and again stopping at a building to walk through it, while Derik and Max had both lunch and dinner.

By nightfall of the second day I was beginning to wonder if my hosts were in fact my captors rather than my saviors. What sick purpose they had in taking me back into the World Outside, to slowly starve me was beyond my comprehension.

Feelings of true anger began to rise in my breast magnified by my hunger that threatened to consume me. I did not want to be angry with these people that had saved me. I tried to stave off my feelings by again imploring Derik for some kind of understanding.

"Why are you treating me this way Derik? I don't understand. You gave me hope when I thought hope was dead. I actually felt safe when you took me to your base of operations, a feeling I was all but certain I would never have again. But now you've dragged me out here to this godforsaken place and are treating me like one of those terrible creatures that we met the first night I was with you. How can you do this to me, I saved your life?"

Not surprised by my accusations Derik did not have to think about his response. "You also saved your own life as well Stephen. I could ask you what your true motivation was."

Exasperated, I continued to vent, 'Then, why did you bother to bring me to your secret hide-out and risk exposing yourselves, especially for someone that you apparently don't trust?"

His response was curt, "We don't make it a habit of taking everyone we find straight to our base. You were taken directly there because you were severely injured and I didn't know if you were going to make it. We were all happy to see that your injuries were not life-threatening, and I will ever be grateful for your contributions to the ensuing battle. But I will not speak further about this now!"

I was taken aback by the forcefulness of his response. I moved as far away from them as I felt I could safely go and spent the time until I drifted into exhausted sleep seething with confused rage.

The next morning I was nudged awake by Max lightly kicking at my feet. I was famished and I felt weak. Crawling onto my feet I watched them eat another meal through a blank stare. Wordlessly, we packed our meager things and were on our way.

The third day passed the same as the others and I found myself sitting on a fallen log looking with tired disgust at the two men I traveled with. For two-and-a-half days I had eaten nothing, although I was given water. The entire day had passed without a single word exchanged.

By the time we laid down to sleep I found I was entertaining thoughts I had never before had. Thoughts of taking food from their packs while they slept flittered across my hunger-wracked brain. I had never stolen before, how could I do such a thing? Was this the beginning of the end for my sanity?

I did not wrestle long with these thoughts. I drifted off to a dreamless sleep without moving from my spot. But these thoughts would continue to haunt me for the next two days.

In all of the fears and horrid visions I'd had regarding the World Outside, I had always unconsciously known that starvation was a distinct possibility. Finding food in a place where none is known to be grown or produced is problematic. What I was surprised about was that it looked very much like my starvation would come at the hands of those I had taken as friends. As time passed and the hunger pangs subsided a little, I began to resign myself to this fate. It was better to die with my honor and dignity, then to become what I would never have wanted to become. I only hoped that an explanation would be forthcoming before the end actually came.

On the fourth day out I found that I was quite a bit weaker and I was growing ill. I had a hard time moving when the morning came and it was time to go. I was accustomed to the lack of sympathy that was shown by my two companions by then. But they were patient as I crawled to my feet and they even adjusted their pace to mine.

In an attempt to get my physical state of being off my mind I tried to converse once again with Derik. The cold hard persona that he had presented previously had softened a little. When I asked, 'Who are you, Derik? I assumed I knew before we set off on this little adventure, but I'm not so sure any more. What's your story?' I was surprised to get a response.

"In my past life I was a Captain in the Marine Corps. I fought in the First Earth War. As you know, most of the fighting in that war was against the aliens. But what most people are unaware of was that every country involved in that war took the opportunity to make small, covert attacks against countries with which they had philosophical differences, while blaming it on the aliens. Well, I'm sorry to say, our country was no different.

"My unit was given one of those tasks and I found myself deep inside a foreign country ordered to fight an enemy that I had not known before. I did my best to follow orders, as did my men. But when I received the order to enter a small village and eliminate all of its residents, I refused. I was court-martialed for my refusal and found guilty of insubordination and failure to follow the order of a superior officer. My fate was sealed before I ever received my sentence. Within a matter of a few days I found myself transplanted from one hell to another.

"I found the World Outside wasn't much different than the war I had been fighting. I had already spent the majority of my time fighting outside the safety of any city force field. The one major difference was the people that then surrounded me. The people that I found in the World Outside were terribly unprepared for the change they had been forced to endure. The Corps had done a good job preparing me and my men for the horrors that we would face, but very few of the people that I encountered in the World Outside could handle what was happening to them.

"Not long after being expelled from the cities, I met Dr. Taylor. We both shared the desire to help the people that we found lead as normal a life as possible. So, with my military training and her skills as a healer, we began to gather the group that you met at the base. Our numbers have shifted over time. Some of our members are no longer with us. But we will press on as long as there are people to help and better lives to build."

I had had enough, I exploded then. How could the same man that claimed to want to build better lives be starving me to death? He seemed to me a contradiction in belief systems.

"What nobility of purpose?! What garbage! Those words sound awfully empty to the man that you are slowly starving to death! I don't get you, I'm not even sure that you are the kind of person I should be with anymore. I was ready to thank my lucky stars that you were the one that found me. But I'm not so sure anymore.

"I've thought about leaving, wondered if I would do better with some other group or even be better off by myself. But you've made me too weak to even be able to leave.

"Maybe dying is the best end for those that find themselves in this place. Maybe I'm waiting to die now, I don't know anymore."

The response I received from Derik was both quick and forceful. "There are two kinds of groups in the World Outside: those that choose to live in chaos and live by the principle of might makes right and those who try to maintain a semblance of sanity.

"Members of the first group run the gambit from simple hobos to those that have descended into cannibalism and even includes humants, who you had the dubious honor of meeting on your first night out.

"It takes a lot of work to belong to the second group. All of the conveniences that existed before coming here utterly disappear in the World Outside. So I say again Stephen, it takes *a lot* of work to keep your sanity here. Before you get lost in fond thoughts for those who would do you willful harm, you must ask yourself, what group do you want to belong to?"

I had struck a nerve as the briskness of his response attested. I decided it best to stop talking then and so we continued our journey.

The absence of food tends to clear one's head and turn your thoughts to matters of greatest import and so I was left with my own deep thoughts for company. The farther we went, the more convinced I became that we weren't actually seeking anything, except maybe my demise. I literally passed out when we stopped that night.

I was the first to awaken on the morning of our fifth day out. Opening my eyes through the weak haze that had taken possession of me, I looked over to see the other two lying on the ground not far from me. Both of them looked ill and when I struggled to sit up it seemed like something was wrong.

Forcing myself to my feet I approached them and could see that each had ashen faces. Looking up at me Derik croaked about some illness that I had never heard of before and told me that if I didn't help them they would die.

Notwithstanding the treatment I had received at their hands for the past number of days, I found myself asking what I needed to do. It was not in me to watch a man die if I could do anything to stop it. I was given a detailed description of a plant that supposedly grew in a field some distance away and was asked to retrieve it. Before departing I was offered a small handgun but I declined figuring if I encountered anyone else along the way I doubted I had even the strength to use it.

Leaving the two lying on the ground I made my way to the other side of town and into a large open field. Too tired and weak to care about being in such an exposed position I looked feebly for the requested herb.

After what seemed an eternity of looking I located the small plant and got on my hands and knees to pull it out. It was then that they revealed themselves to me. I can't recall ever having felt such relief.

While kneeling and tugging feebly I heard Derik's voice. It was not the voice of the sick person I had left back at camp. "Congratulations Stephen; you have passed your NeMEx."

My look conveyed my confusion. Lifting me from my knees and carrying me back to the camp, I was offered the first morsel of food I'd had in days. Practically inhaling it I was more than happy to learn that we were heading back for base, but less so to find that my food consumption would, of necessity, have to be rationed in small bits so as not to vomit it all up again.

My companions took turns assisting me as we walked and the long-awaited explanation of my torture was at last offered.

"Allow me to explain what a NeMEx is Stephen. NeMEx stands for New Member Expedition. It is something that we have to do with all those who wish to become part of our group.

"Obviously many of the people that come to the World Outside actually deserve to be here for committing any number of crimes. Unfortunately, we never know what we're getting when we find new people. We have a short period of time in which to discern the true intentions of those that we find. That's why we devised the NeMEx.

"There are two things that always reveal the true character of a man: money and starvation. Since money has no real meaning here all we have to work with is starvation. True criminals are consumed by self-concern and are not willing to help others. Some are worse than others, some are willing to help as long as their own lives are not at stake; some are never willing.

"I had hoped that you were the man you appeared to be. You put your life on the line to help others that you perceived were being unfair to you. I, therefore, extend the invitation to be a permanent member of our group."

After Derik finished I finally understood and happily accepted the offer.

As we traveled back to base I wondered, what became of those who did not pass the test and with some trepidation, asked, "Has anyone ever failed the NeMEx?"

Looking sadly at the ground Derik responded, "Unfortunately, yes. As hard as it is to get the opportunity to find people to actually give the NeMEx to, a surprising number have not made it."

"What becomes of them," I asked.

"If it turns out that they prefer a life of chaos, and

believe it or not, some do, we simply pick up stakes and move and make it as difficult as possible for them to find us again."

I wondered why anyone would care to find this group again if they chose not to unite with them in the first place and inquired about it.

"Well Stephen, we have a lot of things that other groups in the World Outside would like to have, but don't. It takes dedication, organization, and time to do what we have done. Envy is the biggest problem we have with those who go their separate ways."

He then shared some examples of terrible things that had happened to the group, perpetrated by those who had failed the NeMEx. It was obvious that he struggled and suffered with each loss on a personal level. Still, the leader in him struggled to not let it show. Only then did I understand why he had maintained such emotional distance at the beginning of my NeMEx. Why get close to a person who may turn and stab you in the back?

At one point in our return journey I asked Derik some questions. "It must be awfully difficult to trust another person in a place like this."

"Not at all Stephen, quite the contrary. A place like this brings out the best, and the worst, in people. When you have the trust of another here, it is true and genuine. None of the people that have passed the NeMEx have ever betrayed me."

"You must get angry with the people who don't pass. Do you ever suffer from regret that you have wasted your time with some of them?"

"Anger is a rearward facing emotion as is regret. Finding meaning in life in the World Outside is difficult enough when looking to the future. I do not waste my time with emotions that do not move me forward."

"Do you ever get tired of helping other people?"

"Compassion is an interesting thing. Sometimes it is returned, sometimes it is taken, but it is never wasted.

People are a product of their experiences. Hate begets hate, violence begets violence, and compassion, compassion. You would be amazed how many expressions of surprise I have received from those whose lives have been devoid of the littlest bit of compassion before coming to us.

"The NeMEx has the power to reveal a man's heart, but compassion has the power to change it."

I spent the remainder of my time contemplating what that meant.

When at last we reached the base again I was welcomed with open-arms and the congratulations on passing the NeMEx. I was just glad I was still alive.

I was assigned my own cot and locker and was given a couple days to rest and regain my strength. On the morning of the third day back, Derik was there to awaken me. Motioning me to follow him I arose and dressed quickly. He led me into the kitchen area where I could see all of the others in the group standing in two columns on either side of us. They were all standing at attention.

Before I had a chance to say anything Derik turned and spoke, "Stephen Blake, as the newest member of our group, you have already earned the right to wear the Savior's Beret. Any person within our group that saves the life of another while placing himself or herself in mortal danger while doing so, is to be awarded this beret."

He then extended his right hand towards me, which contained a rolled up black leather beret. Accepting the proffered gift, I looked around to see that nearly every member of the group was wearing such a beret and I felt honored to be among people such as them.

Derik helped me place it correctly upon my head. When I turned to the group some of them saluted, some clapped. My emotions threatened to overwhelm me. But it is a beret and tradition that I will carry with me 'til the day I die.

Chapter 4

"One man's trash is another man's treasure."
Unknown

Time passed after returning from my NeMEx and I was given my own responsibilities for the daily upkeep of the base. I had never been a member of a group before, outside of the engineering club I belonged to in college. But this was different. This was a group of honor, a group I was humbled and proud to be a part of.

I wanted to be a useful member of the group and so I set out to learn and do as much as I possibly could. I was a little worried that I was making a nuisance of myself through all my questions. I will never forget one conversation that I had.

I found myself talking to Clay about the creatures that had attacked us on my first night in the World Outside. I had always known that there were humants in the world, but outside of an entry in an encyclopedia, they were nothing more than the stuff of tall-tales and I really didn't know anything about them.

I knew that the word 'humant' was a term that was applied to genetically altered human-beings; human-mutants, if you will, but I had always wondered why anyone would submit to becoming one. Sure, there are always crazy people willing to do just about any foolhardy thing in order to stand out from the crowd. Yet the humants that had attacked us seemed different to me, mostly because of the one that had cowered in fear.

When I asked him why they had attacked us I cringed at his answer.

"Why? Because the humants were out that night looking for new 'volunteers'" he stated matter-of-factly.

"Volunteers?" I asked with evident dismay.

"Yep, volunteers. There's a real live mad scientist, a genetic-engineer, living on the east coast. His name is Reks Kriton. He is the principle designer and creator – the maker for short – of the humants that inhabit this world. He wanted us all to be among his newest 'creations.'"

A feeling of horror at the thought of what he was explaining filled my gut. I don't think I could have been any more grateful than I was at that moment for the efforts of Derik and his team to save me from such an awful fate. It was a conversation which has haunted me for a very long time.

The next few days passed quickly. During that time I grew to know my 'family' better and better while helping out with whatever chores needed to be done. I began to feel comfortable again, a feeling I had not felt in a long time, and I even began to feel like I was actually part of the group. I spent most of my free time talking with Bill, the karate-man, but I was drawn to know more about Clay, since he almost made me feel like I was with my brother again.

One afternoon I found myself sharing a meal with him. During the short periods we had spoken previously, I had never really had the opportunity to share my story with him. I explained that he resembled my brother very much. Knowing this seemed to make him a bit uncomfortable. I pressed him somewhat so that I might get to know him a little better. Eventually he shared the reason he had come to be in the World Outside.

"I'm a computer hacker. I've hacked 'em all. Heck, I even hacked the government's central computer. That's what got me here. It took 'em a while to catch up with me though. While they were looking, I made piles of money helping people create false ID's."

His abrupt manner of sharing his crimes took me by surprise. Most of the people I had met thus far really didn't seem to belong in the World Outside. My curiosity was piqued by his frankness and I had to ask, 'So, does that mean that you can create any kind of false record, including police video recordings?'

"Oh sure," he responded, "piece 'a cake."

Finishing his meal, and without a further word, he got up and left the table unceremoniously. It reminded me of more than a few meals I had shared with my brother after we had grown into adulthood. Not only did he look like Paul and had his mannerisms, but he was interested in computers as well. It was hard not to feel like I had found something of my brother in that little hideout in the middle of the World Outside.

Sometime after I had arrived at my new home, Derik announced that a scouting party would be sent to the city's edge. Sickness gripped my entire being with just the simple mention of the city. I realized that I had nearly forgotten that I had had an existence there in another life. Feeling as I did, I had to ask the reason why.

"Every week or so the city garbage is expelled onto the ground that surrounds it," he explained. "You would simply be amazed at some of the stuff that people throw out in their trash. We go mainly for food, but often find other useful items. Anyway, I have made assignments for this team. It consists of Mr. Owens, Mr. Olson, Mr. Lawrence, and you."

I was too taken aback to respond immediately. Derik, sensing my unease, continued, "Stephen, eventually you will have to face the fact that you are in the World

Outside, and that the old world threw you out. You need to face the city that did this to you and the sooner you face it, the better. Trust me when I say that this also is something that all of us have had to do as well. I'm sending you with one of my best and he will take good care of you."

I knew who he was referring to without asking and it did give me a certain level of comfort. Still, I didn't know how prepared I was to see the city again and the potential feelings it might create.

I had been given a few meager belongings since my arrival and I packed them slowly. I was in no particular hurry to be underway. My nerves had done nothing but make me ill with worry, but I was determined that I would not let my new family down on the first significant request that had been made to me. The next morning Bill woke me and asked if I was ready. I faked my answer and tried to put on a brave face. Our small scouting group was soon on its way.

Since landing in my pod I hadn't given any thought to the actual distance I had traveled from the city during my brief journey. As it turned out, it was many miles and it took us many days to traverse them in reverse. As we moved we were forced to constantly look over our shoulders and all around us.

During our trek, Bill took the opportunity to teach me the basics of strategic movement. He taught me how to move without leaving tracks and traces. He taught me what things to look out for and even taught me how to tell who, or what, had gone before. It was a lot to take in.

I knew he had an oriental sword but I had not had an opportunity to see him use it. He carried it with him, strapped to his back. Its sheath had a slight curve, which matched the blade within.

Keith was quiet during most of the trip, usually covering the rear. I had noticed early on that he was one of the few that did not have a beret. He was an extremely nervous individual. I wondered how someone like him had ended up in the World Outside.

I noticed him shooting me dirty looks as we moved. He did not seem to like me much and I had no idea why. He kept his distance as much as our stealthy movement would allow and never spoke a solitary word to me.

I was very tired by the end of the first day. I had never been a particularly athletic person and found that the kind of moving we were doing was far more strenuous than normal movement would have been. I knew then that I was going to have to work on my physical abilities or I would end up being an anchor to the group, slowing them down wherever we went. We found some covered shelter and built a small fire that we crowded around that night. I decided then would be a good time to ask my teammates why they were in the World Outside by first sharing my story with them. I hoped that no one would get angry. I discovered quickly that asking someone why they were in the World Outside invited a range of reactions.

As I rehearsed the events that had led me to that place, I wondered if any of them even believed me. It seemed like the perfect 'I'm really innocent' story. Keith seemed less than interested in what I had to say. It bothered me since I wanted to be accepted by this group more than anything.

When I finished my story, Bill, with a knowing look on his face, began to share his.

"I understand perhaps better than most, the brutality of the police in the cities. They have no one to answer to and they know that they are never going to see any of the people that they brutalize ever again.

"I lived in a lower-class neighborhood. It was filled with those that society considers undesirable; people that often found themselves thrown out of the city. There were few things sadder than the families that were torn apart with such regularity in my neighborhood.

"If you made the mistake of arguing too loudly with your spouse, or disciplining your child, you might find yourself separated from them permanently. No one that was taken away in a police car ever returned. We were all poor and none of us could afford the fines.

"One morning my wife and I awoke to find a mouse in our bedroom. My wife began screaming and throwing things at the mouse. I happened to be standing very close to it and got hit by one of the things she threw. Eventually, we got rid of the mouse and things quieted down, but that's when we heard the sirens.

"At first, we figured it was for another unfortunate soul somewhere in our neighborhood, but they steadily grew louder until it became apparent they were heading for our house. We quizzed each other quickly, trying to figure out why they would be coming to our house. It wasn't until the police stormed the front door and informed us that my wife was under arrest for spousal abuse that we figured it out."

"We argued with them at first. Trying to explain what had happened; trying to persuade them that it wasn't as it appeared on the cameras. But they would not listen and they moved to take her.

"I snapped. They would not take my wife away. I fought the police with all the skill and ferocity that I could find within me. They were certainly unprepared for my response as I drove them from my home. I actually thought I might win. Right up until they shot me with multiple stun guns. I woke up in a jail cell."

"You already know that the judges couldn't care less about what you have to say in your defense, only what you have in your bank account. I was quickly sentenced to be sent out of the city. The only good that came of my actions was that the police were so enraged by what I had done to them, they forgot about my wife and she was not arrested."

Then, in a quieter voice and looking at the fire, Bill said, "I miss her." We all sat then quietly for the next few minutes contemplating the roads that had led us each into the World Outside.

I only had to look at Keith for him to begin. He spoke as if he were fulfilling an assignment. It was obvious he was not at all comfortable with what he shared and spoke with an edge in his voice which sounded an awful lot like anger.

"Well, I don't have the tear-jerking, fight-the-powers-that-be story that Bill has. I was a cook in the Navy, stationed on a Destroyer during the First Earth War. But I had no desire to fight in that war though. I don't believe in war and the thought of killing someone, anyone, human or alien, makes my skin crawl. I'm not really sure what it was that I did, but I found myself being 'assigned' to the Navy for some minor infraction in school. I was only seventeen and, within a matter of a few months, found myself on that cursed ship.

"I tried to behave and do my duty. I did my job and tried to stay as far out of the way as possible. I never knew what we were supposed to be doing but we found ourselves sailing on Lake Michigan, down by the Chicago area, outside the protection of any city force field. One night while we were there and while most of us were sleeping, our ship was attacked by the aliens. As you know, the aliens outgun us badly and we were decimated. I found myself pressed into duty, helping the medics treat the wounded and dying on the mess hall floor. The horrors I saw that night will be with me forever.

"For hours I watched men who had lost limbs and other parts of their bodies bleed to death, and I had to clean most of it up. Between trips into that hell I would stop off at the head to puke and try to regain my composure before returning. Each trip I imagined myself in their place, hanging onto life, calling out for loved ones and praying for relief. As the hours passed and the cries of the dying men echoed through the ship, I could take it no longer. Deciding that it would be better to die in the sea than in the war, I made my way to the top deck and threw myself over.

"I floated for what seemed like days. Finally, another navy vessel saw me and picked me up. I thought that my ordeal was just about over, but someone on my old ship had seen me jump and reported it. I never returned to the cities after that. The Captain of the vessel that found me was given the authority to carry out judgment and I was forced off the ship somewhere in the Illinois area where I became a permanent resident of the World Outside. I wandered for a short time until I had the fortune to meet Captain Baxter on one of his garbage runs to Chicago.

"At first I was very reluctant to do anything with him since it was immediately obvious that he had been associated with the military. I'm not even sure to this day why he decided to help me, since I did not arrive in a pod like other convicts but he persisted with kind patience. Eventually, I decided that it was in my best interests to follow him.

"I am grateful that he was one of the first to have found me and did not give up on me. I would very likely have been lunch for someone or would be a humant by now if he hadn't. I still don't have much fight in me but I will never let any of my adopted brothers or sisters down."

By this point his tone had calmed and he looked at the ground thoughtfully. Bill reached over then and patted Keith on the shoulder and softly said, "We know you wouldn't Keith, we know," as if to assure him that he was still part of the group.

Before I could ask, Philip interjected. "I don't really know who you are Stephen. I do not share my stories with people I don't know very well. I recognize that you have been given membership in our group and have even earned yourself a beret. But you must understand that my story is very personal and I do not share it lightly. It is an event that changed my life and I prefer not to relive it when I don't have to."

Somewhat taken aback by Philip's comments I paused for a moment and then began to ask about some of the others in the group that weren't with us. I was stopped short by Bill, "Stephen, you must never ask such things about another person without them present and you must never expect them to answer you if they are not inclined to do so. It is considered highly disrespectful.

"Life before the World Outside does not determine who we are now. There are those that have earned their way into exile and have since changed their ways. That is only *one* of the reasons that some will choose not to share. You must assume nothing. Men are made by what they do, not what they say or who they were." His comments had almost a superstitious ring to them, but I respected them nonetheless and asked no further questions.

It had grown late by then and we took turns standing watch while the others slept. I took first shift since I knew that sleeping would be difficult. Like my NeMEx, it was hard to sleep knowing I was not protected by the secrecy of our hide-out. I had never realized just how dark the night was outside. In the city, surrounded by streetlights and the ever present glow of the force field, it was always easy to see, even in the earliest morning hours. Even the weak lights we used in our hide-out kept the darkness at bay. This moonless darkness was deep and disconcerting. My mind imagined many dangers that possibly lurked just beyond my sight. Despite who I was with, when my shift ended, I was still nervous and drifted off into a fitful sleep after a few hours of lying awake with my fears.

The next couple days passed quicker than the first. As we moved I was dismayed to see the tremendous destruction visible in every direction as far as the eye could see. Nothing had been spared. Damaged buildings and other structures stood in various stages of decay. Nearly all of them had fire damage and large holes in their walls and it had been long enough that plants had grown around and in most of them. I spied people inhabiting many of the structures, but we avoided them as we moved.

The First Earth War had taken a grave toll on our society and many homes, cities, and even a number of important landmarks had been lost. Most of the ruins had been looted and plundered of whatever items of value they might have contained long before our arrival.

As we continued moving, I watched the city grow out of the horizon as we got closer and closer. The gigantic red force field was the first thing that we could see. The next two nights were spent bathed in the eerie red glow that emanated from it. The closer we got, the more nervous I became. The city had come to represent all about society that I hated. Eventually, we reached the edge of the city.

We had to wait until the next day for the garbage dump. It quickly became apparent to me that we were not the only ones that had the idea of coming to forage through the trash. There were many people already there and they continued to come throughout the night and into the next morning. Many of them simply tried to live there always.

Some of the people who came were alone, but many traveled in packs. The night before the trash dump we were all forced to stay up and form a circle. Only then could we keep other groups, showing a little too much interest in who we were, away. Thankfully, none of them got any closer than a few yards after seeing the weapons we carried.

I could do nothing but watch in horror as a pack of cannibals descended upon a single man not far from us. They dragged him away, kicking and screaming horribly, into the distance. To make matters worse, once he saw us he extended a hand and begged for our help. Nervously, I asked Bill what we could do and he simply stated, "If you help him now we will all likely perish. As cold as it seems, you must learn to pick your fights. There are places and times when helping others can be done. There are others, however, when doing so will only mean your demise. Dead men provide no succor for others. There are far too many groups here now to defend ourselves in any other way then in the position we now hold."

As sickened as I became by the things that I had just witnessed I was utterly unprepared for what I saw next. Out of the corner of my eye I spied a quick blur. Looking towards the blur I saw a raggedly-dressed, gaunt child of around ten-years of age. He emerged from the nearby shadows, approached a small pile of garbage, grabbed a handful of something from it, and ate it.

Never once had I even considered the possibility that there might be children in the World Outside and yet there he stood before my eyes. My mouth dropped open in disbelief and I nudged Bill, while motioning to him. Bill simply nodded with sad understanding.

"Yeah, I was filled with horror and pity the first time I saw one out here too. But as horrible as it is, it is not that hard to understand. When you send men and women of varying backgrounds into a world that is as horrific as this, you will discover that they find solace and comfort in each other's arms. And since there is no birth control available, children are simply the terrible side-effect of these couplings. We try to look for children that need our help, but unfortunately, they don't last long and the ones that do have become very good at hiding and are really hard to find. They are the unwitting and undeserving victims of the system as it is." Looking back at the spot I had seen the kid, he was nowhere to be found.

We did not speak the rest of the night. I sat there through the remaining long hours feeling nauseous and disgusted about many aspects of my new life, not least of which were the children. I wanted to help everyone and anyone who needed and wanted help. Someday, I thought, maybe I can actually make a difference.

Mid-morning of the next day, the garbage dump began. Bill motioned towards an amber light, fixed to the city wall, which had begun to spin just a few feet from our position. At the same time, a large metal door began to slide open. Behind the door was the familiar red glow of the force field. Behind that I could see a huge mass of garbage filling a gigantic tube. Abruptly the field went off and the garbage moved forward rapidly where it began to spill onto the ground around the opening.

An unpleasant scent filled my nostrils, keenly reminding me that we had been sent to rummage through garbage. Bill and Keith, raising their weapons, forced the other people back. Bill instructed me to cover them while they looked through the pile. I almost felt sorry for those that would have second choice.

It took a few minutes for the garbage to stop coming. After it was all out the large metal wall behind the garbage pushing it receded quickly. A ragged-looking man ran towards the opening as fast as he could go. Briefly turning to look at him, I watched as he passed the opening of the hole just as the force field re-illuminated. He did not get far though as a second force field, some fifteen feet behind the first, also illuminated. Running at full-speed into it he simply disappeared into thin air. Obviously the city planners had anticipated such an action. Shaking my head sadly I looked at Bill and Keith in hopes that they would be done soon.

Finally, with bags bulging with the most salvageable and useful items they could find, we moved away from the pile to let the others through. Behind us a crowd quickly descended and chaos ensued as the various participants fought ferociously over a few scraps of thrown-out food along with whatever other items of value they found. Taking one last look at the vicious fray, I turned and followed Bill from the edge of the city.

As we retreated from the city's edge I heard a familiar grinding sound and looked up to see a perimeter building's pod bay. Sure enough, a new set of pods were being prepared for departure. I watched with macabre fascination as ten pods fired away from their bays. One of the pods seemed to be malfunctioning however since its engine did not fire fully and it was falling faster than it was moving forward.

Immediately, Bill recognized what was happening and began quickly moving in the direction that he estimated the pod would land. As we moved the pod continued to lose altitude quickly and we were nearly upon it when it hit the ground with an ear-splitting crash.

The glass top of the pod flew away as it had in mine. Approaching cautiously we could see the outline of a woman. She did not move but was breathing shallowly. I could see that she had blood matting in her hair and running down her face. I was amazed she had survived the fall.

Quickly Bill cut the restraints from her, pulled her from the seat, placed her over his shoulders and shouted, "Let's move before anyone else gets here."

We left without another look back.

Chapter 5

"Choose wise thy friends,
for unto them doth we give access to our soul."
Ancient Philosophy

We followed a different path on our way back home than the one we had taken to reach the city. I mused over the fact that in my mind our hide-out had become my new home. I never would have imagined that I would end up living in the lower-level of a run-down war-torn building in the middle of the World Outside. And yet, there I was.

The rubble that we passed all looked the same to me. I was amazed that Bill never seemed to be lost. It was obvious he had spent considerable time traversing these ruins and took us the best ways that he knew.

While we traveled the condition of the woman that we had rescued from the malfunctioning pod grew worse. I didn't have to be a doctor to recognize her injuries were grave and we all worried she wouldn't live much longer. While Bill and the others were busy carrying her along with their packs I was given the responsibility of caring for her. My first aid training had been cursory at best, a fact I regretted just then. Regardless, we didn't have time to give her the care she needed.

She was obviously a beautiful woman. Even through the blood that stained her hair and face, I could see it. She had long dark hair and full lips. I found myself spending long periods of time just looking at her. The effect she was having upon me was different than anything I had ever experienced before.

At times she would have difficulty breathing and we would have to stop to perform rescue breathing. Some of her wounds became infected and her future looked grim. She never woke once during the entire return trip.

Bill and the others took great pains to cover our tracks as we moved silently. On the second day of our return we happened upon an empty pod. It was situated atop a large pile of rubble and had been there for quite some time. Rust lines and spots riddled its surface and plants grew around its base where it rested upon the ground.

Rounding the pod we were met by a grisly sight. Hanging half-out of the top was a skeleton. Around the skeleton's midsection was what appeared to be the remains of the glass top of the pod. Jagged shards of glass surrounded the bones. Visibly deep gouges indicated that the unfortunate occupant of this pod had met a violent end. Behind the skeleton we all could see an unfastened shoulder harness.

Bill spoke briefly then, "I never have figured out why people don't fasten their harnesses when instructed to do so. Those that don't are first thrown through the glass plate and then the plate is sent rocketing up their torso as it is blown away from the pod. They are cut to shreds. Most of them are nowhere near the pod when they die."

Covering my mouth with my hand and shaking my head sadly I realized how fortunate I was to have heeded the warnings. I wondered then if there would ever be an end of the new horrors and disgust I seemed to be experiencing on a daily basis. If there is a Hell, it can't be much worse than the World Outside.

Before we left Bill went to look in the pod to see if there was a survival pack, none of us was surprised there wasn't one. Towards the evening of the second day an explosion sounded in the distance. It emanated from the direction of the city. We had just stopped for a quick meal when it happened. I turned just in time to see a medium-sized ship hovering above the city firing bolts of energy into the force field.

In all of my life in Chicago I had never seen an alien attack. I had read stories in the news about attacks on other cities, and had even seen pictures on television. However, all of the pictures that were shown were from the inside of the field. Small spots in the field would become momentarily darker and then return to normal, but aside from this, it was hard to tell that anything unusual was happening at all.

Viewing the attack from the outside was an entirely different experience. Even from this distance it was easy to see. As the bolts struck the field the energy they contained was immediately dispersed in all directions and spread out to cover the majority of the entire field. The one aspect of the attack entirely missing from the inside was the sounds of the explosions and large electrical charges that filled the air. Their sheer power was evident, even from where we stood.

I had never considered that the force field had been a noise barrier to the things that occurred in the World Outside. Honestly, I never gave the field much thought at all, but apparently it stopped more than I might have even imagined. Though I had little respect for what the cities represented, I couldn't help but be impressed by the awesome sight of a defeated attack.

At some point during the attack Bill handed me a pair of binoculars so I could better see it. I watched with great interest and even found myself feeling a bit of pride that mankind had been able to create such a thing against the alien adversary. Eventually the attack on the city ceased. I watched, expecting the ship to depart into space or something.

Instead, it began flying in our general direction. As it flew, beams of light struck the ground. I could not believe what I was seeing and squinted through the binoculars to be certain. Sure enough, as the ship flew low, light beams struck the ground and the fleeing people that were there. When the beams disappeared, so had the people they had struck.

Dumbfounded I looked at Bill. Seeing my look he simply said, "They take people every time they come. No one has ever returned so we can only guess what their purposes are. But we need to get out of sight if we don't want to find out."

We moved into the nearest structure and found a way into the basement. The sounds of the ship's engines grew steadily louder until it passed over us and slowly receded into the distance. We stayed in our hiding place for a few hours until we were satisfied that it had gone. Only then did we emerge and continue towards home.

We moved for a few more hours that day before breaking for camp. As usual, I was the first one on guard duty. It was quiet. I expected that it would stay that way.

About three o'clock in the morning I awoke with a start to the crack of a bullet. Quickly I rolled over just in time to look up at Bill who had his gun to his shoulder and was firing off into the distance. I looked to see what he was shooting at and was met by the sight of a mob of people. Everywhere I looked I saw them, there had to have been a hundred or so.

Hastily I grabbed my gun and turned to see a number of them within just feet of me. Instantly, without thought, I pointed at the closest one and pulled the trigger. I hadn't fired my gun since the battle with the humans and had forgotten how much power it possessed. My hand flew up and back and I almost lost my grip. Thankfully I didn't and leveled it at the next closest intruder.

Shots rang out all around me then as my companions did the same. Philip had grabbed his weapon and was preparing to fire. But, rather than the crack of a bullet when he pulled the trigger we all heard a sickening 'click', followed quickly by another and another. His gun was jammed.

None of us could disengage from the mobs in front of us to help him. All we could do was continue firing until our ammunition ran out. The mob was instantly upon Philip dragging him to the ground. When the rest of us ran out of ammunition we were forced to fight with our bare hands.

Since Philip had been the first to fall, our attackers where upon him in large numbers. He really didn't stand a chance against such odds. I turned to look as they began dragging him off into the distance.

I glanced at Keith and saw that he too was firing into the mob. A look of terror played on his eyes and I felt sorry for him in spite of my circumstances. His fear escaped his lips as he cried out, but he continued fighting nonetheless. Eventually he too ran out of ammunition. Throwing down his weapon he fought with a spirit that only a man filled with terror could muster.

I stole a quick look at Bill after that and could not believe what I saw. After running out of ammunition he had simply dropped his gun to the ground and had unsheathed his sword. In the short time since I had met him I had never had the opportunity to see him wield it. It was magnificent to watch and I had to actually concentrate on my own battle to keep from being overpowered.

His movements were a blur as his blade cut through the air. He moved that weapon with a speed and precision that did not seem possible. Screams filled the air as he cut them down. Not one of his attackers was able to overcome him as he stood and fought. But I had other worries.

My ammunition spent, I proceeded to fight them as best I could with my bare hands. Luckily this was a form of fighting that I had had some experience with. But these creatures fought with the same abandon as had the group that first met me at my pod. They literally threw themselves forward and I knew I would eventually lose if something didn't change.

I fought for all that I was worth and kicked and hit and scratched and even bit them. Slowly they overpowered me and I screamed in protest. But then, as quickly as it had begun, it ended. The mob retreated into the darkness that surrounded our camp and they were gone.

We all took the opportunity to reload our weapons, but they did not return again that night. I had suffered some minor injuries, mostly cuts, scrapes and bruises. Keith, on the other hand, had sustained more serious injuries. He had more and deeper cuts and had injured an eye. Bill seemed untouched.

I held my gun tightly in my hands and squinted vainly to see into the darkness, afraid that they would appear again. Bill spoke, "Relax Stephen, they won't be back again tonight. Thanks to my screw-up."

Sitting then, but not relaxing the grip I had on my gun, I looked at him with a confused look. 'What do you mean screw-up?'

"Because that was a pack of cannibals. They hunt at night, looking for sleeping people just like us. When they find one or more targets they attack en-masse in order to overpower their prey. Once they have captured at least one person, they always retreat to limit their damage. They have what they came for – a meal," he stated with a distinct tone of disgust in his voice. "I hate to say it, but I have never encountered a pack of cannibals that I didn't lose someone to. If you know a pack is close by, you don't stop moving – ever. I don't know how I managed to miss this pack but I did. I hope Phil will forgive me from eternity."

I was silent, absorbing what I had just been told. We all went about our duties re-organizing the camp silently, numbed by what had just happened; what else could we do? Checking on the woman, I was relieved, and somewhat surprised, to see that she was untouched by the fight. Passing by Bill I couldn't help but notice he had emerged from the battle uninjured. Needless to say, his skills were of great value. Sleep eluded us all for the rest of the night.

Just before daybreak we decided not to waste any more time trying to sleep. My feelings were mixed as we prepared to leave. I had not known Phil and was not experiencing the same grief for him as the others. I replayed the incident in my mind over and over, picturing what he must have gone through after being dragged to his doom into the darkness. How could such a thing ever happen to anyone?

I found myself dwelling upon the comments that Phil had made a few nights before. Why had he been so evasive? What did he not want me to know? The whole day it bothered me until at last, when we had stopped for the night, I approached Bill.

"Since Phil is gone I will never get the opportunity to know his story and I must admit that his strange reaction to our conversation the other night has got me really wondering."

He thought about my request for a short time. "Phil is one of the most unlikely residents I have had the privilege of knowing in the World Outside. His story is one that everyone should hear. I guess since he is not here to share it any longer, I will fill in for him. His story is complicated but I'll do my best to share it nonetheless.

"For as long as I have known Philip he was a very difficult man to know. He was always there for the group and you could always depend on him to keep his word, even if his life would be endangered in so doing. But yet, he didn't talk much and did not share his personal information lightly. There are still members of our group that do not know what I am about to tell you. But by sharing, I hope to honor his memory and perhaps carry on his beliefs.

"In his life before the World Outside, Philip was a very powerful businessman. He had had all the privileges that life could offer a person. He lived in a mansion, drove the most expensive vehicles money could buy, and had his every want and desire met by his servants.

"He hadn't always lived this way, mind you. He was born in one of the poorest neighborhoods in New York City. He was a self-made man. He was shrewd and wise beyond his years and eventually became one of the most influential men in this whole country."

"But throughout, he was a fair and honest man. Those that worked with him loved him and were fiercely loyal. I suppose it was inevitable that someone suggested that he run for public office, and so he did.

"He won election as New York City-State Senator on his first try. The landscape of politics, however, was something he was unprepared for. Never before had he encountered such a group of back-stabbing, self-serving, un-genuine people as he found in the Senate. Honesty, he discovered, was more of a detriment there than being cunning or being able to tell a convincing lie.

"Initially, Philip wanted to leave the Senate as quickly as possible. But, after some soul-searching, he decided that instead he would stay and do his very best to change the institution back into what it was intended to be – a servant to the people.

"He was forced to become a very guarded person then. He found that when he didn't pay close enough attention to the words that he, or even his aids, spoke, they would generally come back to haunt him. That's when he met Caralyn.

"Caralyn entered his life at a social gathering. Phil was instantly attracted to her and their relationship grew over the ensuing months. You might even recall seeing some pictures in the news of them together."

Suddenly, it was all coming together. I hadn't recognized him when I first met him; I don't know that I would have recognized anyone then due to the stresses of my new life. But I wasn't looking for dead men and I thought that the Senator was dead. How could he have been in the World Outside when I thought he was dead? I realized, sadly, that before I even had the chance to know him I learned that our group had included the honorable Senator Lawrence.

I remembered reading stories about the Senator and wishing there were more people like him in the Senate. I also remembered the press reporting on his relationship with Ms. Stone.

*   *   *

I remembered the Senator also. I had even written a story or two about him. My memory was different than Stephen's though. I believed, like my peers believed, that he was a dangerous man. I, too, thought the Senator was dead. But, unlike Stephen, I was relieved when I had learned it. I wondered how such a group as the one that had rescued Stephen could have wanted to harbor such a person.

*   *   *

"Philip dated Caralyn for a few years before anyone even knew about it," Bill continued. "His penchant for secrecy dominated and it followed him into this relationship as well. He became increasingly disenchanted with a government he considered out-of-touch with the people and morally bankrupt in many ways. He secretly started a grass-roots movement whose aim was the restructuring of the government. It was a revolutionary group in many ways, and Philip was its unquestionable leader, behind the scenes. It was known as The

Restorationists. Its members pressed for the return to some of the ancient precepts of government.

"One thing it fought against was the consolidation of power that had created the World Outside. The group believed that such power in the hands of so few was a recipe for abuse. Phil fervently believed that it was the primary reason the Senate had grown so dysfunctional. In too many ways, it had become the rubber stamp for those that possessed the real power. Phil didn't believe the Senate functioned as it should.

"As the movement grew, many of the Senators and even the Prime Minister of the Commonwealth became aware of its existence. Initially it was considered nothing more than a nuisance and was generally ignored. But as its numbers grew into the tens of thousands and acts of civil disobedience were blamed on the movement, it became a genuine threat to those in power and was labeled a traitorous organization by them.

"An organized effort to discover the leader of the group was initiated. But Phil was always able to stay one step ahead of them as they hunted him down.

"Philip grew tired of running. He loved Caralyn with all his heart and decided the time had finally come to settle down and ask her to marry him. On the night he proposed he knew that if they were to be married, he would have to share his secret. Telling her that he was the head of the Restorationists was one of the hardest things he had ever had to do. She simply informed him that she would have to consider his proposal and left. He would never see her in person again.

"Caralyn must have gone directly to the authorities. The next morning the police were at Philip's front door threatening to break it down. Of course, Philip had no idea what was going on and was simply asked to escort the police down to the station.

"Evidently the police were afraid of the reaction that the Restorationists might have to the news that Senator

Lawrence had been arrested. They arrested him only after he was safely behind the walls of the nearest precinct.

"Philip was absolutely stunned. Only Caralyn's betrayal could have caused such a turn of events. He was devastated. As he awaited expulsion from the city, many of his former colleagues came to chastise him for being the leader of such a 'dangerous,' 'malignant,' and 'traitorous' organization. Some could not resist taunting him about where he was heading and hoped nothing but the worst for him.

"Philip actually spent far more time in the city jail awaiting expulsion than anyone else I've ever met. I suspect it was to provide the opportunity to as many as wished to come to see the downfall of the once-great Senator. He suffered awful atrocities in that prison. It is a time that he has never shared with any of us, not even Derik."

As Bill spoke I simply couldn't believe what I was hearing. The news that was shared with the public rehearsed the details of a terrible accident in which Senator Lawrence had been killed. When I heard it I was actually a little saddened by it. Of course, the news report never mentioned the Restorationists. Before then I had never even heard of them and I wondered if they still existed.

"When Philip was finally sent away in his pod the humants found him first and took him to their compound out east. Of course, most everyone who finds themselves there are turned into humants, but when Reks Kriton discovered that he had the great Senator Lawrence among his prisoners, he had him brought directly to him.

"You see, when Philip was still a Senator he had chaired in a tribunal of a certain Dr. Kriton. Kriton had been accused of numerous crimes, among which included such things as kidnapping, illegal gene manipulation, human mutation, and reckless disregard for human life. He decried the doctor in front of the entire tribunal for his many atrocities and was instrumental in getting the good doctor expelled. It is not hard to imagine why Reks would have been downright gleeful to have Philip in his prison.

"When Philip was finally brought before Reks he would discover new horrors that he could never have even dreamed of. Reks gleefully informed him that he was to become a humant and was immediately whisked into surgery.

"I have had the opportunity to speak to a handful of humants in my time in the World Outside, and none of them remember the ordeal of becoming one, except for Phil. Reks thought that it would be particularly fitting, and cruel, to keep him awake during the procedure. He was fully conscience throughout, but unable to move or speak. He could do little else but watch in disbelief as his intestinal tract was removed and replaced with a new one that had been 'cultivated' for a certain purpose. A purpose he would learn as he lay recovering from the surgery.

"Reks couldn't even wait until he had fully recovered to gloat. He entered the small room were Philip lay motionless and spoke. 'Senator Lawrence. *Senator* Lawrence? I think not. How does *slave* Lawrence sound? I have replaced your digestive system with one which can only survive on a substance that only I know how to create. From this day forward, you will be dependent upon me for your very existence and if you were ever to make the mistake of running away, you would die within a few days of *very* painful starvation. It seems appropriate that you and I should spend some quality time together don't you think…slave?' He then left cackling like the madman that he is.

"Philip was forced to spend the next two years as Reks's personal assistant. He was forced to observe numberless procedures on other unfortunate victims and was filled with horror and sorrow each and every time. Towards the end of this period, Reks even began asking him his opinion on what should be done to his new victims, but Philip never responded to any of these questions.

"Some two years after arriving at Kriton's compound he was actually sent on a mission to collect new 'volunteers' with a group of humants. He went along in body but not in spirit and refused to help the others. The leader of the humants became so enraged at Philip that he attacked him, severely injuring him. You know this humant. It is the one that you shot the first night that we met, the one that got away."

My head was swimming in the sheer volume of information I was receiving. I had so many questions I didn't know where to begin. But Bill was not yet finished.

"Philip laid in the spot where he fell for two whole days, waiting and wanting to die as the pain began. That's when Derik found him. He tried to nurse him back to health but found that he was not having any success, Phil just grew worse and worse. Eventually the pain of starvation became so great that Philip took a chance and shared his problem with Derik.

"Derik took compassion on Phil and, against the advice of many of his companions, took a small team to the supply depot of the Kriton compound and stole a few years' worth of the nutritional supplement that would sustain Philip's life. Lately, Phil's supply has begun to run low. We've discussed the possibility of returning for more of the supplement but Phil was torn about whether anyone else should risk their life for his benefit. He probably would have wanted it to end this way, he really didn't want anybody to get hurt, or worse, for him. He was a good man and we will all miss him."

In the short time I had known him, not once had I even slightly suspected that one of the people I then associated with was a humant. My brief exposure to humants had left me believing them all to be evil, vile creatures. And yet, I found myself looking back on the one humant I had seen in the battle that had been afraid. Had he been forced into that fight by somebody else? I questioned Bill.

"I thought all humants worked for Reks Kriton, and even if they don't, I would never have trusted one. How did a humant find his way into our group?"

I could tell that my questions regarding this fallen friend made Bill uncomfortable, but he endeavored to answer me just the same.

"All humants are victims, just like you or me, only on a more heinous level. And although they present an evil picture when they are attacking you, they are not all evil. As adept as Kriton has become at changing bodies, the one thing he has had difficulty controlling directly are minds.

"Not every humant that is created ends up fighting for him, more than you know are executed for failing to follow his orders without question. Those that do fight, do it for various reasons.

"I assure you that Reks has spent many years trying to find some genetic method to control the minds and spirits of those unfortunate enough to find themselves within his grasp, but he has mercifully been unable to do so. But, minus this, he has found other, just as effective, methods for control.

"Most of us are keen self-preservationists. Well, this tendency does not stop when one becomes a humant. The vast majority of those who fight for Reks do so because they fear him or need him for survival. Too many armies of the past have been filled by people like this, people who feared their leaders more than they feared being in the army. It is hard to consider such an enemy as this as evil, even those that no longer look like men.

"Reks has been known to take entire families whenever he is able. When this happens, often one is forced to fight while the others are held as a prisoner to inspire compliance. These humants fight fiercely and are, many times, the most dangerous opponents. It's simple, if they fight hard, their loved ones live; if they don't, they die.

"The horrors that are inflicted upon those that enter his compound are impossible for those who have not experienced them to understand. Some of those who survive the ordeal fear that they could never be accepted by anyone outside the community of humants again, particularly those that undergo radical changes. Others simply stop living, for all intents and purposes, and become soulless soldiers for Kriton.

"One of Reks's favorite tricks is to make his humants physically dependent upon him for their very lives, just like he did to Philip. And again, just like Philip, he makes sure that if they ever find the means to leave him, their lives would be filled with grueling agony until death finally releases them. For them, death is a welcome change. Heck, the number of humants that commit suicide nearly matches that of those that stay with Kriton. Few are prepared for the mental tortures that accompany their change.

"As you might imagine, some of his unfortunate victims simply go insane, while others truly learn to enjoy the work that they do for Reks. But, for whatever reason humants find themselves fighting and dying for that man, it is hard to see them as anything other than the victims that they are.

"I have lost count of the number of times now that I have had to enter battle with a group of humants. Yet still to this day, I leave those battles feeling I have killed at least one unwilling participant."

We had to stop our conversation there; it was time to move on. I replayed his words over and over again as we walked, thinking of the implications of what he had said. We all sort of drifted into a melancholy silence as we trudged onward towards home.

Eventually my mind drifted from humants to the principles that drove the Restorationists and on to the awesome physical skills I had seen Bill display. Moving closer to Bill I asked, "Have you ever thought about teaching someone how to fight like you do?"

Without looking at me he responded, "Only children can learn those ways of fighting effectively, for it takes a lifetime of learning. I do not believe that a full-grown man or woman could learn it well."

I pondered his words but did not entirely agree with them. I do not believe there is anything a person, properly motivated, cannot learn. More than once I had seen the magnificent things Bill could do. More than once he had saved the lives of those around him. I wanted to learn this more than anything I had ever wanted to.

I kept at Bill as we continued, sharing my beliefs with him. All the while he remained silent, but listened to my repeated requests. A short distance from home, Bill stopped us and asked Keith to keep an eye on our lady guest and to radio us if anything happened. Then, heading towards a small pond in the distance, Bill motioned for me to follow him. I almost tripped in my eagerness.

At length we reached the water's edge where Bill asked me to kneel. "Power comes from knowledge and knowledge comes from belief. Do you believe that you have the desire necessary to become a *true* warrior?" To which I responded in the affirmative. Then, without warning, Bill grabbed me in a powerful hold, took hold of my head and plunged it into the water.

Immediately I began thrashing about wildly, but there was no way I could break Bill's grasp. I don't know how long he kept my head submerged, but it seemed like an eternity. I took water into my mouth as I thrashed about and I could feel the pressure in my chest increase as my body screamed out for air. And still he held my head under the water

At the very same instant I was certain that I could bear no more, Bill pulled my head from the water. I sat on the shore for a minute coughing, sputtering, and regaining my breath. I looked at Bill then with incredulity in my expression but said nothing, wondering if I had crossed a line by asking too many times.

Bill allowed my thoughts to go wild for a few minutes while he said nothing. I knew instinctively that I should not speak first and so I waited for him. At long last, he finally did.

"Stephen, to learn those things that have been entrusted to me takes dedication, an understanding of those things not possessed by common men, and a desire equal to your desire to breathe just now. For without a desire of that magnitude, this will all be for naught and you will have wasted both of our times. Ponder my words during the remainder of our journey and if, when we have reached home, you still feel that you have this desire, than I will teach you what you wish to know."

I had never wanted anything as badly as I wanted to breathe at the moment that I was ready to abandon myself to a watery grave. It was a powerful object lesson that would have a profound impact on my life. I knew that if I could learn the things that Bill could teach me, there was nothing I could not do.

Sitting there, with water dripping from my face, I wondered what he meant by *true* warrior. I discovered a piece of myself that day, on a bleak plain beside a dirty pond in the middle of the World Outside. I don't think I could have been more committed than I was at that time.

With those thoughts in mind I entered my new home a new man with a new outlook on life. I was no longer the person that had entered the World Outside. I was becoming someone else.

Chapter 6

"I am not teaching you how to fight and kill,
I am teaching you how to live and die."
Bill Owens

The two weeks immediately following our return from the city's edge were uneventful. The silence that accompanied the quiet times in the World Outside seemed to match the chaotic tumult it also provided. It was an odd place. I began to see why some people just couldn't take living there and did inconceivable things to escape it.

I made myself useful helping with more and more of the necessary chores, trying to find my place within the group. But amid my efforts I made sure to find sufficient time to look after our female guest and I spent a lot of my free time attending to her. Even unconscious, her beauty literally radiated.

Under the care of Dr. Taylor, her condition continued to improve daily. I had never seen medical care like that offered by the doctor. With precious few of the items that are commonly found in a hospital she nevertheless successfully treated most of the injuries and ailments suffered by our little group.

Much of what she would apply to wounds or ask us to swallow certainly didn't look, smell, or taste very appetizing, but the results were hard to argue over. I was told that no one had yet died from an illness or an injury that hadn't immediately killed them.

She made use of a vast array of items; common household things became her medical equipment. When she ran low of her 'medicines' she, along with a guardian, would disappear from an hour to a couple of days in order to restock. Her skill always impressed me.

After about a week under the doctor's care our guest's eyes fluttered and she finally awoke. At first, her reaction was a mixture of confusion and fear. She didn't speak right away. Though I wanted to reassure her that there was nothing to fear, all potential members are strictly off-limits to all but Derik and the doctor.

When Derik entered the room to introduce himself and our group a number of us crowded together near the medical area. We were like kids trying to see a parade over the heads of those standing in front of us.

As he talked to her a terrible realization swept over me. I hadn't realized until just that moment that I had been so swept up in the beauty of our guest that the idea of a NeMEx for her had not even crossed my mind. My heart dropped as he mentioned it to her, at the thought of someone so fragile experiencing what was so recently etched into my memory. Vivid recollection of the hunger and fatigue I had suffered during my own NeMEx came to mind.

At length he finished speaking to her and turned to leave the area. When he asked me to accompany him on her NeMEx I was momentarily speechless. She seemed so delicate. I had just finished worrying and wondering if she would fully recover from the condition in which we had found her. How could I watch her suffer further anguish, partly at my hand? Silently I nodded my assent, unwilling to deny a request made by Derik, though I wasn't sure I was up to the task.

I watched her from a distance as Derik gave her a couple of days to regain her strength, trying to find some objectivity for what lay ahead. I felt guilty even before we left. She did not feel the reassurance I had in the group nearly as quickly as I did. It was a little while before she was comfortable enough to even share her name: Ashleigh Voss.

Despite my struggles to maintain a sense of objectivity for the upcoming expedition, I was drawn in by her almost immediately. She had a mesmerizingly beautiful voice. Whenever she spoke I found myself feeling that an angel had paid a visit to the unfortunate denizens of hell. It actually made me somewhat angry and confused. I was acting like a heart-sick teenaged boy. I had to get control of myself.

Derik noticed my interest in our guest and took me aside. 'Stephen, I've noticed that you seem to have something more than a passing interest in Ashleigh. I cannot have the person which accompanies me on any NeMEx be anything less than absolutely dedicated to the goals of the expedition. That person must be ready and willing to abandon the subject of the NeMEx on a moment's notice, *without* looking back.

"I know it sounds harsh, but as you learned during your own NeMEx, it is for the best. You cannot save those that do not wish to be saved – no matter how badly you may want it to be otherwise."

Then, looking past me and into the room where Ashleigh lay asleep, he said, "Yes, she is very beautiful, but remember, exterior beauty is of little value when it wraps a heart of black. Only by opening a book can you truly know what's inside.

"Philip Lawrence paid an awful price for the love he extended to Caralyn. She was not what she appeared to be. I sincerely hope you find in Ashleigh everything that your heart now desires. But, right now I need your *total* commitment to her NeMEx. Do I have it?"

Sighing deeply I knew what I had to do and that Derik was right. I assured him that I would fulfill my duties as expected and that I would be ready on the morrow when the time came to leave.

It was apparent to Ashleigh right away that this was not an ordinary trip. She expressed her concern about the purposes of the trip and seemed perplexed that we would leave the safety of the base.

I could hear my own questions replayed in hers as she asked what we were looking for. And my heart went out to her when she said, "Have I done something wrong? You saved me and have treated me so well, even though none of you know anything about me. I hope I haven't offended anyone."

To this day I am not sure how Derik maintained his composure with all of the people he took on a NeMEx. He had been on so many, nearly every one. Some that he took he now trusted with his very life, but too many others, far too many, had tried to stab him in the back, or worse.

Regardless, characteristic of the hard, yet wise, man that I was coming to know, he answered without undo emotion, "No, we just need to find something and we need your help to find it."

The first night out was one of the hardest I have ever experienced. Like me, Ashleigh did not say anything about being left out of the meal. But when she turned and quietly wept, it tore my heart out. It made eating my own meal difficult, to say the very least. I knew why I had to eat it and what the purpose of it was, but I went to sleep that night with an upset stomach. I could have eaten the best meal of my life that night and it still would have set uncomfortably in my belly.

When our food was gone she approached us and tried to start a conversation. I knew that neither Derik nor Max had spoken to me on my first night out, but I had not been given any rules for a NeMEx so I found myself talking back.

It was obvious that Derik did not believe that speaking to the subject of a NeMEx was a good idea, but one thing led to another and eventually the topic of why she was expelled from the cities came up. I listened intently, between looks of concern and disapproval from Derik. When she started speaking and mentioned Dr. Taylor's name, Derik softened – a little.

"I understand that you were one of my rescuers, Stephen. You have my thanks forever. Dr. Taylor told me all the things you did for me while I was in a coma. She told me about all of the time you spent talking softly to me, even when I couldn't respond. She also told me that you spent many a sleepless night worrying over me, even though you didn't know anything about me. I can't begin to tell you how that makes me feel. It's been a long time since I have felt important to anyone and I would like the opportunity to get to know you better. I thought the best way to do that was share with you a little about who I am.

"My parents were wealthy and they tried to buy my love, but I never had much of a relationship with either one of them. What little I might have had pretty much died after they divorced. I bounced between each one throughout my teenage years, never really settling in any one place. I had no real opportunity to develop friendships, but it seemed that no one ever wanted to know me beyond my looks.

"It was an empty existence and I created a shell for myself where I lived. I never realized how naïve I was until after graduating from high school. I attended the local college where I got engaged to the first boy that I dated. I realize in retrospect that my standards for a husband were pretty low, but I didn't really have any good comparison to look at. Nonetheless, we were soon married and I was eager to begin life as a wife and mother.

"My new husband got a job in a faraway city and began commuting. Monday through Friday he spent at the office, returning only on the weekends to me. He was supposed to have been looking for an apartment for us so that we could be together, but he kept telling me he was having trouble finding one. It wasn't long after he started working that he began acting suspiciously. Eventually, he even found reasons not to come home on the weekends.

"It went on for so long that even through my willful blindness I became concerned that our marriage was in serious trouble. I decided the best thing to do was to find an apartment myself so I could move to the city where he worked. Even after I had no trouble finding one I fooled myself into believing that I had just had better luck than he had had.

"He seemed unusually surprised when I showed up in the city where he worked with a new apartment. He feigned happiness about the change and things seemed to be better for a little while. After a time, I found myself pregnant, even though we had taken all precautions to prevent it. I was ecstatic but my husband did not share my enthusiasm *at all*. I rushed to the doctor's office to verify the news but my joy was dashed when I was asked to produce my Pregnancy Permit. I did not have one since it had been unplanned and since I had none I was scheduled to have my pregnancy terminated.

"It is amazing how fast and fully positive emotions can be replaced with a gut-wrenching despair. When I refused I was quickly placed under arrest. As I would learn throughout my brief experience within the justice system, women are allowed to opt not to have their child aborted but would, after the birth, be expelled from the cities. I was escorted from the clinic to a holding cell and was given the opportunity to pay my fine the next day.

"I would not have suspected illegal pregnancies to be classified as such a seriou crimes and yet when I was told what the amount that my fine would be I knew it was out of reach for most people. I knew my husband's new salary was ample enough to cover it, but when I went to pay it I discovered that he had removed all of the money from our joint accounts and was nowhere to be found.

"I panicked as I realized that I did not have the money to pay the fine. I'm embarrassed to say that I reacted in stereotypically female fashion and I slumped to the floor and sobbed when I was sentenced to be expelled into the World Outside. Unlike other prisoners, pregnant women are kept in an area of the city jail that is more like a clinic than a cell. They are kept there until their babies are born. After that they're expelled at the next possible opportunity, even those that have suffered complications. I have no idea what happens to the babies that leave the prison.

"During the eight months I spent there, my husband never visited and aside from the disinterested sterile visits from the doctors, I was almost completely alone. My parents did manage to visit once, but during the visit my mother became so hysterical that our visit was terminated and they were forbidden from returning. The only other visit I got was from my husband's lawyer to serve me with divorce papers and to inform me that he would be taking custody of our child as soon as it was born. As twisted as it sounds, I found some comfort in the knowledge that our child would at least be with one of its parents.

"I needn't tell you that it was not a good eight months, and had I not been on suicide watch, I probably would have killed myself. I had nightmares every time I slept and wondered who my baby would grow up to become.

"It was a strange waiting period. One minute I had the typical mother excitement at the prospect of bringing a new life into the world, especially when I could feel it kick or saw it on an ultrasound. While the next minute I would fall into a deep depression in which I would remain for days at a time.

"When at last I went into labor, I had more than one reason to cry. My physical pain was lost in the soul-wrenching despair that I had. In a matter of hours I knew that my baby and I would be separated forever. The tears that ran down my face were not the first that the prison's doctors and nurses had seen I'm certain.

"All I could do was sink back on the birthing table and stare blankly into space when they immediately whisked the baby from the room without even letting me see it. All I have as a memory of my child is the sound of its cries as they faded into the distance. I was given one day to recover; after which, I was taken to a pod building and loaded onto a pod. The rest you know."

When she finished she lowered her head and cried softly. I had no idea how to respond to what she had just shared. There were no words that would do. I simply put my arm around her shoulders and hugged her. She buried her head into my chest and cried with abandon. Even Derik did not wear the somber look he typically wore.

She wept for a while. I remained silent, allowing her the opportunity to speak first. "As I rode that pod I pondered unbuckling the seatbelt. All I wanted to do was die but something told me not to. When I woke up from my coma I was actually angry that you and your group had not let me die. But I've come to realize that you all are what I so desperately sought from my husband: a place to belong and be needed. I thank you both from the bottom of my heart for saving me and I thank you for listening."

I felt too overwhelmed then to adequately respond and made up some feeble excuse to leave to regain my own composure. Sleep would not come that evening.

Early the next morning an indignant Derik woke me roughly. "Stephen, you're coming apart on me. Your feelings for this girl are dulling your senses. I think that maybe we should return to base so I can get somebody else to help me."

The thought of leaving Ashleigh in the hands of anyone else greatly troubled me and I objected as strongly as I could, ensuring him that I was not swayed and that if the time came that we would have to leave her I would do just that. Problem was, I wasn't sure I believed my own words so I don't know why, or even if, he did. Nonetheless, he accepted my asserted dedication as genuine and we continued on our way.

The whole of the next day passed in silence. Moving by hand gestures, we made our way into areas that I recognized from my own NeMEx. By the rate of our progress it was obvious that Ashleigh had not fully recovered from her expulsion ordeal. As Derik and I sat for dinner that evening she leaned onto a wall a little ways from us and spoke not a word.

Her face was quite pale and Derik rose with concern and went to speak to her. When he asked if she were alright she feebly responded that she was sure that we had a good reason for the things that we were doing and that she trusted she would not come to harm in our care.

It was Derik's turn then not to get any sleep and I watched him toss and turn as he wrestled with his thoughts. By the next morning, to my surprise, he ended the NeMEx and we found ourselves heading for home.

When I inquired of him the reasons for ending the NeMEx he said, "I have been on expedition with more than a hundred people. I keep a NeMEx journal and I have recorded them all. I believe that even those who turn on me in the end deserve to be remembered.

"Of all the people I have met in the World Outside, I have never met anyone quite like Ashleigh. She possesses an innocence like nothing I've ever seen. She has no guile and does not belong in such a horrible place."

Then turning, Derik put a hand on each of my arms as he grasped me, looking into my eyes. "Take care of her Stephen. The World Outside will consume her if you do not stand in its way. Together, maybe we can keep the stains of this place away from her."

Of all the skills Derik possessed, and there were many, I would have to say that his judge of character was unmatched by any other. My feelings for her would grow from that day forward and I did everything I could to honor his charge.

Returning early from the NeMEx brought some excitement to the group as it had never happened before. I was not around to hear Derik's explanation to the others but I assume it was similar to mine.

I took the opportunity then to begin my training with Bill in earnest. I tried to split my time between my training and visiting with Ashleigh but Bill would have none of it. Ashleigh seemed to sense the importance of the training I was receiving and encouraged me to take full advantage of it. But it did make focusing pretty difficult in the beginning.

I learned quickly what was important and what was not. The very first question out of my mouth annoyed Bill, bringing a disapproving look to his face.

"So, what belt are you Bill? You must be some kind of black belt to do all the things you do."

Responding dryly he said, "I have never measured myself against an article of clothing."

Not quick to pick up on the direction of the exchange I then asked, "What are we going to be studying then: karate, kung-fu, tae-kwon-do?"

Patiently he responded, "I am going to teach you what I know. Does it make a difference what it is called? Will you suddenly lose interest if it does not have a name that sounds impressive?"

Realizing that knowing it was more important than naming it, I simply nodded my agreement. He began by teaching me effective methods of meditation.

I must have been difficult to bear at first. I whined about the meditation like a kid, seeing little point to it. Bill simply said patiently, "Robots, despite their massive gears, raw power, and impressive weaponry, are useless without the proper programming. Basic self-defense is the rudimentary control of the principles that I will teach you.

Only through understanding both the physical *and* the spiritual aspects of what you seek to do, will you be able to go beyond rudimentary control to mastery."

We spent a good deal of time training for things that didn't seem to have anything to do with knowing how to use a sword and how to fight. Among these items was Bill's Bushido, or the Way of the Warrior; the Warrior's Code for short.

Bringing me a large piece of thick paper and a pen, Bill instructed me to make a poster of the principles contained in the Warrior's Code. We discussed each principle in great detail and slowly the poster was filled.

Years after, I still do not completely understand the wisdom contained in the code, nobody can in this life, but I will endeavor to summarize the code the best I can.

Principle number one is rectitude. This was a hard one for me to get at first. The short description of the principle is rightness of principal or practice. What it means is that we should always do things the right way for the right reasons or don't do them at all.

Law in the World Outside is fundamental and harsh. Might makes right is more than just a saying. There have been many, many times I had the opportunity to be among the mighty, making my own laws. One of the more compelling things which stopped me was this principal. It has served me more than I ever thought possible before writing it on that poster. It has been a guiding principal for those things I have done over the years and I believe that is the reason it is principal number one.

Principle number two is courage. As defined in the Code, courage is the ability to confront fear, uncertainty, and pain without losing your resolve. Without resolve, and a purpose for which to maintain it, courage is nothing more than foolish bravery. As I would learn courage is certainly not an absence of fear but rather the willingness to persevere in the face of trouble and danger. In short, courage is simply control over fear.

Principle three is benevolence. All I had to do to understand this principle was to think of Derik. Benevolence is defined as goodwill and charity. I have always substituted compassion, as it was described to me on my NeMEx, in the place of this principal. And as Derik taught me, compassion is never wasted when it is given.

The next principle is respect. I had some trouble with this one at the beginning. To me, there were truly some people and creatures that did not deserve, or even care about, my respect. But this was a biggie with Bill; respect was especially important for your opponents. He taught that not only did you respect your opponents for their abilities, but also their purposes, even when you didn't agree with them. They, like us, all had reasons to do the things they did. Were their reasons any less legitimate than our own? It took me a long time to learn that to give respect does not mean we have to agree with the opponent to whom it is given.

Principle five is honesty. This was a straight forward principle for me. Honesty meant your word could be depended upon.

Principle number six is honor. As with respect, I had a hard time understanding the importance of what seemed an ancient concept. Even the very mention conjured up visions of honor-killings and ancient warriors killing themselves over honor. Bill acknowledged that honor had caused many a man to do foolish things, but in the final analysis it is the measure of a man's trustworthiness.

Explaining further, Bill tried to convey that honor is the non-physical, yet far more important, reward that a man gets for living the way of the warrior with rectitude. But honor is a two-edged sword since honor for its own sake becomes glory, which can be a problem in and of itself.

One concept of honor that Bill wanted to impress upon me was that honor is *never* obtained through acts of revenge and that honor does not and cannot come through meaningless killing.

Honor is a frustrating concept when it is practiced only by one. In times past, honor was important to both parties of a battle. Now honor is only a way to measure rectitude in keeping the code. It is one of the most important principles, and one of the most difficult to understand and master.

Principle seven is loyalty. Loyalty should never be given as a free gift, but must be absolute once it is earned.

The last principle is wisdom. Wisdom went hand-in-hand with rectitude. They were bookends of the code. While rectitude meant doing the rights things at the right times, wisdom meant knowing the difference.

Our training progressed at what I considered an excruciatingly slow pace. I did not then understand the value of the things being offered to me. When at long last I found myself requested to do such things as walk thin beams and hop from the top of one small surface to the next in order to learn balance and control, I finally lost my patience.

Confronting Bill I blurted out, "I'm sick of this Bill! This isn't true training! I was drawn to you because I saw how you used your sword, why aren't we practicing with them?"

The forbearance displayed by Bill during this period of our training was commendable. Without a rise in his voice he simply looked at me and said, with great emphasis, "I am not teaching you how to fight and kill Stephen, I am teaching you how to live and die. Until you understand that concept we will not move beyond this portion of your training. I was not even allowed to touch a sword for the first two years of my training. You must earn the right to wield one."

Sufficiently chastened I was silent then. Each morning Bill and I would retire to a different part of the city where he would instruct me. I tried to be appropriately contrite then and asked his forgiveness.

Only after adequate time had passed did I gather the courage to ask what he meant when he told me that he was teaching me how to die. In answer he replied, "Rise and retire every day as if it were your very last opportunity to do so. Expect that you will die in every battle and die only for that which warrants the giving of a life."

As with most things that I learned from Bill, only after experience did I really understand what he was teaching me.

While I training with Bill, Derik took the opportunity to introduce me to some of the other weapons used by our group. He taught me how to disassemble, clean, and reassemble my personal weapon and I had target practice as often as was practical with our limited ammunition supply.

I listened intently to all of the lessons, regardless of who was teaching them. I was an eager learner. I believed that the more I knew, the more useful I would be to myself and to the group. The training I was receiving was comprehensive.

I hoped that, through my training, I would be able to do as Derik has suggested: keep the stain of the World Outside off of Ashleigh. It became one of my primary motivators to endure it all.

A few weeks after arriving in the World Outside the duty of night guard fell upon me. I was tired from the day's training and was looking forward to some quiet time to gather my thoughts. I was feeling comfortable and happy in my new home. The members of the group even felt like something of a family to me. Unfortunately, my time of quiet was brief.

Chapter 7

"There is no dishonor in abandoning an indefensible position."
Bill Owens

I had spent a few weeks in the World Outside without any trouble. It had been so quiet that it almost felt like I had simply continued my old life in this new place. With the safety and security I found within the group, together with the duties I had been given, it would have been easy to fool myself into believing I had simply moved to a new city to take a new job. I had even found a good book in the group's meager library that I curled up with as I prepared to take my turn standing guard at the front door.

Sometime around two in the morning I heard a loud thump from somewhere outside our hide-out. Looking away from my book I glanced nervously in the direction of the sound. I knew that sometimes the night winds blew the abundant rubble around that filled the streets above. Thumps and bumps in the night were not generally something to be concerned about.

But when the thump repeated a second time, only louder, it quickly became an item of grave concern. Letting my book slide off my lap, I grasped the handles of the periscope that had been placed at the guard station. Biting my lip I put my eyes to the lens only to see approaching trouble. A familiar fear, one I had almost forgotten, grasped my entire being.

Approaching our position quickly was a group of six humants. Behind them, and a little harder to make out, was a much larger group. Each group seemed to be looking for something. I wasted no time pulling the cord that set off the alarm in the quarters below. Half a minute later the smaller group of humants had found the trap door and had fired a hook through it, pulling it open. Seeing me on the small perch behind the door, they rushed in towards me.

The humant experience I had endured on my first night in the World Outside had left a deep scar on my emotions. Despite the safety I had been feeling only minutes earlier, I was momentarily frozen in place as terror gripped me. I had to will myself to keep breathing; it seemed that my heart was blocking my windpipe.

I knew that if I didn't react quickly I would not survive, but control of my body did not seem to be mine. Then, gritting my teeth with determination, I forced my arms to move. Bringing my weapon to my shoulder in what seemed like slow-motion I aimed and pulled the trigger. I doubt I could have accomplished even that simple move had I not been training. Bullets flew from the barrel and two of the humants fell immediately. But then, between shots, the whole building rocked with an explosion.

While the small group at the entrance engaged and distracted us, the larger group had located the hole that had been made by the awful humant with the axe that had attacked us on my first night in the World Outside. After the battle, we had tried to cover the hole so that it could not be easily found again. It was nothing more than a temporary cover and other concerns had taken precedence over a more permanent cover. Once the large group had found it, they had blown it open.

A shower of debris rained down on my teammates beneath the hole followed soon after by a tangle of ropes. Humants en masse then descended upon my tired and ill-prepared family. I could hear gunfire below me but I had my own problems to worry about.

I never really got a good look at the two humants that fell first, but I will never forget the four that followed. The next two had deformed figures: they had miscellaneous bulges, bumps, and even a few extra eyes and limbs in places where they shouldn't have been. Their bodies had patches of long, straggly hair and their skin looked like leather that had been stretched on a frame to dry. Each one was at least seven feet tall and they lumbered towards me.

It is hard to explain the other two humants. The first one had the size and shape of a regular human; however, its body was covered by what looked like small spikes. These ranged from small quarter-inch protrusions to large six-inch-long spikes. They were made of hardened flesh and were colored the same but they glistened slightly like they had been covered by a thin layer of oil.

I had to resist my temptation to stare at it as it approached. It looked very much like a cross between a porcupine and a human being. But I had to pull my eyes from it in order to fight the others.

The other humant that approached also had the head, torso, and legs of a normal human, but where arms should have been were a pair of what could only have been described as tentacles. But unlike the tentacles of sea creatures, these tentacles had no visible suction cups. As I would find out later however, they were there, but instead of hundreds of larger ones, there were instead millions of ones that were nearly too small to be seen by the naked eye.

I continued firing at the humants and with the third and fourth humants down, I swung my weapon towards the spiked one to take aim. But before I could fire I felt intense pain burn through the shoulder of my firing arm. No sooner had the bullet left the barrel then I felt another sharp pain in my side, just under that shoulder.

Instinctively I fired a second time at the same moment that yet another spike penetrated my thigh. Agonizing pain tore through my body and my knees began to buckle. Unable to support my own weight any longer, I fell to my knees and looked down at my leg. I could see a spike protruding from my thigh. My mind struggled with the fact that this humant was actually firing his own flesh spikes at me.

My strength was rapidly leaving me and as I fell backwards, I felt yet another spike pierce the bottom of my jaw. I could feel the very tip of the spike poke the bottom of my tongue as it lodged into place. Blood filled my mouth and I collapsed, but did not pass out. As I would learn later, the spikes contained some sort of muscle paralyzing agent and I was unable to move. With the blood collecting against the muscles I used to breathe, that did not want to work, I struggled with what strength I had left just to keep breathing.

Paralyzed and unable to move, I could do little else but watch with renewed horror as the tentacled humant approached me. Moving to the edge of the perch, where the tunnel descended into our hide-out, he grasped an ankle in each tentacle and yanked me violently from the floor. Flinging me outwards he released me and I flew through the air, hitting the side of the tunnel before dropping hard onto the floor some distance below.

The fall worsened my ability to breathe as it knocked the air out of my lungs. Gasping, I watched the humant jump off the perch and land beside me. Then, grabbing both my ankles again, he swung me over his head one full turn before releasing me. His tentacles allowed him to gather considerable speed before throwing me and every so often I could actually hear my bones crack as I landed.

I was losing the fight with this humant and I feared that my nightmares might come true. Visions of my first few minutes within the World Outside flooded my mind and the terrible thought of becoming one of Reks Kriton's newest 'volunteers' made my soul scream out in anguish. But I had absolutely no control over my body and could do nothing as he swung me about like a rag doll.

Because of the tranquilizing effects of the other humant's spikes, I was not aware that every place the tentacles touched my skin, they scraped the top layer off and blood flowed from each wound. The little suction cups worked the same as hundreds of little jagged edges scraping across my skin.

I lost track of the number of times he swung me about, all I remember is that when it was over one arm, a leg, three ribs, and my collar bone were all broken. One eye was swollen shut and it would not open again for many days. And at some point during the beating, a spike had perforated my abdomen. To put it mildly, I was in very bad shape.

Somehow my mind still registered that a battle was raging around me but finally, after what truly seemed like an eternity to me, Derik made his way towards me. My beating ended with two quick shots. I groaned as he hoisted me off the floor. If I had been able I would have enjoyed a chuckle as he muttered under his breath something like, "We've got to stop meeting like this."

Carrying what was left of me towards what was left of our medical area, he carefully laid me onto a cot. Feebly glancing around as he carried me, I could see through my one good eye the many humant bodies strewn about the room.

My heart sank when I noticed one of the group was among the bodies. Squinting, I could not make out who it was through the haze that now blurred my vision. I hoped against hope that he, like me, was only injured, but I would learn later that we had lost Max Harrd. When the venom from the spikes began to wear off it grew progressively harder to see and I could only hope that no one else lay upon the floor, beyond my vision. And even though he was not really my brother, I found myself particularly worried about Clay. My mind conjured up pictures of him, lying in unnatural positions upon the floor.

These were the visions in my mind as Derik laid me upon that cot. Just before I passed out I could see Dr. Taylor and Ashleigh as they entered the room. I could see some blood on Ashleigh's face but could not tell if it belonged to her. Concern gripped my heart, but my wounds finally overcame me and I lost consciousness. I took the visions of my fallen comrade, the humant monsters that had attacked me, and my concern for Clay, Ashleigh, and all the rest of my friend's into my nightmare filled world to keep me company for the next five horrible days and nights.

Terrible visions were all I had then. I relived every awful thing that I had seen or experienced since coming to the World Outside. Terrible things happened to me, to my new family, to Ashleigh, and to my little brother Pauly in my dreams.

I saw Paul being accused of horrible crimes, beaten by guards, and thrown into the World Outside. I could see his pod ride into hell in vivid detail and the humant welcoming party that was there to greet him. My mind envisioned a gigantic black fortress wherein dwelt the evil Reks Kriton, and it was there that my brother was taken.

Always it was a dark and moonless night. The dark had a life all its own. In those terrible visions Paul was subjected to every terrifying form of surgery that my mind could devise. No once, not twice, but numberless times. And of course, since Philip Lawrence had been kept awake during his unimaginable ordeal, so too was Paul.

Every time I would scream out in anguish, but never could I do anything about what I saw. It was one of the most soul-wrenching miserable times of my life. I cried out to the God of heaven to save me from that never ending nightmare.

At long last, I began to awake. Intensely bright light flooded through the crack in my still-good eye as I strained to open it. After spending nearly a week in my self-imposed hell, the angel that awaited me was Ashleigh. The smile she gave me when she saw that I was waking up lifted my soul and gave me a reason to fight all that much harder to come back to the real world.

After I had recovered somewhat, Dr. Taylor took the opportunity to share that Ashleigh had returned the favor I have shown her during her coma. Not once had she left my side. She held my limp hand and would whisper to me from time to time. Some precious few of her words penetrated my darkness.

At times, in the middle of whatever sordid horror I was experiencing, Ashleigh's soothing voice would break through the darkness and bring a moment of respite to my soul. When I learned that she was actually speaking to me during those times, I knew that I was falling in love with her.

It took a few more days before I had the strength to move. Derik was pleased to see me up and about but I could tell that something was troubling him when he asked if I was well enough to participate in a group meeting.

We all sat around the kitchen area while Derik stood before us and began to speak. "Over the past few weeks our group has suffered the loss of two of our members. The first, Philip Lawrence, on a supply run to the city's edge, and now the second, Max Harrd, during our last battle with the humans.

"They were both good men, men of courage and honor, men that I was honored to call friends and men that will be sorely missed. At times like these the costs involved in belonging to this group may seem high, but it must be considered in the light of the costs to one's body and mind to belong to any other group in the World Outside.

"As many of you know, the humants are not known for striking with such precision in the same place twice. Yes, they often haunt the same swaths of territory in search of their victims, but even then they don't usually hunt in the same areas of that territory very often. What we have seen here indicates that the humants have discovered our hide-out and will no doubt return given enough time.

"I realize that this has been one of our best and most comfortable bases of operation. I also realize that we have remained at this base unmolested for the longest period of time of any base we have yet occupied. But, as much reluctance as I have in saying so, the time has come for us to abandon this base and move on to a new one."

I looked around the room to see the reactions of the others. All of them were indicating their understanding and agreement through nods and verbal indicators; most of them looked sad.

"I have heard that there is less humant and cannibal activity the farther north you go," Derik continued. "I realize that this means we will have to deal with weather that can be more bitter than what some of us are accustomed to, but I would rather deal with a little bad weather than what we have to deal with here.

"It is therefore my proposal that we move our base of operations to Duluth. It was a large city in what was formerly the state of Minnesota. It has access to one of the Great Lakes. I have heard that there is a sizable group of people there that defend against humant and cannibal attacks for the common good, very much like what we do. I would like to find this group and possibly become associated with them in some way. But, as it has always been with decisions of this magnitude, what say you?

"Those in favor say aye."

The room filled with the sound of the word 'Aye.' There was no need for an opposition vote.

"It is settled then. We begin our preparations tomorrow. But don't take too long getting ready. Remember, the humants know where we live now and will be back sooner rather than later."

By the next morning our hide-out was buzzing with activity. People were busy packing their personal belongings, along with the belongings of the group. Every so often members would disappear to the surface with a box and return empty-handed. I wondered where they were taking all of the stuff.

Unfortunately, I was not much help to them. I was restrained in what seemed like one big cast. And although my cast was actually a flexible body-sized splint simply moving in it made me very tired. I was relegated to the position of cheerleader, sitting on the sidelines and encouraging those that could work. Thankfully, no one seemed to mind.

As I sat watching the others my thoughts drifted to Max Harrd. I had seen him in my nightmares more times than I could number, lying on the floor. Everyone had a story to tell and I wondered what his was. After dinner that evening I found myself sharing the table with Bill and decided to ask him about it.

His brow furrowed slightly at my request and he groaned somewhat. After a few moments he began. 'Well, if anyone in our group really deserved to be in the World Outside, Max was that person."

I was shocked, although I shouldn't have been. The reality of statistics eventually impressed upon me the fact that a good number of those in the World Outside deserved to be there. But I did not have time to ponder this as Bill continued.

"Max was a soldier's soldier. He joined the military as soon as he was able and lived for the fight. It didn't take long for him to figure out that the regular army wasn't hard enough for him, no pun intended. He applied for and was accepted into the Special Forces.

"I heard a couple of the stories from his special ops days and the things they had those guys doing would curl the hair on the back of your neck. Anyway, Max loved it. He even got himself assigned to a special unit of the Special Forces. They went and did things that no one else would, or could, do. I guess it's safe to say that Max kind of liked killing. He took his job real serious. I will say that he was one of the most intense fighters I have ever seen and he fought until the bitter end.

"On the final mission that Max made as part of his unit I guess he killed a few more people than was necessary, quite a few more. Max discovered then that even the Special Forces have a tolerance threshold and he was court-martialed and expelled from the city.

"It was a devastating blow for Max to be thrown out of the Army, the only place that he had ever called or considered home. Obviously he had little trouble taking care of himself in the World Outside, he had seen much worse. But he was a lost soul. He met Derik during a trip to the city's edge. He noticed Derik's military uniform immediately and went to talk to him.

"Max once again had a home. He swore allegiance to Derik and this group and served with honor from that time on. He taught us a lot about moving with stealth, about modern weapons, and about small group close-quarter combat. He even taught us about camouflage. But still, he relished participating in death. As a fellow warrior, I am sad to see him go, but as a human being I am ambivalent."

He left me then confused, sitting and wondering what kind of person I was becoming. Would I be remembered with fondness or disdain or maybe even ambivalence?

The hours passed while our home grew more and more empty until the last few items lay strewn about, awaiting their evacuation. As these last items were removed to who-knows-where, I was instructed to lay on a stretcher and I, like the boxes I had seen over the previous day, was carried from the hide-out.

Once on the surface I was carried to an adjacent building. We entered the building through a small side door. As my eyes adjusted to the light within I could see the outline of an ancient semi-truck. Attached to the truck was a trailer that had once been used to haul livestock. Plates with small eyeholes had been welded onto the side of the trailer and the inside had been rearranged to allow for the hanging of hammocks. There was plenty of space left over for storage. In the corner of the building was a much smaller tanker truck.

I had never seen a vehicle that used a gasoline powered internal-combustion engine before. I had heard enough from the others by then to know that in order to fill an entire tanker truck with gasoline – diesel gasoline no less – would have taken months. To use such a precious commodity as that fuel indicated that our trip was indeed important to our group.

Derik climbed into the cab of the semi-truck and Bill climbed into the smaller one. I was carried onto the trailer as both engines were started.

Chapter 8

"What lies within is not necessarily what lies without."
Unknown

It was a particularly painful journey for me. I had not yet had sufficient time to heal from my injuries and I could often be found gritting my teeth, gripping my hammock bar, or praying in order to deal with the pain. I never realized until then just how nice skimming along on a layer of air could be. It certainly was more comfortable than bumping along the ground on old rubber tires filled with air.

Ashleigh eased my pain somewhat, wiping the sweat from my forehead, stroking my hair and rubbing my head during the excruciating headaches, and giving me something other than my discomfort to think about. When occasion permitted we took the opportunity to come to know each other a little better. Of all the souls I ever met in the World Outside, she was one of the few that truly did not belong there.

The World Outside does not care what souls it receives, it is merciless to them all. Our trip was long, bumpy, and cold, but uneventful. We passed multitudes of small cities on our way. They all told the same story, all filled with destruction.

The sheer magnitude of the devastation that we witnesses took its toll on Ashleigh. She had not had the opportunity to see its terrible spectacle since she had awoken from her pod ride in the group's hide-out and even her NeMEx had been cut short. It is impossible to describe just what the World Outside looks like to someone who has never seen it for themselves. It was easy to believe that there was no place the wars had not touched.

Strewn amid the ruins we passed were the skeletons of thousands long dead. And among them roamed those damned to live among them. More than once Ashleigh had to turn away in order to weep quietly. I did not want her to lose the innocence both Derik and I could sense within her and so I would simply hold her close when she would let me. No words could soothe the awful things that we saw on our trek.

Before that trip I believed I had become fairly hardened to the visions and experiences within the World Outside. I was wrong. I had almost as much trouble with the things we saw as Ashleigh did, but I dared not let on to her.

As we moved further north, we saw fewer and fewer people as we had suspected we would. Evidently ease of survival, at least as far as weather was concerned, kept people in the south.

It took many days to get there. We traveled on old highways where feasible, but often found ourselves traveling in the wilderness. These times were especially painful for me as they were the bumpiest. I lost count of the number of times we had to remove debris from the roadway or make a path through the overgrown vegetation before we could continue.

From time to time we found ourselves at the edge of large craters, left-overs of the wars. Thankfully, only one could be classified as truly mammoth. These would require backtracking and finding a new way. Many times our backtracking took only a few minutes, but the gargantuan pit required an entire day. Progress was dishearteningly slow.

As Minneapolis grew near, we made a large detour around it. Numerous groups, of all manner of people, would camp around the cities, sometimes miles out. And since many of these groups were dangerous, we were forced to make wide swings in order to avoid them.

Our detour took us many days out of the way. But avoiding those groups was one thing we could all agree on. It is shocking the level of ignorance that I had while I lived within the city. I never would have suspected just how many dangers lurked just beyond the city's edge. Until I was sentenced to go there, the World Outside was not a topic of thought or concern.

At long last we could see Duluth in the distance. It was not a large city, even in its day, but we could still see the high-rise buildings of downtown and the huge warehouses along its lakeshore rising over the horizon.

I was excited to see the place where the people Derik spoke of lived. I must admit that as we approached it was somewhat anticlimactic. It looked no different than all of the other places I had been able to see. It, like all of the others, was burned-up and badly damaged. I could only hope that our trip had not been in vain.

We entered the city and made our way through the streets heading towards the shoreline. We didn't really know where we should be going but as we continued we noticed a number of heads quickly emerging from windows and doors of buildings, watching our progress. It soon became apparent that there were far more people here than any of the other places I was aware of.

We continued driving until we had reached the center of the city and parked once we had located a lot of sufficient size. As we pulled into the lot the air hissed from the air tanks and we cautiously emerged from the vehicles.

Those with me helped me from my hammock and we met Derik at the trailer door.

Within a few minutes of our arrival a small group began to form around us. Each individual within the group carried a weapon. They considered us with suspicion as they spoke quietly amongst themselves. Against the instincts he had developed from years of exposure to the World Outside, Derik instructed us to stay calm and not take a defensive stance. The sounds of a dozen cocking weapons filled the air when Keith raised a hand to his face for a scratch.

Sensing the mounting tension, Derik stepped forward and with a loud voice announced, "My name is Derik Baxter. I am here with a group of people that have traveled from Bloomington, Illinois. We are neither cannibals nor humants and we come peacefully.

"We have come because we have heard that there is peace and order to be found here. If this is true, we would very much like to become a part of your community and we offer our talents in building and maintaining such a place. We wish to speak to your leader."

Murmuring among the assembled group increased noticeably after that. A few stress-filled minutes passed before a man stepped forward and said, "My name is Porthos Higbee and I am the leader of this group."

Derik approached him and offered his hand. Uncertain, Porthos gave Derik a long scrutinizing look before finally accepting it. At length they spoke with each other for a number of minutes, after which Derik returned to our group. "We are welcome here."

We spent the next week finding a suitable empty building for our needs and moved ourselves into it. We discovered early on that there were a large number of people living within the city. No one was quite sure why the people had begun to gather to Duluth as a refuge, but it didn't really matter. They had found what they were seeking once they had arrived.

There were still a large number of buildings that remained unoccupied and we chose one of the larger ones located downtown as our new base. It was built of stone, barely damaged, and it looked like it would serve our needs particularly well. Derik was very excited about his find and we all shared in his enthusiasm.

We stayed to ourselves mostly since we did not have the NeMEx to weed out bad recruits. Regardless, we came to know Porthos Higbee and many of the other residents. The group formed a loose association of people that fought together anytime the common good was in potential danger. Other than that there was little other interaction.

I was surprised that such a large group of like-minded individuals had found their way to this place and I was further surprised that, without a formal link, they had all decided to fight for the common good. Most of the people that we met were good people and we never asked any of them why they were in the World Outside. Whatever reason had brought them to Duluth, they were there to help themselves and the others have a different life. And yet, there was no close bond between any of the disparate groups that made Duluth their home.

After a couple of weeks Dr. Taylor called us all together for a meeting. She had a grave look on her face as she began to speak. "This community faces a serious threat to its existence. As some of you may know, after offering our services to the people we found here they were particularly interested in me once they learned I was a doctor. Well, there's a reason for that.

"Seems that this place has more than its fair share of medical issues. What place in the World Outside doesn't, right? Having such a large concentration of people in one area, without any organized method to feed them, has created a problem. Many of the residents are starving to death. This is a problem we don't usually see because the cannibals really prevent such large gatherings of people, but they don't generally come this far north.

"I don't know what to do. There simply is not enough edible plants, animals, or cities close enough to feed everyone here. Some of the residents fish with homemade poles out on the lake, but most of them don't know how. That alone is a big problem, however, there is a far more insidious problem: nearly everyone that I treated suffers from a severe bacterial infection.

"These people draw their drinking water directly out of the lake. I took a number of shoreline samples and they all tested positive for the bacteria. Heaven only knows what kinds of contaminants these lakes have been exposed to over time. None of the cities have had to deal with this problem since the water that they draw from the lake for drinking is filtered and treated before it enters their water systems."

I knew immediately what she was talking about. Part of my duties as a Hydrological Engineer was water treatment for drinking purposes. In fact, at one time I had been the weekend on-site supervisor for Treatment Plant #3, which drew water from Lake Michigan for Chicago. I knew some of the terrible things we took out of that water and some of the bad things that could happen from drinking contaminated water.

Scientists had discovered that applying a force field, using varying combinations of frequency and power, worked better than a physical filter ever could. Anything could be removed from the water. But all impurities that weren't burned by the force field were simply dumped back into the lake.

Dr. Taylor continued, "A disturbing number of the people I treated have since died. Many others will soon. Unless we find a fresh source of water for these people, they are all going to die. They will simply dwindle until there is no one left, including us."

We were all silent, but I had an idea.

My healing progress had quickened after finally getting

off of the bouncing truck and I was back on my feet within a week. I was stir-crazy by then and had spent the majority of my time exploring the city, especially the lakeshore. I felt most at home there since that was where I had chosen to spend my career.

As soon as Dr. Taylor had stated that a fresh source of water would have to be found, I remembered an old water treatment plant I had found during my explorations of the city. I had been particularly interested in that plant; it had been an opportunity to take a look into the past and see how things were done in the old days. Like the building we then used as our new home, the plant was in excellent condition, nearly untouched by the wars. I knew immediately that this plant could be the answer to the problems the city faced.

Excited, I stood to share my find. "I believe I may have a solution to the problem that Dr. Taylor shared. In my explorations of this city I came across a water treatment plant based on old technology. I have never shared this before but I was a Hydrological Engineer in my life before the World Outside. Among other things one of my jobs was to purify water and make it safe for drinking.

"I spent a considerable amount of time at the plant this last week, trying to figure out how it worked. I believe that with some planning and a healthy portion of elbow-grease, we can actually make it work again.

"Because there is no electricity we will have to rig a system in order to provide pressure through mechanical means, but I believe that we can do this. It will take a lot of work and I will need all the help you can spare in order to make it happen."

Immediately Derik stood, "You've got it Stephen, anything you need." Then, turning to the rest of the group he said, "Group, give Stephen whatever help he requires. This really needs to happen."

Despite the immediate support I got from our small group, selling the idea to Higbee's group turned out to be more difficult than one would have imagined. Their group was not unlike ours, finding their origins in the desire to escape the prevailing atmosphere of the World Outside. Migrating north to escape the humant and cannibal predators they had found their way to Duluth. The primary difference between us and them was that they were fanatically loyal to Porthos while we had a bit more democratic approach to things.

Despite his claim to be leader, no real formal leadership existed then in Duluth. Relations between the various individuals within our two groups was amiable and whenever major decisions needed to be made discussions between Derik and Porthos usually accomplished the desired objective. At times when Porthos felt things were not going as he believed they should, he would simply refuse Derik any support. Thankfully, Derik was a skilled diplomat and these times were few.

For reasons beyond me, Porthos was initially hesitant to go along with my proposal. He was almost superstitious of anything that had the appearance of having come from the city, and bringing an automated water plant back on line certainly qualified in his mind. I have no idea what Derik said to him but he eventually capitulated to the idea and I was given the green-light to continue.

Drawing up the plans for the plant took a little longer than I had anticipated. Two weeks had passed before I was even ready to begin any actual work. In the meantime, we found other people within the Duluth group that had industrial work experience and some old tools and equipment that would be necessary for the requisite changes.

It was a chilly October morning when work at last began and things steadily progressed. It took a long time for us to make the necessary changes since we were working with old outdated tools and spent almost as much time fixing them as we did actually working on the plant.

But finally the plans were implemented, and the day came that we opened the valves to let the water in; but, as with most everything else in life, it did not work as planned. I was forced to make modifications and since working complicated mathematical equations by hand is time-consuming, progress was painfully slow. Days dragged on into weeks.

It was a very frustrating period of time for me. I did not want to let the people of Duluth down, but I must confess that I was beginning to wonder if my plan was ever really going to work. Ashleigh cheered me on during these low points. When she assured me that I could do it I always tried to believe in her words. They usually gave me new vigor for my efforts.

She never forgot the sights she saw on our trip to Duluth and her way of coping with being in the World Outside was to lose herself in the service of others. I never met anyone who didn't like her. She inspired me to double my efforts.

It was during my time working on the plant that I met Alan Foster. Since I was a relatively insignificant technician while working in the city, I had never had to tackle problems on the scale that I found myself facing. I simply became overwhelmed from time to time and had to leave the city in order to clear my head.

Of course, it goes without saying that Ashleigh did not like it whenever I left the confines of the city. She was simply terrified of the things that she believed existed outside of it, real or imagined. Despite my assurances that I would be safe, she cried each time I left, making it increasingly difficult to find the clear head I went to seek.

But on one particular venture outside the city her lectures for my safety become particularly poignant. In all the time that we had been in Duluth, I had never encountered a single humant. For that matter, no one had and so I felt relatively safe during my excursions into the countryside surrounding the city. So, packing my bags, I departed one cold morning.

The cold that permeated the north on those fall days was biting and I often sought out any available old farm building in order to get out of the wind. Over time I found myself returning to one farm in particular for my periods of solitude and it was there that I headed.

As I approached the farm I caught a glimpse of someone quickly entering the front door of the large barn where I often went. Drawing my weapon I approached a barely visible side door that I had identified some visits before and began to search the building.

He was not at all hard to find. He was cowering behind a large crate with his back to my position. Advancing upon him quietly I ordered him to freeze. I told him to place his hands on the back of his neck, and lay upon the ground. He complied immediately and without resistance laid face down.

Keeping my aim upon him I ordered him to roll over. I knew the instant he did that he was a humant. His nose had been removed from his face and two large slits occupied the place it should have been. His eyes were completely black. Needless to say, I was stunned.

I demanded to know what he was doing there. But rather than answer me, he simply covered his face with his hands and began to weep loudly. Unsure what to do, I stood there for a few minutes as he regained his composure, eventually speaking to me.

"Look what he's done to me! How can I ever face another normal human being again? I have become a living, breathing nightmare!" He motioned to his face as he spoke. The emotions that filled his statements struck me forcefully. I found myself thinking of the humant victims described by Bill.

"General Kriton is an evil man. I cannot do what he demands of me. He demands horrible things. Just the thought of them makes me ill. I clearly had to leave, so the first chance I had I took it. I knocked out my leader and ran as far and as fast as I could. When I saw you I was frightened, so I tried to hide in here."

Unable to determine his true intentions, and surprised that a humant was actually displaying remorse for simply knocking someone out, I waited to see if he would continue.

"I came as far north as I could go. I heard that no one else really lives here, the conditions being so harsh and all. I wanted to get as far north as I could and then wait to die. I didn't figure on meeting anyone here. What are you going to do with me?"

With my gun sight dead center of his forehead I realized that I had not even begun to contemplate what I would do with him and was unable to answer right away. Humants still inspired the deepest dread within me then, but his eyes conveyed true fear and self-loathing. I found compassion welling up in my heart for the pathetic creature. Despite his appearance, I knew that he was as much a victim as I. How could I victimize him further?

Quickly I assessed my options. I could have simply let him continue on his way and finish what he intended to do, die. But I could not do that to another human being, even one that had been altered. He deserved a better life too, didn't he?

I found myself telling him about the city of Duluth and offering him refuge there. I couldn't believe what I was saying. But this had to be the true meaning of compassion, didn't it? Looking at me with a mixture of genuine surprise and gratitude he said, "Really? Even the way I look?"

I told him that there were people of every kind in Duluth and that I was certain he would be welcome. I hoped he believed the words; I wasn't sure I believed myself. Tentatively he stood then and introduced himself.

Needless to say my mind-clearing excursion was cut short as I returned to Duluth with Alan following close behind. He never stopped thanking me as we moved, but I hoped that the assurances I had given him would be true once we arrived.

I was filled with trepidation as we entered the city. What would Ashleigh say? Half-a-dozen times she had warned of just exactly what had happened. Would she be understanding or would she slap me in the face for finally realizing her fears?

I figured that introducing him to my group, a group that had once included a humant, was the wisest step. It was a rough start as their initial acceptance of him was based entirely upon their trust in me. They all figured that if I trusted him, so could they. Thankfully, Ashleigh had a similar reaction, just grateful I had returned safely.

Some of the other people that lived in Duluth were not at all happy about its new resident. Some would ridicule Alan mercilessly, some even threatened him, but most simply just avoided him. Thankfully, none of the threats were ever carried out. During those times in which he felt overwhelmed by the comments and threats, he would seek me out. I tried to make him feel better and feel like he still had a life worth living, but that is a tall order for a self-hating humant in the World Outside.

When my words sounded hollow to me I worried how they sounded to him. I knew little about him at the beginning and trying to convince a humant that his life was worth as much as any other's certainly had its challenges. Things became easier as we came to know one another.

As time passed, Alan proved to be a hard worker. I learned that he too had been an engineer in his previous life and so I was able to use him on the water treatment project. There was initial skepticism on the part of some of those laboring with us, but over time Alan became as much a part of our community as anyone else. He stopped being a humant in my eyes and became another member of the team.

We discovered that he had an ultra-sensitive sense of smell. He could tell simply by smell if a given sample of water was fresh. His presence alone increased the pace of the work on the plant manifold.

Work continued as changes were made. We moved from plan A to B to C and on through the alphabet. But as the months passed from October into November and on into December, I began to wonder if any of my plans were ever going to work. Somewhere into plan Q the valve was opened, water flowed through the system, and fresh water at last emerged out the other end.

A large group of people had assembled each time a plan was tried, only to be sent home with spirits low. This time was different, a cheer went up and then everyone present had a glass of the freshest water that they had had since arriving in the World Outside. The effects of the clean water on the health of the city's residents were soon evident. I became something of a celebrity within the town.

Our water problem had finally been solved, but without a supply of food that could sustain the ever-growing population of the city, fresh water would quickly become meaningless.

Chapter 9

"True greatness is never achieved,
it is only found by those not looking for it."
Unknown

Much of the focus of the city's residents had been on the water. Without drinkable water, too many lay sick and dying. Only after the water had flowed was any serious attempt made to address the food issue and since I had handled the water problem successfully I was 'volunteered' by the city leaders to deal with the next. I spent a week ensuring that the water plant worked as it was designed to before turning it over to a manager that I had selected.

Solving the water problem had been one thing, after all, I had worked as a Hydrological Engineer, but I didn't even know where to begin to solve the food problem. Pondering all of the potential solutions I could possibly think of, I asked Derik to assign me a group to scout the area around Duluth. I wanted to locate any available farmable land while I formulated other possible ideas. The group he gave me was small; it consisted only of myself, Bill, and Miguel. We were all eager to solve this problem and departed right away.

Other than the few times I had left the city while working on the water plant, I had not left for any significant period of time, but I knew that this trip was going to be considerably longer, possibly even months. This responsibility was far greater than anything I had been asked to undertake before then.

It was difficult for Ashleigh and me. We both understood the dangers inherent to trips beyond the relative safety of the city. Each time I had left in the past she was always there to greet me upon my return. But she was far more worried about this trip.

On the day we were to leave she came, tears streaming down her cheeks, as we packed our final equipment. I began to speak but was silenced by a light finger on my lips. She spoke softly without looking at me.

"Do you remember when I shared my family's tradition of giving a lock of hair for good luck?"

I said "Yes."

"Do you also remember when I told you the only man that would ever hold one within his hands was the man to whom I had wholly given my heart but that I could only hope and pray that I could find such a man?"

Again, I said "Yes."

Then, looking up at me, she grabbed me by the neck and pulled me to her, kissing me with a desperation that she might never see me again. While we kissed she pressed something into my hand. Then, turning quickly, she rushed into the building without looking back.

I didn't need to look to know what she had given me and a lump filled my throat as I opened my fingers to see the small lock laying in my palm. Leaving then was a sober affair as we wordlessly left town.

We were not entirely sure what it was we were looking for as we left Duluth, since none of us had ever even had a garden before, but hoped we would know when we found it. We spent days scouting the surrounding land and did find a small bit of suitably clear farmland, and even some farm equipment that we thought could be restored back to operating condition. But overall we found ourselves ever more frustrated over the precious little that we were finding.

Even the little land that we found would be unusable until the next spring, which was some four to five months away. We needed a quicker solution.

The air that we worked in and surrounded us was cold. Only after entering the World Outside had I had the opportunity to see my breath for the first time and it had fascinated me at first. As we walked I watched my breath billow out in large clouds and dissipate slowly as it escaped my lungs. Before that day I had only seen snow once, in the zoo in the cages of the cold weather animals, but I had never touched it. So when a flake fell lazily towards the ground in front of my eyes I was more than a little excited.

The moment I noticed it was snowing I stopped abruptly and shouted to Bill and Miguel excitedly about my new discovery. Their reaction was less than ecstatic. Looking upwards to see the snow begin to fall they agreed that shelter would have to be found. Looking towards the horizon we spied a medium-sized old barn. Motioning for me to hurry, we moved towards the structure.

I watched them move out with some confusion, but quickly followed. It did not take me long to understand their concern. Snow soon began to fall with greater and greater speed. It began to collect upon the ground and the flakes stung my face as they struck me.

Soon the snow began to blow about us, dancing through the air. It grew dark as the snow continued to increase and the blowing snow made it difficult to see more than a few yards into the distance. We would not be able to see the barn much longer.

The wind roared about me, piercing my clothing. I hastened my steps, realizing the life-threatening situation that was quickly developing. It became so miserable so fast that the barn, it seemed, was moving away from us. At long last we arrived and, going inside, pulled the barn doors closed behind us.

The wind whistled as it blew into the barn through the numerous small holes in its walls. Although the barn provided us shelter from the snow and stopped the majority of the wind, it was still extremely cold as we pitched our tent within. We huddled into our sleeping bags, teeth chattering.

I could not believe how cold it got! We discussed the possibility of building a fire but thought better of it within the old wooden structure. We only left our bags to relieve ourselves. For the next two days the snow fell and the wind blew and all we could do was wait for it to stop.

We didn't talk much the first night, we were all too exhausted from our day's journey. I thought about Ashleigh as I tried to stay warm. I hoped she wasn't worried about me. It turned out that the same blizzard that fell on us that night also covered Duluth. Without power, the water purification plant had to be turned off to prevent it from being damaged by the freezing temperatures. We weren't the only ones that struggled through the storm to stay warm.

With the swelled numbers that had made their way to Duluth, few were prepared for the bitter cold that kept the undesirable elements farther south. Ashleigh kept herself busy helping as best she could. But as the weather began to take its toll, and she could see the results, her heart filled with great concern for the welfare of me and my companions. Nonetheless, she worked throughout the night comforting as many as she could, getting frostbite as she did.

It took Dr. Taylor some real effort and time to help her recover from the cold damage she suffered that night. But the people of Duluth were grateful for her efforts and even gave her a nickname that she came to be known as from then on: Snow Angel.

People deal with being in the World Outside in various ways. Too many allow it to steal their humanity only to become what they feared most before coming to the World Outside themselves. Ashleigh covered her fears about the World Outside by helping others find their own oasis. By giving others the hope that a life can still be lived, even in the World Outside, she was able to believe herself. She is still the Snow Angel to the many people she has helped over the years.

Back in the small barn where we had taken refuge, Miguel talked quietly to me about her. It was obvious to everyone in the group that I had more than a passing interest in her. He wondered why I hadn't made our relationship more serious. Pondering his words I guess I had let the cares of trying to make Duluth as successful as I possibly could impede on my time with Ashleigh. I decided that night that I needed to do more once I returned from our expedition.

We all fell asleep together that night without posting a guard. Without a word we all knew that for anyone to have found us in the middle of the blizzard would have been a miracle.

The next day we stayed within our little tent. Luckily we had sufficient provisions for our needs. About mid-morning we checked our situation, had a small meal and began to talk. We had little else to do and since neither Miguel nor myself had heard the other's story, I started by sharing mine. Bill just quietly listened to both.

When I finished Miguel shared his important story. His experiences would be important later.

"A long time ago I worked for a company named Evertech as Chief of Security. I had spent some time in the military and with various police departments. I never made it very far up the chain-of-command in any of the places where I worked. I guess you could say that if I saw a problem, I wasn't afraid to voice it. I wasn't real popular among the head honchos. I've never been real clear on why Evertech gave me the job, but since working with the police and the military had worn me down I decided that I would probably live longer, and be paid better, if I transferred to the private sector.

"I spent nearly ten years working there, constantly refining their security policies. When I took over security the place was a shambles, by the time that the new CEO arrived I had things pretty much the way I wanted them. The new CEO was rough around the edges and took an immediate dislike to me.

"Whatever other problems she may have had, she did bring new business to Evertech. She was one of the first executives to get her hands on alien technology – obviously an item of extreme security. I found out about the alien device from the security memo she sent to me. Not a memo to initiate a security plan; no, rather a memo telling me how security was going to be handled on the project.

"I'm being kind when I say that her plans were atrocious and would almost certainly have led to a breach of some kind. It was all I could do not to blow-up at her during the meeting where she poorly feigned interest in what I was saying. I left that meeting in a huff and went home to cool off.

"The day following the meeting I received notice that I was being transferred to another division within the company. No explanations were given but I knew right away why it was happening. I sat in my office the rest of that day fuming and pondering. By day's end I knew what I was going to have to do. I requested vacation in order to plan. I had no intention of accepting the transfer.

"I wasn't thinking clearly then, I was pretty angry. In hindsight I really don't know why I believed that my plan would result in any way other than it did. All I cared about was proving that I was right so I planned to break into Evertech's facilities and steal the alien technology. After that I was going to return it in order to make my point.

"By week's end I had completed my planning and was ready to make my move. I have to admit that it was not the cakewalk my planning had indicated it would be. In the short week I had been away the new CEO, and her new hand-picked Chief of Security, had implemented a number of new policies and procedures. Regardless, this didn't stop me, all it did was slow me down.

"I won't bore you with the details of what I did, let's just say it consisted of a lot of hacking together with some old fashioned lock picking and small explosive devices. Once I had reached Evertech's main vault I grabbed the alien device and made a quick getaway.

"The following morning I brazenly walked into the CEO's office, placing the item upon her desk arrogantly. Unmoved she looked from the device to me."

"Mr. Sanchez is there something I can do for you?"

"A bit stunned by her nonchalance I said, 'I just wanted you to know you were wrong about re-assigning me. I wanted you to see how easy it was to break into Evertech to steal the alien device under your security plan. I hope now that you will take appropriate measures.'

"She responded with obvious disdain, 'You underestimate me Mr. Sanchez. I never fail at anything I set out to do. You were the pawn in my plan that allowed me to find the flaws in the system. And you played your part so well. But now that your usefulness is at an end I terminate pathetic little employees like you all the time. You're not as good as you think you are. You only got away with this because I let you.'

"She had me then; I didn't know how to respond. My self-assurance had gotten the better of me and I had grown careless. While I watched and guarded Evertech's interests I had not done the same for myself. I was so stunned that I didn't notice when she reached down to press the security button under her desk."

"'Who do you think runs this company Mr. Sanchez, me or you? It simply would not do for me to allow you to dictate policy to me. I learned a long time ago not to leave loose ends untied.' Reaching into a desk drawer she pulled out a small pistol. 'You see Mr. Sanchez, the only way for me to be absolutely certain that you will never have the opportunity to be a thorn in my side again is to have you thrown into the World Outside, and I can't think of a better reason then theft of government property.'

"I knew then that I was in serious trouble so before she could get a fix on me I bolted to the side and then over her desk, knocking her to the floor. Her gun skidded away from her as I grabbed the alien device and exited through an air duct.

"As Chief of Security I spent hours poring over the air ducting plans of Evertech's building, looking for weaknesses. I knew where the remaining ones were, at least I hoped I still did. Thankfully, the one I wanted to use to escape had not yet been fixed so I made a quick exit and hurried away.

"The police cameras made movement difficult. Although I could disable them for short periods I knew that it would be just a matter of time before they would catch up to me. Days and hours began to blur together and I became exhausted. It was a game I was destined to lose so I took the device to a place where I knew it would never be found and went home to take a nap. I don't know how long it took them but eventually the police arrived to break down my door. They cuffed me and hauled me away."

As I listened to him I realized that I had never considered the possibility that the police cameras could be disabled. And if they could be disabled surely they could be tampered with in other ways. Clay had once told me that police recordings could even be forged. How could a so-called perfect system of justice have so many imperfections?

Miguel continued. "By most standards I was quite wealthy, however, there are some crimes whose fines are not meant to be payable. This was one of them. The politics behind stealing government property, especially alien technology, was stacked against me.

"They tried their hardest to find out where I'd hidden the alien technology. They sent their best to beat it our of me. There was a few times I almost broke. But in the end, I was condemned to the World Outside. Honestly, I'm surprised they didn't kill me. Like you, Derik and his group were the first to find me upon my arrival in the World Outside.

"I have spent the years since wondering what it was that I took from Evertech. Would it have made a difference for mankind or was it the equivalent of an alien rivet? I guess it doesn't really matter since I will never see it again. But if I ever do get back into the city, I sure would like to find out what it does."

We were all unusually quiet for the rest of the day as we listened to the howling wind. I pondered Miguel's words. The more I learned about the system, the more I knew how badly broken it was. Could a person find a way back into the city? And, if so, why would they want to?

Finally, the wind died down and we could see streams of sunlight pouring through the numerous holes in the walls. My first experience with snow turned out to be a blizzard and it was an experience that I would not soon forget.

We struggled against the snow that had piled up on the barn door with no success. Looking for other exits we climbed into the hayloft and found a pair of doors unblocked by the snow. Opening them we could see that the snow had blown against the front doors into a heap a few feet high. Looking at us with a grin, Bill leaped from the opening and landed waist-deep in the bank. Unhurt he moved slowly to the side and motioned us to follow.

Looking at each other and shrugging our shoulders, Miguel and I both jumped at the same time, landing a few feet apart. Although the weather outside had warmed slightly, I was quickly reminded that it was quite a bit colder outside of the barn. Removing the snow from the barn's front doors we retrieved our items and were on our way.

We spent more than a month scouting, mapping as we went. There was precious little ground not covered by snow. It was difficult to identify potential farm ground, but it was even more difficult trying to stay warm while watching for trouble. Every night as I laid in my bag trying to keep warm I understood why the groups of cannibals and humants just didn't go there. Without a plan for survival, it was unlikely to happen.

With our supplies running low and exhaustion slowing our every move, we considered abandoning our mission when we entered the burned-out town of Two Harbors in what was once Minnesota. As we made a brief sweep of the city I spotted it off in the distance. There, moored to a small pier, was a fishing boat. Excitedly I called to my companions and we all raced to the pier.

It had obviously been well-used in its day and it was nothing to look at. Nevertheless, I raced up the plank and onto the deck. Raising our weapons and proceeding with caution we made a thorough sweep of the vessel. Making my way to the engine room I found an engine that was in surprisingly good condition. Examining it closely I believed it could be started with just a little prep work. Leaving the others to nurse it if necessary, I proceeded to the wheelhouse in order to give it a try.

Amazingly I found a key inserted in the ignition. Flipping a few switched I was my amazement grew that the batteries still had a hint of power. Grasping the key between my fingers, I held my breath as I turned it. The engine protested on the first few tries but thick black smoke spewed from the exhaust on the fifth and I was rewarded with a deep rumble as it came to life for the first time in who knew how long.

I was joined quickly by Bill and Miguel. We were all as giddy as children over our new find. We agreed that we should try to get it back to Duluth. Luckily the water was not yet frozen by the pier so Miguel went to cast us off as I pulled back on the throttles. I couldn't help grabbing Bill in a hug as the boat glided backwards smoothly through the water. Turning the wheel I advanced the throttles and we begin moving slowly forward.

We proceeded south-west, following the coast closely, moving towards Duluth. We didn't dare lose sight of the shore; we didn't want to get lost in the middle of the lake. I kept a close eye on the engine gauges as we progressed and was pleased that it continued operating without incident. Less than an hour after our departure we could see Duluth in the distance. We were eager to share our find with those we had left behind. But I was more than eager to see Ashleigh after such a long time away.

No one expected us to return via the lake so it was not surprising that only a single shore guard was there to greet us. Bill offered to stay with the boat while Miguel and I went to tell the others. I couldn't contain my excitement any longer as I jumped over the side and onto the pier. Both of us literally ran back to our base, arriving breathlessly. I searched in vain to find Ashleigh.

I doubt we made a whole lot of sense to our little team at first as we struggled to speak while trying to catch our breath. But eventually the words 'fishing' and 'boat' emerged through the heavy breathing and the implications of what we were saying began to sink in. Enthusiastically the entire group went to see the boat floating next to the pier.

After taking a quick tour of the craft Derik put his hands on each of my shoulders, looked directly into my eyes, and said, "You did a good job, Stephen. Good job all of you. There are no words which can adequately express our gratitude. You have saved the lives of everyone here." There are precious few times in my life that I felt better than I did at that moment.

After the initial excitement had finally died away I found Ashleigh doing what she does best, helping other people. When she at last spied me among the people surrounding her, we ran to each other. There are few times in life more rewarding than returning to your loved-ones after a time away from which a return is uncertain. We were inseparable for the next few days. But I knew that the boat needed to be repaired and made ready for service.

Pooling the talents of the group and what resources we had, we spent the next few days repairing the fishing nets and practicing our seamanship. I had always been interested in boats, both with and without engines, and had even spent a weekend or two sailing on the small lakes within the city. I had studied the theory behind long-distance navigation at sea, but I had never been beyond sight of the shore.

When Derik had learned that I had been an amateur sailor he made me the skipper of our new ship. Its name had been worn away by time and so we decided that she needed a new one. When I suggested what it should be we all knew we had a name: Hope.

Before we spent any serious effort trying to refit the craft for service again we caught and tested some of the fish in the waters just off Duluth. We wanted to ensure that they were free enough of bacteria or other harmful contaminants to be edible. We all waited for the test results with the same fervor found at sporting events. Some of us even cheered when they were pronounced clean. So the refit proceeded.

I spent many a sleepless night trying to recall the things I had read about sailing, writing them down as they came to mind. I knew that if I got it wrong I might never see land again. I wrote down as much as I could remember. I tried to impress upon anyone who would listen how potentially dangerous and life-threatening the first voyage could be. Regardless, Keith and Clay volunteered to join me as my crew. I was touched and terrified all at once.

But for a moment of confusion in which I became convinced that we were lost at sea, the first voyage went as planned. The nets worked as they should have and we brought back a boat full of fish. At last the Duluth group had water *and* food. With the exception of small plants and rodents here and there, my meals had consisted of things that had been discarded by others. For the first time possibly anywhere within the World Outside, a group of people had the means to eat food and drink water that was completely fresh.

I suppose I got credit for the food source since I had led the expedition that had found the boat, but I never felt that I merited the attention I got because of it. If I had felt like a celebrity before with the water plant, I only felt more so then. I didn't give it much thought though, I was too happy with the progress that was being made.

The news of our city began to spread slowly then. Our numbers grew as people from far and wide began to make their way to us. It seemed that many people were seeking the kind of life that we had found in Duluth.

As they came they all spoke of the fresh water and the ship that fed thousands. They also came with a name on their lips: Stephen Blake. I have never understood why I got credit for the things that took place there in the beginning, but they all seemed to want to meet me.

As the arrivals continued, it became apparent that some organization would be required. Rules had to be made and a leader would have to be chosen. Without the infrastructure required to take an accurate vote of so many, the relatively few original residents of Duluth decided that Derik should continue to serve as he had unofficially done for so long. This, as agreed, would continue until such time that the infrastructure did exist.

Some vocally called for me to be the leader, but I felt unqualified to assume such a position. I could not take credit for those things for which I was given so much. Only with the help of numerous individuals had the water plant been a success and my involvement in the discovery of 'Hope' had been a complete coincidence. At times the attention made me uncomfortable, so I tried to be helpful as much as possible while staying behind the scenes.

Some vocally called for Porthos Higbee to be the leader. We all understood the loyalty that they felt to the man which had helped to provide a refuge from the World Outside; the first man to come to Duluth. Many felt it unfair that the original leader of Duluth should be deposed by an outsider. Tension grew between the factions and concern that our tenuous haven would prove temporary frightened some.

Although I suspect that Porthos felt the same as his followers initially, I believe that in the end he decided that the survival of the infant city was more important than his desire to be leader. The World Outside simply had to have a place to escape to. Extending a hand in solidarity and friendship, Porthos was given an active and visible role in planning and building the city.

February arrived with a fresh coating of snow. Things in Duluth were progressing nicely. Aside from the occasional disagreement, to be found in any large group of people, things were peaceful. The people had as much fresh water as they could drink, full bellies, and were happy. Ashleigh and I spent as much time as we could together and came to be known as a couple. It was a good period of time, a time it was possible to almost forget where we actually lived.

One morning a young man I had never before met was brought to me. Keith introduced him and told me that he had something very important to share with me. I asked him what he had that was so important. When he began I had no idea just how radically the path he would set me on would change my perception of the world.

"My name is James Dylon. I was stationed at the military base in Grand Forks, North Dakota before it was destroyed by an alien attack. I worked for the National Security Agency for a Colonel Bock. I never knew his first name. Anyway, I know that they kept some sort of alien weapon there. They were testing it when everything was stopped short by the attack.

"They tried to evacuate but few escaped. After that, the military leaders abandoned the entire base and everyone that had survived the attack. We became part of the World Outside because no one cared enough to send out a rescue party to search for survivors. I've survived now for quite a few years but I have never heard of a place like this before now. I've come to swear my allegiance to the man who has built this place and become part of your group if you'll have me. Any man that can find order and even some happiness in the midst of this hell, deserves my loyalty."

Three things hit me then as I realized that he was referring to me. One, I found myself shocked that an entire base was simply abandoned along with the soldiers and airman serving there; two, for the first time in my life, another person was actually swearing their allegiance to me; and third, there was possibly an alien weapon in a place not too distant. I didn't know which one to respond to first.

Thanking Mr. Dylon, I told him that membership in the group was had for the asking by those who managed to get there and were willing to contribute to the common good. Further, I asked him if he could and would lead me to the base in Grand Forks. Without hesitation he indicated that he would be pleased to accompany me to the base and then thanked me. He was taken away and given food, water, and a place to stay. I knew then that if I could get my hands on the weapon that might be there, things could be very different. Laying out a map on a nearby table I began to plan, I had no time to waste.

Chapter 10

"...Ignorance is bliss..."
Thomas Gray

Planning the trip to Grand Forks was progressing smoothly. Derik and the rest of the group were eager to determine what actually waited, if anything, to be found at the military base. However, since all available fuel was being used to power the fishing vessel and since walking would take an inordinate amount of time, another method of transportation would have to be used: horses.

I was less then ecstatic at the mention of horses. My deficient experience with them consisted of visits to petting zoos and riding stables. At each place I had been convinced to take brief rides, but each had ended with soreness in inconvenient places. My back hurt just from the mere suggestion that I ride for multiple days. Right away I protested that I knew nothing about riding and that in the time it would take to train me I could walk there and back.

Horses were a new aspect of our time in Duluth, prior to then we walked everywhere we went with few exceptions. Derik, who to my surprise had gotten a horse of his very own, had spent considerable time familiarizing himself with the skills necessary to ride safely and effectively. I had even encouraged others to utilize them in order to conserve fuel but had no intention of ever actually using one myself. I was confident there would never be a real need for me to ride one.

When I shared my concerns with Derik, he laughed a bit. But when he realized I was serious, he would hear none of it. I would simply have to learn along the way. It seemed that Keith had had some applicable experience and was to be my instructor. My relationship with him had not improved much since arriving in Duluth, instead it had only given us the opportunity to avoid each other with greater ease. I needn't tell you how *happy* we both were at the prospect of working so closely together for the length of time it would take to get there and back.

Derik also assigned Miguel and James Dylan to accompany us. Miguel would have to extricate the alien weapon from the vault and Mr. Dylan was there to lead the way. Derik did his best to spare Keith from mission service, he knew the toll it took on him, but since he was the closest thing we had to a horseman, there was little choice since I was not the only one not familiar with them. As with all other missions, Keith became ill at the mere prospect of going on a mission and prepared with something less than enthusiasm.

Once again, I found myself being separated from Ashleigh. My service to the group and to Duluth came with a price. I had returned her lock of hair after returning from my last extended expedition. I knew what she was giving me as she pressed it into my hands. Closing her hands around mine, she looked deeply into my eyes and said, "Come back to me." Then, without looking back, she turned and ran back into the gates of the city. Rubbing her hair softly between my fingers I watched her until she disappeared into the streets of the city. I mounted my horse then and turned towards the West.

Riding the horses was even more uncomfortable than I had feared. Straight away my back began to ache. Try as I might there didn't seem to be any position in which I was comfortable. It became a matter of pain management.

Although Keith seemed to actually enjoy watching me suffer, he did offer me advice on appropriate ways to ride and control my animal. Perhaps I did not understand what I was told, or maybe I'm just not cut out for horseback travel, but it was only slightly more tolerable after that. I sought opportunities to talk to the others. This, I found, was the best method to keep my mind off of the pain. Of course, after a while, my backside was just numb.

Of all the people I had come to know outside of Ashleigh, Keith seemed the most out-of-place in the World Outside. From the terror during my first battle to his continued abhorrence of violence, I wondered how such a person came to be there. I knew how hard he struggled at times to do what was asked of him and yet he never once shirked. Whatever our differences were, he had proven difficult for me to know. I decided to approach him on one particularly long, painful ride.

"What was it like to float at sea for days, unable to see land on any side? Even though I worked with water in my former life, I'm not much of a swimmer and am somewhat scared of water. I cannot imagine what you must have been thinking when you found yourself there."

Not expecting me to try a conversation with him, he looked at me with surprise, surprise that I was speaking to him. But turning to look ahead as we rode, he responded thoughtfully after a bit.

"I expected to die when I hit the ocean that day, maybe even wanted to just a little. All I wanted was to escape that hell, so I had given no thought to removing my life-jacket before jumping. So, instead of sinking, I found myself floating. I guess that the shark repellant the navy has installed into all its life-jackets must have worked since I never saw one. However, escaping the ship gave me a renewed desire to live. But all I could do was float on the waves and watch and pray for a ship to pass by.

"The next few days afforded me the opportunity to ponder all of life's big questions and to wonder what kind of life I had led. I was cold, tired, and hungry. More than once I made the decision to release the latches on my jacket and sink into a watery grave, but something always stopped me. When I saw the ship that rescued me I knew that fate had given me another chance.

"When I was sentenced to the World Outside for desertion I learned that there are fates, and places, worse than death. The horrors on that ship I escaped have paled in comparison to some of the awful things I have seen here. No person should have to live in this terrible place.

"Had it not been for Derik and his group I am quite certain I would be dead, or worse, a humant. In him I found a man worthy to follow. I do not have the abilities that so many of the others have so my contributions are limited but I do the best I can.

"I'll admit that when I met you I did not like you one bit. You showed up one night and by the very next day had earned a Savior's Beret. You and I seemed a lot alike, no heart for contention or violence, so when you stepped right up and shot that humant, I guess I became jealous of you. Jealous of what I hadn't had the courage to do myself. I can't honestly say that I would have been able to do the same. I like to think I would have but we'll probably never know.

"I've watched you since then and since we moved to Duluth. You have the courage of a warrior but your heart is filled with mercy and compassion. It has been a struggle to watch you accomplish so much. But what you have accomplished, I didn't think was possible. Despite Derik and his group I was pretty certain it would be a terrible struggle to just exist until the day I died. But you have built a city out of rubble and created hope out of despair. Maybe I can be a part of creating a better place for people to live, a place that is in, but not part of, the World Outside. Believe it or not, you have inspired me to believe in this better world, Stephen, and I will follow you towards that goal wherever it may lead."

When he finished he gave me an intense look so I would know he meant what he had said. Then he encouraged his horse to move a bit faster and moved away from me. I was speechless. At last I could feel the ice that had existed between us melting. I was very pleased that others were getting the vision that I had and I sincerely hoped that Keith would find the purpose that he sought.

After many days we arrived at the front gate of the base. It, like all of the cities that we had been through, had been ravaged by destruction. Following James' lead we made our way towards a large building that was mostly undamaged. It was built of strong materials and the sign on it announced it as the Headquarters of the Missile Wing. We rode up to the building, dismounted, and entered the front door which leaned against the entrance by a single hinge, leaving Keith to look after the horses.

Progress was slow, hindered by the volume of debris within. We located the nearest stairs and began our descent into the darkness. Leading the way by lantern, Mr. Dylan brought us to a large, thick, metal door. It was not locked but had rusted into place. Together we managed to pry it open and entered the room beyond. Light flooded into the area illuminating what had remained in darkness for many long years.

Looking about I could see the usual office accoutrements: desk, filing cabinets, computer, and telephone. Immediately apparent in the midst of these surroundings was the skeleton that occupied the chair behind the desk. Most of the skeleton was held together by a military uniform, its head rested on the collar of the jacket that it wore and the headrest of the chair.

Approaching apprehensively I looked closer and noticed a large hole in the right temple of the skull. Its right arm hung over the arm of the chair and dangled close to the floor. There, lying where it had fallen, was a pistol. It was evident what had taken place. I leaned closer in order to see the nametag, which read: BOCK. Multiple ribbons decorated its chest and there were eagles on each shoulder. Despite working for him, James had only met the Colonel once and knew next to nothing about him. Whoever he had been, he was high ranking and highly decorated.

A large vault door occupied nearly one whole wall of the room and I knew we had reached our destination. Miguel set to work immediately working on the locking mechanisms. We all hoped we would find the alien artifact for which we had traveled so far. I knew a door of such magnitude would take some time to open and since Mr. Dylan assisted Miguel, I was left with my thoughts and the skeleton for company. Miguel had informed me that we would probably be there for many hours and so I sat as far across the room as possible from the skeleton and stared.

Eventually my eyes wandered from the skeleton and onto the walls of the room. There were college degrees, award letters, and calendars. Prominently displayed in the midst of them all was one large poster. It had a faded picture of a dying tree on it, covered with lines of script. Curious, I stood to get a closer look. The title on its top read: "The Tree of Liberty." I read on:

"God forbid we should ever be twenty years without…a rebellion. The people cannot be all, and always, well informed. The part which is wrong will be discontented in proportion to the importance of the facts they misconceive. If they remain quiet under such misconceptions, it is a lethargy, the forerunner of death to the public liberty…And what country can preserve its liberties, if their rulers are not warned from time to time, that their people preserve the spirit of resistance? Let them take arms… The tree of liberty must be refreshed from

time to time with the blood of patriots and tyrants."
–Thomas Jefferson

At first, I didn't remember ever hearing of a person named Thomas Jefferson, but then I recalled he'd had something to do with the old Constitution of the United States, before the Commonwealth had been formed. We had briefly covered that portion of history in class at school. I had never read words such as those. Reading them again I carefully removed the poster from the wall and rolled it tightly. The words rang loudly in my head as I nestled my find tightly under my arm. I would come to memorize that quote. It was then that I noticed all the papers strewn about the Colonel's desk.

Most of the papers were insignificant, but before his final act the Colonel had taken the effort to make a small pile of a few. Some of the items were articles removed from their respective newspapers, some were memos, and a few had handwritten notes on them. Starting at the top, I began to read each one.

*   *   *

At last Stephen reached down for the pile of papers he had placed beside his seat at the beginning of our interview.

"I made copies of all the things that I read that day. I must keep the originals at all cost. They opened my eyes to the *real* world. Never again would I live in blindness."

He hesitated before offering them to me.

"Paithar, I must warn you. What these papers reveal, were never meant for our eyes and I can assure you that great measures have, and will be, taken to keep them a secret. Viewing them is a one-way road. If you do not wish to see them, I will continue the interview without them. But you must decide for yourself."

*   *   *

His was not the first warning I had ever been given by an interviewee, but it carried a certain poignancy that I had hitherto not seen. Never had I wanted to know more than I wanted to know then. Instinctively, I knew that I was indeed stepping onto a strange new road. I wondered if it was truly one-way but I just had to know for myself. Taking the first offered paper I read eagerly.

"You might recognize this one Paithar."

I did indeed.

Earth Attacked by Enemy from Space!
By Paithar Ranston

Yesterday morning at exactly 6:06 a.m., EST, the world learned that we are not alone in the Universe. Explosions ripped through nearly every major city in the world causing immeasurable damage. Thousands of cities were targeted and destruction was wide spread as major highways, airports, and other important infrastructural items were attacked. Known casualties now exceed a million and are expected to climb into the tens of millions.

Previously unknown and undetected, aliens filled the skies with their large metallic circular-shaped ships as they assumed strategic positions throughout the globe. They moved quickly from city to city, leaving devastation in their wake. Within just a few hours, much of the Earth's metropolitan areas had been laid waste. Among the cities decimated include: New York, Los Angeles, London, Moscow, and Tokyo.

Wildfires ignited by these attacks have combined with the flames rising from the cities to fill the atmosphere with ash. Many of the fires are spreading noxious chemicals and the effects of such widespread, blanketing fire is, as yet, unknown. Dramatic shifts in weather patterns are

---

predicted.

Hospitals and morgues have run out of space. A national disaster has been declared and the country has been put under martial law. Looting and crime are rampant and all citizens are ordered to remain indoors.

A military retaliation was not immediately forthcoming as the capabilities of the enemies were entirely unknown. We have since learned that missiles, including nuclear weapons, are completely ineffective. Neither the Pentagon nor the Department of Defense are available for comment. President Johnson, in a statement to the world, stated, "All efforts to communicate have failed. This first attack was a decisive strike designed to destroy our economy and disable our military. All feasible measures are being taken to recover and bring what forces remain to bear upon this enemy."

While some regional skirmishes have occurred, most of the remaining countries have united under a common banner. All of the world's forces have been put on the highest alert.

He continued, handing me two more articles, making sure that I read them in order.

Most Costly War
By Gaven Reed

Military and civilian casualties have steadily increased as the First Earth War, as it has come to be known in the short time it has lasted, continues unabated. Property damages have exceeded a trillion dollars while the war rages on. Random attacks in places spanning the globe have gone unanswered. No pattern for these attacks has been determined and no safe place for shelter has been found.

As Earth's larger cities have been decimated, ships have moved onto medium-sized and smaller cities and even into the countryside, destroying crops and food-processing facilities. Shortages of all commodities have made the situation worse and bickering among the various nations over dwindling resources has increased.

As of today, the death toll for this war has surpassed all other wars combined. All of Earth's weapons, including nuclear, have proven to be ineffective against the alien ships' defenses. While resources are funneled to appropriate programs, efforts to identify enemy weaknesses and to develop new weapon technologies have slowed.

Ever larger groups have begun to assemble to protest what they perceive to be government inaction to the aliens. Groups have formed around most world Capitals. They contend that without centralized control of Earth's resources and coordination between all available forces, it seems unlikely that we will ever prevail. Military and police forces stretched thin have not been able to respond to the rising protests.

It was proposed that a global government be formed temporarily in order to deal with the alien threat during a clandestine meeting of the United Nations. A vote is scheduled later this week on the proposal.

RESISTANCE TO GLOBAL GOVERNMENT

Yesterday, the war against the aliens lost one of its leaders as General Thomas Henry fell, following intense fighting. Few survived the encounter and many of them will have scars for life. U.S. Forces were again forced to retreat in the face of what seems insurmountable odds. There is no denying that the situation looks grim and options are sparse. As Thomas Paine once said so long ago, "These are the times that try men's souls."

His words found their genesis in the struggle of the early colonies against what must, to them, have seemed equally insurmountable odds. Independent States, working together, accomplished what few thought possible. We face a similar decision at our crossroad in history.

Why is it that, to some people, the only way to effectively respond to an emergency is to increase the size of the government while simultaneously giving them more power? Perhaps it is because it has worked out so well throughout history.

Demands for the formation of a new government that spans the entire world are now being made. This is a truly terrifying prospect and one we should approach with great soberness of thought. Power, once given, is rarely returned. As King George, upon hearing that George Washington would voluntarily give up his authority and return to his farm once uttered, "If he does that, he will be the greatest man in the world."

Unfortunately, desperate people make foolish choices and very little opposition to this new government is being raised. Although we all fear the same thing, we mustn't create a new evil in order to deal with a different one. Diplomacy and the willingness to work together as fellow nations of this planet can work, as it did for the colonists of the young United States.

Benjamin Franklin once said, "They who can give up essential liberty to obtain a little temporary safety, deserve neither liberty nor safety." We must learn from history so that we do not repeat it. When you create a monster to deal with another monster, once you have accomplished your goal, you must then deal with the monster you have made. We must not create this monster!

I recognized the source of the second article as an underground newspaper. I have never given it much credence since most of its 'articles' read more like editorials and most, like this one, were from anonymous sources. I was surprised that an Air Force Colonel would have such an article among his things. But as I continued reading it began to make sense. After the articles, Stephen handed me an official looking document.

TOP SECRET

M E M O R A N D U M

From: Committee of Strategic Direction & Oversight

To: Zone Administrators

Re: New Policy Implementation

Recently General Thomas Henry was killed in action during a battle with the aliens. He had gained notoriety as one of the most effective leaders in the conflict and his loss has been reported by nearly all of the world's notable reporting agencies. Polling has indicated that over seventy-five percent of the population is familiar with the General and is aware of this incident. Reactions to this news has generally been anger.

Managed decisively and appropriately, this incident is the opportunity the committee was seeking for effective implementation of the Comfortable Fear Policy. History has shown that isolated incidents such as the death of General Henry are forgotten by large populations relatively quickly without some effort to keep it in the news. We must capitalize upon this crisis with haste as time is of the essence.

Accordingly, the following steps are to be taken as soon as it is feasibly possible:

---

1. General Henry must be framed as a martyr in the cause against the aliens. His death must be portrayed as a national tragedy, requiring a radical response. He needs to become this generation's Horst Wessel in order to stir up emotional support for the cause. Intimate details regarding General Henry and the impact his death has had on his family must be disseminated as widely as possible.

2. Numerous small groups supportive of the Committee's goals exist in various parts of the world. Coordination between these groups must be cautiously regarded. Only groups with strong acceptable leadership should be given the financial and logistical support to facilitate growth, as needed. Only approved rallies and group gatherings should occur and police intervention, where it is available to Committee use, should be utilized to disband unapproved gatherings.

3. New group membership should be encouraged by exploiting all available means. Supportive media personalities should be asked to participate and those that are unsupportive should be encouraged (through threat or bribes) to not create obstacles for Committee goals. Those that directly oppose these goals should be marginalized or removed. Removal must be handled in a manner as to not arouse suspicion.

4. Groups which oppose Committee goals must be derided as out-of-touch. Members of these groups must be targeted for personal attention. They must be portrayed as radical and even dangerous to the personal safety of their neighbors. Insults and personal attacks must be utilized for the purpose of enticing these groups to violence. Forceful removal by arrest of members of these groups will help maintain control of these groups. Marginalization should be accomplished through editorials, news stories, and through personal association by individuals sympathetic to the Committee's goals.

5. As part of implementing this policy the Management Group shall be created and tasked with the development and management of fear of the aliens. This group's primary objective is to cultivate a culture of fear through constant yet unobtrusive reminders of the threat posed by the aliens. Xenophobic tendencies should be encouraged and suspicions that certain individuals might possibly be alien sympathizers are effective tools for fear management. Fear should be based upon vague but believable threats and must be managed in such a way as to ensure continued manifestations of this fear. Under no circumstances should the populace be allowed to believe that the aliens are unable to defeat the Earth. **Fear must always exist**.

6. No effort, beyond simple control, should be made to deal with the alien threat. Progress in weapons and defense technologies appear to present the potential to maintain a stalemate with the aliens. **This is desirable** since this would create a certain level of fear in the populace that could and should be maintained indefinitely. Once this stalemate is reached, constant reminders that this safety was achieved **and can only be maintained** through a strong unified government must be given. At the same time, any other potential solutions must be labeled as dangerous and must be portrayed as making the alien problem worse.

7. This group will remain independent of all other government departments and will report directly to this Committee.

TOP SECRET

I found that I had covered my mouth with my hand as I read the memo from a Committee I had never heard of; a Committee with a troubling name. Was it real? It seemed impossible to me that such things could exist without my knowledge. I had never heard of Horst Wessel named in the memo, but I would later look him up. He had served as a martyr for another people in another time. There didn't seem to be a great deal of similarity between Horst and General Henry, other than being military men, but I was beginning to wonder if the people they served as martyrs were all that different.

Following this memo, Stephen handed me an article. The article was very disturbing when I noticed that it followed the memo by merely a week's time.

Progress in Everything but Government
By Karen Carton

As citizens of the planet Earth, we have been the recipients of advancements undreamed of in ages past. Technology has allowed the human race to accomplish feats that would have been considered magic, or witchcraft, in days gone by. We have enjoyed advancements in all areas of our lives, from communications to transportation and medicine. But the government that we labor under remains a relic of the past – and it is high time that we relegate it to the history books from where it came.

Proposals for the formation of a common global government have caused ripples in predictable pools. If irrational belief could make the sky fall, it would be falling in large chunks. Calls for resistance to this 'New World Order' have some scrambling for their history books in an attempt to give us a tired lesson on the history of our nation, yet again.

History is not what we should dwell upon now, rather it is the future we must now concern ourselves with. It is difficult to believe that the founding fathers would counsel against marshaling of the Earth's resources in order to defend against an enemy superior in every way that counts.

Rather, they would likely encourage us to fight for the same things they fought for – the rights to be who we are and to defend our families.

If we were faced with the challenge of curing a dreaded disease or sending an important message across the ocean or even traveling there ourselves, would we look to the past for the answers to these problems? Progress is a blessing which allows us to adapt as we grow to find new answers to new problems.

The war continues to rage around us and men and women are lost each and every day. The armies of a multitude of nations fight disparately and little is being accomplished. By joining the Federal Commonwealth of Nations we will not lose the United States, instead we will simply become a part of a larger picture and will play an important role in making new history in defeating the alien invaders.

Now is the time to be courageous and throw off the shackles that history has bound us with for far too long. Now is the time for us, as a nation, to grow up and to rise to the occasion and meet the challenge now before us. Together we will survive; alone we will perish.

I remembered reading this article and feeling drawn to its logic when I read it for the first time. But, now, I almost felt betrayed by the author. Was it simply propaganda, controlled by the Committee's Management Group? I knew from history what happened in the next article, but I had to continue reading, hesitant of what further discoveries awaited me.

Broader Powers for the Former U.N.
By Kaylynn Ayers

Following months of defeat at the hands of the aliens,

the former United Nations formally re-organized itself into The Federal Commonwealth of Nations in order to provide for global governance and a unified response to the alien invasion. Demonstrations in support of the new government have been occurring since the war's inception and the creation of the new government came amidst cheers and great applause.

Nation-members recognized the new government by signing its Charter. While maintaining national identities, each member will be able to contribute more effectively to planetary defenses and development. This new form of government is a federal form of government and will function very much like the United States with each nation now filling the role of a State. The Capital of the new Commonwealth will be located in Paris, France.

Little change in the daily life of respective citizens of members-nations is expected. While new upper-level governmental agencies have been created to provide more central control of vital resources, little to no change is expected at the level of the Member States.

Representatives of the various nation-states will be selected by the leaders of those members to serve in the Commonwealth Ministries and since voting will still be handled on national and local levels, where applicable, no significant changes will be required.

As I read, it was as if the government I had grown up under, the same government that had given me a feeling of safety and security for so many years was changing before my very eyes. Following the article, Stephen gave me another memo. Scrawled in handwritten text a large "NO!" partially blocked the contents of Section 2.

TOP SECRET

FEDERAL ENFORCEMENT AGENCY
Special Projects Group

M E M O R A N D U M
From: Special Projects Group Director

To: Colonel Thomas Bock, USAF

Re: Change of Duty Assignment

Colonel Bock, you are hereby assigned to duty at Grand Forks Air Force Base (GFAFB) in North Dakota, U.S., to serve as Commander of a special projects group that is being formed at this time. Your personnel roster will be forthcoming. Upon arrival you are to present yourself to the base population as Captain Jared Hill, a missile officer. The Base Commander and the Missile Wing Commander have been notified that an operative of the Office of Special Investigations (OSI) has been placed within their organization. They are unaware of your function or mission but have received orders to provide office space and research facilities in the bottom most sub-level of the missile building.

During your initial mission briefing you were made aware of facts regarding the battle with an alien craft over the city of Fargo, North Dakota. Absent from the official record is that during the ensuing pursuit the alien ship was severely damaged and parts of it fell away from the craft and were subsequently recovered. These are currently secured at the underground facility located at GFAFB.

STATEMENT OF PROJECT OBJECTIVES

1. You are to determine the constituent elements of the

craft parts and determine if any are capable of energy production. You are to determine if any of the parts present potential weapon or defense systems capable of interface and utilization with current Earth technologies. An emphasis should be put upon locating defensive field generators.

2. If it is determined that any of the parts represent potential weapon systems you are authorized and ordered to procure test subjects from the surrounding area to determine functionality and effectiveness of any such weapons. Two Special Agents from the Special Projects Group have been assigned to your command for procurement of these test subjects.

3. You are to develop operating procedures and instructions for use of and, particularly, mass production of, any weapons and/or energy production sources identified from the parts.

You and your team are the only ones that are aware of your functions at the base and all information appertaining thereto is EYES ONLY and is *not to be discussed* with any office other than the Directorate of the Special Projects Group. All results and hypothesis are to be promptly submitted to the Directorate of the Special Projects Group.

General Geott Absiba
Military Adjutant
National Security Agency, Special Projects Group

TOP SECRET

I began to realize that my breathing and heartbeat had increased, as if I had entered a haunted house. Like the haunted house, I knew I was going to be frightened by what was contained within it, but this knowledge alone did little, if anything, to dull the fright when it actually occurred. I accepted each new proffered document with increasing hesitancy, but with growing interest. Next was an article from a fellow reporter I knew well. Once again, I wondered what propaganda had been allowed to creep into the piece.

First Earth Victory
By Nurrem Josten

After years of defeat at the hands of our alien enemies, Earth enjoyed a spectacular victory over an alien mother ship today during a battle over the city of Washington, D.C. The military, using new weapons and defenses previously unknown, was able to withstand the barrage from the alien's energy weapons at the same time returning fire with similar-firing weapons of their own.

Meeting the mandate placed upon it at its inception the young Federal Commonwealth of Nations enjoyed Earth's first military gain. Feeling that the enemies have enjoyed the ability to strike with impunity for far too long, the new citizens of the Commonwealth of Nations met the news with joy and enthusiasm throughout the world.

A large military presence had entered the city in an effort to attract one of the alien's ships. No one expected an often unseen large mother ship to descend upon the city where it opened fire. Emerging from an underground bunker the Federal military, shielded by what appeared to be a red glowing bubble, returned fire.

Sustaining damage the alien vessel attempted to flee, but continued hits from the Commonwealth Military's new weapons forced it down. However, before any portion of the crash could be salvaged a second mother ship arrived and destroyed it, ensuring that Earth scientists would be unable to study it.

Many now feel that the tide of war against the alien

invaders has taken a decisive and desperately-needed turn in our favor, thanks to the new Commonwealth.

The next thing that Stephen offered me was a handwritten letter. I assumed it was addressed to Colonel Bock from its contents. Paper clipped to the letter was a small brochure. It was a schedule of events for a convention in which Senator Lawrence was the keynote speaker. The schedule line for his speech was highlighted with a bold color. Following this was another letter, again addressed to the Colonel but from a different source.

Tom,

I hope all is well with you since your move to North Dakota. It sounds like you are excited about your new assignment, even if it is in North Dakota. But your excitement regarding your other new find caused me to receive your last letter with some concern.

I must confess that I don't understand the alarm you seem to have about the Commonwealth. A consolidated government will make prosecuting this war more efficient and might even give us the power to turn the tides. Your stubborn refusal to stop talking about this subject is going to have a detrimental effect on your future. And for what? Fear of that small group coordinating efforts in Paris? Remember, the Central Committee does not have direct control over the local governments of any of the Member-States. So what are you afraid of?

This brings me to your newfound interest in Senator Lawrence. I believe he is only making a show out of his distrust of, and opposition to, the Federal Commonwealth. His poll numbers are terrible and he will not be in the Senate much longer. His speeches are nothing more than emotional rhetoric; a pathetic attempt to save his failing

Senatorial career. If you value your career, don't tie yourself to this sinking ship, even by accident. Avoid him. You are not the only one to have reservations about the new government. But don't forget that progress in the conflict against the aliens was the sole reason making the change necessary and the results are hard to argue with. We've now had our first victory of the war, a victory that wouldn't have happened without the Commonwealth. Don't believe what you hear from people like Senator Lawrence, that all of the Member-States will be ultimately absorbed into the global government. Only the fear mongers, conspiracy theorists, and those that can't think for themselves really believe that.

I believe that you could become a General and that you have the potential to go very far. There is even some talk, in small circles, about General Bock. Where you go from here is really up to you but you have got to stop railing against the system.

I've been your friend for a long time and so officially I don't remember any of our previous communications on this subject. But I simply cannot receive any more letters like the last one. As your friend I am begging you, PLEASE stop this insanity. Embrace the future instead of fighting it!

Your friend,
Jack

Dear T.B.,

I have enjoyed our fruitful association these past months. Your dedication and willingness to contribute to the cause of the Restorationists have been admirable and I am honored to be able to call you a true friend. Too many surrounding us simply do not understand what is going on around them. We think very much alike and you are awake to the problem. I would never have imagined we could have accomplished so much in the few short months since the convention. I am grateful for the fortunate opportunity we had to meet there.

Since our first meeting I have come into possession of two documents that we must discuss as soon as it is possible to do so. I have attached a copy of each to this letter. The sheer magnitude of their contents is unbelievably astounding and each has the capacity to topple and completely dismantle the Commonwealth, standing alone. We must move purposefully and carefully as they will, no doubt, do *everything* within their power to prevent any of this from coming to light. But we must make the public aware of these documents as soon as feasibly possible.

We must not associate the Restorationists with the release of this information. If they are linked, I have no doubt that all of the group's leadership will be arrested and the reaction will be swift and ruthless; because if the Commonwealth is allowed to implement these policies, we will be all but powerless to effect any further meaningful changes.

I do not know if we will be able to meet or talk again, the consequences of the release of this information is volatile and hard to predict. God speed Tom and keep you in His care until we meet again.

Your friend,
P.L.

After reading these letters I simply had to take a break, sit down, and collect my thoughts. I knew I had to continue but I sensed that what was to come would alter my perception of my reality. I paused momentarily before committing to this change.

Chapter 11

"Sometimes we should fear what we don't know..."
Senator Lawrence

I knew that I needed to continue to read, but I was filled with trepidation. I wasn't sure that my break had been long enough, but, at last, I continued. The press certainly painted a pretty portrait of the new Federal Commonwealth of Nations. I had read dozens of stories similar to the next article Stephen handed me. But as I found my perception of reality evolving, I read it with a much different eye than I had so many times before.

New Management, New Results
By Gaven Reed

Almost from the first day the Federal Commonwealth of Nations took control of the war effort, things have been different. Some said that assuming effective control of the multi-nation bickering military forces could not be done. But with the establishment of a uniform training system and the abolishment of all nationally-unique military items, the Commonwealth has managed to mold and forge a

---

better, more efficient military. And since that day we have seen less and less of the aliens.

As we watched, magnificent cities rose from the ashes that had become the grave to so many. Cities like New York, Chicago, and Los Angeles have been reborn, surrounded by those dazzling red force fields taken from the aliens. Beautiful buildings, magnificent parks, and all the amenities that any person could want have filled each one.

At long last the alien weapons can no longer kill or injure. Rarely are city residents even aware of the attacks, so good are the fields. People are free once again to go about their lives, to find happiness and to not be afraid. No longer must school be taught by anxious parents hiding in a bunker. At last, hunger means a trip to the neighborhood grocery store rather than a sleepless night.

Truly we have re-discovered a way of life forgotten through the conflict with our alien enemies. I salute the courage of the founding members of the Commonwealth for standing up and saying enough is enough. Long live the Federal Commonwealth of Nations!

The tone of the article almost made me physically ill. It sounded like pure propaganda. How could I have been so blind for so long, I asked myself. I prided myself on my journalistic ability to find those stories that were not easy to get. But the magnitude of what I just plain didn't know anything about grew, it seemed, with every new document Stephen handed me.

TOP SECRET
Central Committee Eyes Only

**Federal Commonwealth of Nations
Central Committee**

Statement of Federal Objectives

In order to establish, promote, strengthen, and facilitate the Federal Commonwealth of Nations, and to achieve a harmonious balance of power between the Commonwealth and the aliens, the Central Committee has enacted the following objectives. All objectives will and may be enforced by whatever means necessary.

1. Establish a central office for the Commonwealth in Paris, France. All Federal authority will be vested in the Central Committee to be located in this office. Each continent, including Asia, Africa, North America, South America, and Australia shall establish and maintain a Federal Office. (Europe shall be covered by the Paris, France office.) Each of these offices will report directly to the office in Paris, France.

2. All individual interest in property, real or otherwise, is hereby abolished. Granting of trademarks, patents, and copyrights shall cease immediately. Central control of all of Earth's natural resources is an absolutely essential element to maintaining control. All businesses (whether corporations and corporate-derivatives, partnerships, or sole proprietorships) are hereby nationalized and will be used for the good of the whole. Individual incomes will be based first upon position within the government structure and then upon need. Variations of income shall not be common knowledge and high-level government operatives shall be physically segregated from others so that this is not apparent.

3. School programs and curricula will be determined by the Department of Information. There shall be a common curricula throughout all school systems. An essential element of this curriculum is the management of history. In the United States and throughout countries with similar

historical figures, founding individuals must be portrayed as repressive of the indigenous populations. Their presence must not be completely removed, but they must be marginalized as relics from another time that have little to offer modern society.

4. Population growth must be in harmony with Commonwealth goals. Population management must include control of radical groups and individuals. Media outlets of any sort must encourage commonality while simultaneously discouraging individuality. Activities of individuals must remain in harmony with the stated goals of the Central Committee; however, these goals must be disseminated through local branches of government to remove the appearance of central control. Uncontrolled individualism will engender chaos and endanger the common good and must be strictly monitored and controlled. Those individuals that do not conform must be first, ostracized, and then removed if unsuccessful. As part of population management, strict control must be maintained over the availability and administration of medicine, in whatever form it is available. Euthanasia and suicide shall be made legal.

5. Religions that teach belief in vague and distant deities and discourage rigid definitions of deity shall be supported by the state. Religions that teach strict doctrine and require substantial commitment to religious tenets shall be submitted to intense ridicule. All religions should be homogenized into essentially one religion.

6. Control of travel between cities must be maintained through a permit system. The government shall construct and limit access to a system of tubes, through which vehicles will travel between cities. Citizens must apply for and obtain a pass from their local government office in order to use this system.

7. Morale of the citizenry is essential to the continuance of the Commonwealth, therefore all reports of the war, human suffrage issues, and government actions must be approved by the Department of Information before dissemination. Only licensed journalists will be allowed to make and submit reports through a central control point of dissemination. Underground and electronic boards must be monitored and strictly controlled; removal of such boards should be avoided however unless absolutely necessary, as it would arouse suspicion. Also, commentaries on the virtues of living within the city-system shall be broadcast on a regular basis.

8. Installation of a monitoring device will be completed in every existing room within every structure within every city in the Commonwealth immediately. Furthermore, installation of these devices shall be mandatory in each room of any and all newly constructed buildings. These installations are to be checked and certified by government-approved inspectors regularly. This monitoring system will ensure the compliance of all citizens with these objectives and will maintain strict control and management of criminal activity. Police at the local level will be given access to criminal information pertinent to their area only. Media presentations explaining the merits of the system and the eradication of crime are to be broadcast to all citizens.

9. Each city will be enclosed by a force field. These fields will prevent the city from any further damage from the aliens. The area outside of the cities will be used to place unproductive or troublesome citizens. Criminals, regardless of the level of their crime, will be assessed fines. Those unable or unwilling to pay applicable fines will also be expelled from the cities. All sentences for these individuals will last for life. No one shall ever be returned

to the cities. Sentence Givers are encouraged to use the monitoring system and the sentencing laws liberally to relieve the overpopulation that will exist in some areas.

10. Absolute and total control must be maintained over the procurement and dissemination of any alien technology recovered from captured alien vessels. Persons involved in this process must also be controlled. Methods of control may include, but are not limited to: psychological (brain-washing), chemical, and emotional (threats to loved ones). Should any person in this area become even a slight security risk, they are to be removed at once.

11. Citizens that are being protected from attack are more amiable to the idea of limited personal freedoms and so it is upon this principal that all objectives must be presented. No direct effort shall be made to end the war with the aliens. Maintaining the current stand-off while keeping large numbers of citizens from being killed or injured is and will be the main objective of the Central Committee.

TOP SECRET
Central Committee Eyes Only

Flashes from history of some of the world's worst governments began to fill my mind. I couldn't believe that I was comparing the government I thought I knew so well to them. Feeling the protection of the force field certainly lulled me into a sense that I had nothing to worry about. But not everybody liked the benevolent government the Commonwealth wanted to appear to be. Thankfully, there were those that could see it for what it was. The next thing that Stephen offered me was a government report about the Restorationists. It was the group, I recalled, that was led by the late Senator Lawrence.

It was a group that had certainly gained the attentive focus of the new Commonwealth. From the report it seemed that the Restorationists were singly responsible for the creation of the Department of Information Management. According to the report, the influence of the Restorationists was growing at an alarming rate due to its charismatic leader. If one were to believe the content of the report, the Restorationists were one of the most radical and dangerous factions in existence.

Following the report I read a memo ordering the placement of an operative, as girlfriend, with the Senator. As soon as I read this memo, the blood drained from my face. The Commonwealth had been so threatened by the Senator that they had placed that woman that had caused him so much grief at the end of his time before being expelled from the cities. How long had she had to keep up her ruse? I wondered if he'd ever suspected she was not what she portrayed herself to be. I was sad to know I would never be able to ask him.

The next document Stephen proffered me was a handwritten letter from Senator Lawrence to Colonel Bock.

My Dearest Friend,

It has been an honor and privilege to have known you and to have served the interests of freedom in our struggle against the Commonwealth. You have been an asset to our cause and you can continue to be an asset to us in your current position. I understand why you feel that you should join the Restorationists in your heart. But you are of greater value to us as a silent outside brother-in-arms. Besides, publicly aligning yourself with the Restorationists will ruin your career. I question neither your true belief nor your willingness to contribute to the cause, but remain patient and steadfast my friend. I pray that one day we shall celebrate together the restoration of true principals of governing a free people.

On another note, I believe the surveillance that the government conducts has increased significantly recently. I do not think we will be able to talk again for a while. Until then, God speed my friend.

Signed, your friend,
Phillip Lawrence

I sighed in the knowledge that they probably never did have the chance to speak together again. The next letter was a hand-written note. I recognized the handwriting as that of Colonel Bock. It was written to the members of the Restorationists. How many of them actually had the opportunity to read it was impossible to know.

To my fellow members of the Restorationists:

Today we have been dealt a great blow. We have lost one of the great leaders of history – our friend and fellow in our fight to retain our freedom, Senator Phillip Lawrence. They say that he is the victim of a dreadful accident, but I do not believe it! But whatever has happened to our companion in our struggles, he is gone. They are counting on his disappearance to discourage us from carrying on the fight.

WE MUST NOT LET THIS HAPPEN!!

We must now use the sting of his loss to always remind us of those things he taught us and we must continue to spread his words as far and as wide as we can. They will try to stop us but we must not let them! Remember always the words of Thomas Jefferson: "Freedom is lost gradually from an uninterested, uninformed, and uninvolved people."

STAY STRONG NOW AND FOREVER!

The Colonel's words stirred my soul. I wondered if any Restorationists still existed. I doubted that even the Commonwealth had the power to eradicate them all. A strange correlation exists between powerful entities, like the Commonwealth, and those they seek to control and suppress. The harder the efforts to suppress the greater the resistance. Had I known what I was learning now, it was quite possible I might have been a Restorationist myself. And still, the shocking revelations continued. The next thing Stephen offered me was a partial memo. It was missing the heading but seemed to contain most of the rest of its original contents.

Successful implementation of the Alien Accord will require profound changes. This accord can be effectively implemented with the establishment of a single, comprehensive policy. The official title of this policy proposal shall be: POPULATION PLANNING & CONTROL. However, it shall be known to the public as the RESOURCE SUSTAINABILITY PLAN. This policy has six parts that should be implemented in order, as follows:

1. Earth's natural resources must be comprehensively and secretly managed. Strategically-selected population groups are to be denied sufficient resources for all members within the group to survive. Media attention must be drawn to these groups to highlight this shortage. This will work to develop a perceived shortage of Earth's resources. A perception that can, and should, be reinforced by

providing whatever information will be effective regarding the use of these resources during war prosecution.

2. After this information campaign has been allowed to progress to a pre-determined saturation level, the policy will be made public as a method of dealing with this "growing problem." This will make widespread public acceptance of the policy more likely and should isolate dissidents that publicly oppose the policy easier to locate so that they may be dealt with. This policy will fully implement all current and future population management regulations promulgated from the Central Committee.

3. After widespread public acceptance of the policy has been achieved, resources must be further restricted to create a semi-panic condition within the populace. Timing will be extremely important at this stage. A sufficiently panicked populace will allow for the establishment of city enclosures with a large percentage of persons remaining outside of the enclosures. If the populace is allowed to achieve too great a level of panic, this could induce riots and would require the expenditure of unnecessary resources.

In order to implement this new policy the Federal Enforcement Agency must be created. This agency will be tasked with enforcement of this new policy and must be given the necessary authority to do so. Upon acceptable implementation of Step 3, this agency must then disseminate the following Memorandum to all Group, Division, and Section Commanders.

"City overcrowding and homelessness have become significant issues endangering the further safety and well-being of society-at-large. In order to deal with these issues the Federal Commonwealth of Nations has implemented a zero-tolerance rule for law offenders and the Crime Fees for crimes often associated with homelessness have been raised. Police departments have been instructed to remove all 'street people' upon contact and Federal Enforcement Agents are encouraged to take whatever measures are necessary to ensure that those persons thus removed are unable to pay the fine(s).

Likewise, all military group, division, and section commanders are granted the authority to act as judge regarding the soldiers, sailors, and airmen in their respective commands. All court-martials may be conducted on the level at which they are initiated (i.e., at the group, division, or section level). Superior officers should be informed of these proceedings within forty-eight hours of completion, however, all judgments of military officers will stand as ruled, without scrutiny. Summary court-martials are encouraged.

Questions regarding this policy should be addressed to the Office of the Director of the FEA.

4. After the cities have been sealed-off an extensive monitoring system must be put in place. This system must create a network that does not leave any places unmonitored. This system will make convictions of individuals for criminal activity far more efficient. All individuals convicted of any crime whatsoever will be fined. Those unable to meet the fine will be ejected from the cities.

5. An ancillary policy will be the Bankruptcy/Conviction policy. Individuals will be targeted for bankruptcy followed by conviction. This will ensure these targeted individuals are unable to pay their fines. No particular level of care need be implemented in carrying out this policy since all those that fall under its purview will simply be ejected from the city and will be unable to bring any appeal in the court system.

6. As the POPULATION PLANNING & CONTROL

policy progresses, the aliens, pursuant to the Accord, will provide staged victories for the Federal Commonwealth. This will help to create a perceived balance between the alien and Earth forces. At this point, resource management may be altered in order to create a more comfortable docile population, after a sustainable population number has been achieved.

Had the Commonwealth really entered into an agreement with the aliens that had caused such destruction to the Earth? I didn't want to believe it and yet the reference to an Alien Accord in the memo made it impossible to deny. I sat silently pondering what possible reasons would have been sufficient to entice *any* resident of Earth to enact such a policy to support an accord. Stephen sensed my shock and was silent for a few minutes, letting it sink in.

*   *   *

I had as hard a time as you coming to grips with all of this. It is never easy to lose the reality you thought you had for so long. Especially when it is replaced by one like this.

*   *   *

The last two things he gave me to read were articles. I had read one of them before since I had known its author, but the last one came from another underground paper.

Resources Stretched Thin
By Angelise Norris

With one-week remaining until the date for field activation, numerous people have not yet moved into the cities. But despite the debate that rages over the reality, and the morality, of the slated closure, too many will find themselves excluded from the civilized world when the time comes. Since all cities have plans to implement the policy of expelling criminals into the world outside of the cities, things are expected to deteriorate quickly and these criminals will become neighbors to those unwilling to make the move.

Government assistance for those unable to make the move has been typically slow, but the flow of people remains unabated. From the time the Commonwealth announced its intentions to close off certain cities from the remaining world, people have swarmed by the hundreds of thousands. With such an influx, it has not taken long for food and living space to become a problem.

Increased demand for these commodities has caused prices to sky-rocket. Many people have found themselves unable to afford their basic needs. Mobs of the homeless already mill about the streets and still more arrive each day.

Panhandlers and beggars have appeared; a natural extension to the homeless. Food pantries are empty; stretched to their limits trying to help. Looting and burglary have increased exponentially. The government is studying the problem.

Local groups have petitioned the government to increase the fines for vagrancy and panhandling. Most would be unable to pay, thus sending the majority back into the world that they made an effort to escape. Support for the idea is on the rise.

Another solution, a little less radical, is an increase in tax. Additional tax revenues could be used for building new high-rise apartment complexes and new hydroponic growing farms.

But whatever the solution, the time for the virtual 'door closing' arrives in a week. Once these doors close, they will never open again.

GOVERNMENT *SURPRISED* BY RIOTING AS CITIES ARE CLOSED

At last the day we have been promised would arrive, a day we were warned about has come. The last of the megacities, handpicked by the Commonwealth to survive has finally activated its protective shield. Two mutually exclusive worlds now exist on Earth – the haves and the have-nots.

Like too many times in Earth's history, we now have those that have food, shelter, medicine, along with all of the other needs we take for granted, available to them. They are the haves. But millions of people, with a terrible portion of them simply unable to move into the cities for reasons beyond their control, have now become the have-nots.

Families, friends, and loved ones now permanently separated must find a new life in whatever world they find themselves in. For some, this reality is too much to comprehend and they have taken to the streets to express their anger and fear for those they are separated from. All the while the government representatives express their surprise that any of the Commonwealth citizens could be anything less than grateful for the many things they have been provided.

Most of these riots have been disbursed, however, some of these rioters have been arrested and those that are do not return to riot, or do anything else for that matter. I suppose these rioters are the fortunate ones since they will be reunited with those they left behind in the world outside of the cities soon enough.

With frightening effectiveness, the Commonwealth has successfully contained the majority of these riots. They are rare now but not entirely unheard of. It is as though we have sent those that are left behind into a war in a faraway

166

place and do not know what has become of them. Unfortunately, our minds fill in the blanks in the face of the unknown but we cannot afford to indulge our fears. Whatever is the ultimate outcome of the field separation, we must never forget those we lost when they finally come on, the day our entire world changed.

My head was swimming as I finished the final article. I couldn't help but feel as if I were living in a foreign world, a world I could no longer call my own. Stephen's words took on a whole new meaning and importance then.

*   *   *

It's too bad I never had the chance to know Colonel Bock, I think I would have liked him. I don't know what happened after the last letter he wrote to the members of the Restorationists, but the Commonwealth terminated his military commission and stripped him of his rank. To be honest, I have always wondered why he was still there in that office. I suspect it wasn't long after he got notice of this that he took his own life.

He must have committed suicide immediately preceding the alien attack since he still sat in his chair at his desk. It almost felt as though that office had been sealed off to become his tomb. It was a tomb that held incredible secrets.

Sometime later Miguel opened the vault and retrieved the large case that held the alien artifact. By then I had spent three long hours pondering the words that I had read. Silently, we returned to our horses and departed. I was so lost in my thoughts that as I watched the large building recede into the distance, I was unaware of the physical discomfort that my ride was causing me. Finally, I looked ahead and decided that somehow, someway I was going to make a difference in the world.

Chapter 12

"Roses have thorns, and silver fountains mud;
Clouds and eclipses stain both moon and sun…"
William Shakespeare

I had difficulty concentrating on much during the return trip. As the documents I had read haunted me, I spent the majority of my time looking into the sky wondering what purpose the aliens had that the Commonwealth had agreed to support. I was in mourning for the world I thought I had known. I rarely spoke a word.

During the remainder of the trip I thought of ways that I could make a difference; to the people that were now coming to Duluth looking for a better life, and to those that still lived within the cities.

A lot of people belonged in the World Outside for the things they had done, but there were so many that didn't. I felt like our efforts were inconsequential in the face of those things I had read at the base. How could I, or anyone for that matter, fight against such powers? Not only did we face the alien threat, whatever it represented, but our government was against us too.

After what seemed like an eternity we arrived back at Duluth. Ashleigh was there to meet us but our reunion was unusually quiet for the both of us. With few words she followed me as I somberly returned to our headquarters to unload the case containing the alien weapon. I handed it to one of the members of our group as we walked into the building. I watched as it was taken away to be put into safe storage. As time and resources permitted I knew that it would be researched and I hoped that it would prove useful.

Grasping my hand tightly, Ashleigh stayed by my side as we received welcomes from everyone that passed us, but I noticed right away the conspicuous absence of Derik. Every time he had sent a group out on a mission, any mission, he had always been there to greet them upon their return, without exception. He was always filled with concern that everyone was all right and that the mission had accomplished whatever goal that had been set for it. Yet, he was nowhere to be found.

Finally I looked at Ashleigh and I could sense that something was wrong. I feared for the worst and when I asked her if she knew where Derik was her eyes fell to the ground and she was silent for a moment.

Then, looking up, she said, "You should probably see for yourself Stephen. He's in the infirmary."

The infirmary was our equivalent of a hospital that Dr. Taylor had set up for the use of the citizens of Duluth. I hastily made my way there.

As I entered the room, I immediately saw Derik lying on a bed in the far corner. His face looked gaunt and his breathing was labored. I hurried to his side and spoke his name quietly.

Opening his sunken eyes he gave me a smile that I could tell took a great deal of energy from him. And before I had a chance to ask him what was wrong, he spoke softly.

"Was your mission a success Stephen? Everything go well? Anybody get hurt?" he said slowly.

Nodding, I shared our success with him and tried to keep my explanation brief. He looked at me with interest in his eyes and then smiled again.

"I'm glad to hear that," he responded. But before I had a chance to ask what was on my mind he continued, "I suppose you're wondering what has happened to me."

All I could do was nod to his question.

"The same hour that you and the others left to go to Grand Forks someone brought a new arrival to me. Like so many of the others that have come, this one had important news to share. But this particular news had importance only to me.

"Right away I thought that I recognized the person. I soon learned that I had indeed known him. I have crossed the path of many groups since the time that I came into the World Outside, some good, some bad. He came from one of the good ones.

"In the beginning, I moved from group to group, looking for one that I could feel at home in. None of them ever felt quite right so I resolved to make my own. Anyway, I spent a few months with this one group. People would come and go from it. There was never a whole lot of stability within it.

"One day a young woman showed up and I have to admit that I was immediately taken by her. I did all that I could to get her attention and to impress her. One thing led to another and we found ourselves swept up in a relationship that was filled with passion and love for one another.

"As you know, I was raised in a devoutly religious family. It has always been a part of me and only grew stronger in the World Outside. I never doubted that I would marry the woman that I fell in love with and I wanted nothing more than to be married to her.

"Unfortunately, marriage is a lost institution in this place and although I have known many couples, none have existed under the vows of marriage. I realized that I would either have to abandon one of my core beliefs to the World Outside or I could search high and low to find a priest, or some other religious leader, to marry us. It was the hardest thing for which I had sought but when I found one, we were married right away."

I simply could not believe what I was hearing. Not once had I ever even suspected that Derik had a wife. I had always assumed that he, a career military man, had simply never had the time to marry. And finding one after expulsion was unheard of.

I had also always assumed that certain parts of 'normal' life were, by necessity, left behind when entering the World Outside. Certainly I would have included marriage on that list. Yet here was a man that I respected as much as anyone can respect another and he had found a way to be married to his love. He continued.

"At last I remembered from where I recognized the man that they brought to me; he had been one of the few at my wedding. He had good news and bad news.

"You see, many years ago, during an outing one night with that group, an outing that included my new wife, we were overtaken by a large group of cannibals. Among others, my wife was lost to them and I screamed for all I was worth as I watched them take her.

"My life was ruined. I had no reason to live, but I did not have it in me to take my own life. I drifted away from that group then; the memories that their association brought to me were too painful. One day, I was simply gone.

"As I listened to the man he reviewed for me the events that had led to my leaving that group. Fresh pain filled my heart where scars had been. But as he continued he related subsequent events that I did not know. Not long after I left the group, never to return, my wife wandered back into the camp. She was dazed and injured, but alive…and pregnant.

"I stood in stunned silence. Had I actually left my wife behind? So it seemed. Eight months later she gave birth to a son. She died during the birth, but my son still lived in the old city of Springfield, Missouri. I knew at once that I had to go. That same day I prepared and departed alone. I realize that that was against my own rules. But I was simply overcome by my emotions and I could not wait even a second to leave. My wife was gone, but I had a son, and I had to see him. I left quietly then, without anyone knowing I had gone.

"I took one of the mountain bikes so I didn't have to worry about fuel and I knew that my horse would be missed. I moved swiftly, stopping only once for rest. When I reached the group late the second day, I was absolutely exhausted. I fell asleep just outside the camp and woke early the next day to the sounds of gunfire.

"While I slept a group of humants had come upon the camp and was attacking. Rising quickly, I joined the fight. I looked about as best I could and recognized a few of my fellow fighters, as they evidently did me. As I looked, a young man emerged from one of the shelters to join the fight.

"He was about five and a half feet tall. He looked just like his mother, it was unmistakable. He hefted a weapon that was nearly as long as he was tall. I paused momentarily to look at him and that's when it happened.

"One of the humants jumped onto my back throwing his arm around my neck. Before I had a chance to react he leaned forward and sunk his teeth into my shoulder near my neck. Pain ripped through my body as I collapsed. I laid on the ground as the remainder of the battle raged about me. Thankfully, a shot stopped that humant from finishing the job.

"When the battle was over the group approached me cautiously. Some of them recognized me, most did not.

Some of those who did took me into one of their shelters to tend to my wound. I passed out and slept for a few hours. When I came too I anxiously shared my reason for coming and at last I met the boy who was my son.

"We did not know each other and, even though we shared blood, he did not share any of the feelings that I then felt. Our first exchange was painfully brief.

"I wanted to know him, to protect him, to love the son that I had never known but I knew that the area where we were was too far south to provide for any level of safety. I gathered the leaders of the group and explained about Duluth, offering a place to all willing to journey back with me.

"Most of them eagerly accepted my offer and by the following day we were on our way back here. My condition continued to deteriorate as we traveled and I had to be carried the remainder of the way. We got here just a few hours before you did."

My heart had filled with emotions as he had talked. I wanted to share those things that I had found in Grand Forks beyond just the alien artifact. I wanted to meet Derik's lost son and wondered if Derik would be alright. But it was obvious that his tale had taken all of his strength and he passed into a fitful sleep. I went to find Dr. Taylor, leaving Ashleigh who held Derik's hand as she patted it softly.

The infirmary, or hospital to most, was a busy place from the time of its inception. Never had I entered the place without being filled with awe over what Dr. Taylor could accomplish for so many with so little. I did not really know her, but I had always been impressed by her. I found her tending to a patient at one of the many beds that had found their way to the hospital. I waited for her to finish and then approached.

She could see the concern on my face and did not have to be told what I wanted. Taking me aside she held my hand and looked into my eyes.

"I'm sorry Stephen, but Derik is not going to live much longer. The humant that bit him had some kind of venom that I have never encountered before. I have no remedy for it; I've tried everything I know how. You should take this opportunity to say goodbye to him. Everyone but you and the group that went with you have already done so. Go now."

Running my hands down my cheeks, my heart sunk at her words. My leader, my savior, my friend was dying and I was supposed to say goodbye to him. I was never any good at saying goodbye, even when leaving on relatively short trips, how was I supposed to do this now? It didn't matter, my friend was dying and I knew that I had to be at his side when he passed.

I drug my feet returning to his room. I wanted to postpone the inevitable. I finally summoned up the courage to go back. Seeing me at the door, Ashleigh stood, gently placing Derik's hand onto his chest. Coming to the door she leaned in to give me a quick kiss and hug before leaving herself. Although I wanted her with me, I knew this was something I would have to face myself. Steeling myself, I entered the room and crossed over to the side of the bed.

I was relieved to see that he was still breathing when I got there, albeit shallowly. I sat and looked at him for a while thinking of all he had come to represent to me. He was the kind of man that I hoped to be, the kind of leader loved by those who followed. He had always looked to the future and found brightness there. He was fiercely loyal and a man of his word. And he didn't let the World Outside ruin him the way that so many others had.

As I sat pondering these things, his eyes fluttered open and focused on me. He tried to sit up but lacked the strength. I helped him and he looked at me with seriousness. Then, looking to someone on the other side of the room, motioned weakly for them to come forward.

Two people drew near: a man and a boy of about twelve or thirteen. After delivering the boy to the side of the bed, the man departed. The boy did not look happy, indeed if I had had to guess his feelings at that time it would have been a mixture of confusion and disgust. Derik spoke.

"Stephen, this is my son, Aurris. In this life I will not have the opportunity to know him, but I must know that he will be safe here. I want all that a father can want for a son, but cannot give it to him. Stephen, when I am gone I want *you* to look after him. Treat him like you would your own son, teach him what I have taught you and whatever else you deem of value."

He reached his hand towards me then and with a tear on his check said,

"Stephen, there are few people that have earned my respect in this life, you are one of them. You are a natural-born leader; you must lead these people into the new world that we have envisioned together.

"As you know, relationships are all that truly matter in this life and I know that I could trust you with my life. When I am gone all that will remain of me will be my son, and this I leave in your care. Take care, my friend, and never forget me."

His eyes closed then and his grip loosened and his hand fell from mine. He was gone. I sat in silence for a moment and turned to look at the boy. He did indeed look like his father. I was unsure what to say to him.

"Your father was the greatest man that I have ever had the privilege to know. He had a lion's heart and you have his blood in your veins. I will never be the man that he was but I will endeavor to teach you what he would have you know and help you understand who your father was." I placed my hand upon his shoulder and looked him squarely in his eyes. I left then.

I found Dr. Taylor to tell her that Derik was gone. As I did I broke down and wept quietly. Gene, without a word, simply put her arms about me and hugged me while I cried for my friend. After a few minutes she led me to a quiet chair in a corner where she sat me down and went to assist yet another person.

I sat there for a time regaining my composure. I watched Dr. Taylor as she continued helping people. She was tireless and I wondered how she did it. Slowly I arose and approached her. I thanked her for her compassion and said, "someday you will have to tell me how you do it."

She responded that if I had a minute she would be happy to do it then. She knew that if I had something else to think about, it might make Derik's death a smite less painful. Happy to have something else in my head I readily agreed and we went to the small room that she used as her office. Closing the door she sat across from me.

"From my earliest memories I've always wanted to help people. As I grew I took every first-aid course that I could find. Half of these courses were part of a camp that I attended and so I began quite early to learn natural and alternative methods of treating people. At first, my knowledge was limited to first-aid but eventually I learned how to treat various illnesses and diseases.

"As soon as I was able I entered Pre-Med in college; finishing that I continued on to medical school. I learned the accepted methods of treatment there, but never forgot the natural things that I had learned along the way. After four long years of school, and the residency that followed, I was finally the physician that I had always wanted to be.

"I entered a clinic then and started working in earnest, spending all of my spare time camping in what little wilderness was available within the cities. I continued studying natural methods of treatment and soon had become the foremost authority on these methods. However, I soon learned that knowing this was a mixed-bag, not everyone agreed with the methods that I used and I became somewhat of a pariah.

"It was during this time that a governmental policy letter was issued that forbid the treatment of people that were not in the health system. Such a policy, by design, must include the poor and the homeless. Most of the doctors complied with the order, a few, including myself, did not.

"I, along with a few doctors of like mind, set up a clandestine clinic that poor people could come to. They came in droves and we took turns staying up at nights to treat them. Some of their conditions had progressed past the point of no return. Many of them were children. My heart went out to all of them. I yearned to do something more.

"Then one day at work the police showed up and I, along with all of the doctors that had staffed our secret nighttime clinic, were arrested on the charge of 'malpractice.' Our intentions made little difference as we each plead our case. Within a few days we lost contact as we each were expelled into the World Outside.

"My pod was met by a group of people that existed somewhere between sanity and the chaos of the cannibals. It is hard to explain them, they didn't have me for dinner, but they lived only a few feet away from insanity. Once they learned that I was a doctor I was forced to treat anyone and everyone that they deemed deserving, and I had to comply. Also, being a woman, I became the source of pleasure for too many men to count them all. I began to feel less than human. I was nothing more than a pack-animal that served various 'purposes.'

"After a while of this I found myself in another group when the one that I had previously been in was attacked and taken over. Once again I became a physician against my will. Although I had taken the Hippocratic Oath, I knew that some of the people that I found myself treating would end up killing many other people. For the first time ever, I did not want to help everyone that I could and did not want others to know that I was a doctor. I determined then to escape and so one night slipped away.

"I wandered for weeks then, avoiding all of the groups that I encountered along the way. I foraged through whatever garbage I could find in order to sustain myself. I could feel my grip on reality loosen and I questioned my sanity. I wondered if being dead would be better than the life I had. I stopped eating and drinking and found a place where I could curl up and die. That's when Derik found me.

"One morning I awoke to see a large man standing above me. I was so far gone by that time that I didn't know whether I was dreaming or awake. It felt surreal and I watched as if from outside of my own body as he bent down and picked me up and carried me in is arms.

"Looking up at his face through the fog I thought I could make out some of the features of his face. Seeing me looking at him he retuned my gaze with a broad smile. I lost consciousness somewhere along the way but when I awoke I found I was lying upon a cot covered with comfortable blankets. The man was still there. Lifting me with strong arms he helped me take a few drinks. At length he began to feed me. I hadn't the strength to do any of it myself, so at the beginning he did it all for me.

"As my condition improved he would ask me how I felt. Never once did he ask me what I could do for him. His concern for me was genuine. I could not believe that such a man could exist in such a place. As I watched him care for and help all of the others, I grew to love him.

"The people that Derik attracted to him were people like you and me. They are those who seek to lead a life that is tainted as little by the World Outside as possible. At last I had a group of people that I could feel good about treating and so I became a doctor once again. I don't have to tell you how useful my natural medicine training has been here.

"The people here in Duluth have been so appreciative of what I do for them. Many of them even bring me things in gratitude. I feel needed here. I thank Derik for that and will miss him as much, if not more, than the rest of you. Although he gave a piece of his heart to all those willing to accept his help, only one had, or would, ever have it all; and she was dead to him. We shared a lot, as much as two people can that do not declare their feelings openly to one another. My heart ached to be his and my arms ached to hold him tightly, but in the end our love remained unspoken."

She buried her face in her arm then and cried. It was my turn to wrap my arms around her and hug her until she finished. We would both miss Derik terribly, but we simply had to press on. Pulling ourselves up then and wiping the tears from our faces we parted and went our various ways.

The mood within our little group for the next few days was glum. The passing of Derik hit everyone hard. We rarely exchanged words, and then only when absolutely necessary to accomplish our duties.

A few days after returning to my duties I learned that the people of Duluth had accepted a couple more humants into their numbers. Both had arrived separately requesting asylum. Each had escaped from their group and, hearing of the better life that could be had in Duluth, had made their way there. Impressed by the hard work and industry that the people had seen in Alan Foster, few questioned the new arrivals.

At the beginning everything went along fine as each humant went about their assigned duties well enough. Until the night that two Duluth residents went missing. No trace could be found of their whereabouts, they had simply vanished. I worked with one of them and he had become a good friend.

At first, I wondered if they had been taken by the aliens; after all, I had seen people vanish in their beams. Still, I had never heard of anyone being taken from the inside of buildings and both of the people that were missing had been asleep in their beds. It didn't take long for the suspicions of the city, and of myself I confess, to turn to the humants. Some of the others even began to question Alan. Tensions intensified and we believed it was best to place the humants in 'protective' custody to protect them and us from each other.

We formed a search party, split the city into sections and began our search for our lost citizens. Progress was slow as we painstakingly covered every square inch of the city. At length we found them, or what was left of them, about two weeks after our search had begun. Their bodies had been shoved into a large metal sewer pipe in a particularly dark and dreary part of the city. We also found a piece of clothing from one of the new humant arrivals.

Abject rage filled my whole being. Since I had been the first one to accept a humant into our midst I felt personally responsible for the actions of the others. With the cloth in my tightened fist, I hurried to the cell that held the humant that it belonged to. With grim determination I drew my gun as I entered the cell. Crossing over to the humant prisoner I pressed the barrel to his head and began to speak loudly.

"I have only one question for you, you vile creature, why!? You came to us looking for a new life, and we took you in. How could you reward such generosity with this kind of treachery?'"

In response he placed his head in his hands and let out a sigh that came from deep within his soul. It took a few moments for him to speak.

"I didn't mean to kill them, really! It was an accident." Then, lifting his face from his hands and seeing the puzzled look on my face, he continued.

"When Reks turned me into a humant he put poison into my hands. All I have to do to kill a man is touch his bare skin. Because of my deadly touch, everyone avoided me, my life became very lonely and empty. Even the other humants avoided me. When I heard about this place I just knew that I had to come. Even if I was killed on sight, just the mere possibility that I could find something of a normal life inspired me to take my chances.

"The willingness and open-heartedness of the people here to accept me and the others like me, touched my heart deeply. I had begun to believe that compassion was dead in this world. I really thought that I would be able to avoid touching anyone once I got here. I even wore gloves whenever I left my new home. Things were going better than I ever thought they could again.

"Not long ago I was assigned to work with one of the people that fell prey to my poison. We finished our work and I went home, but I guess I must have impressed my coworker since he and his companion came to visit me.

"I was so stunned by the knock that I heard on my door that I forgot I had removed my protective gloves for the night. Still stunned I approached the door apprehensively, cracking it open and peering out. I couldn't believe that someone, anyone, had taken the time to visit me. We looked at each other silently for a couple uncomfortable seconds before he asked me if I was going to invite him in.

"So desperate had I grown for companionship that without thinking I opened the door wide, inviting them in. As he came in he reached out and grabbed my hand with his to give it a shake. Horrified, I quickly snatched my hand from his, but it was too late. I watched as his face quickly contorted into a look of complete confusion and pain."

"Sensing that there was something wrong the woman that had accompanied him reached out and tried to remove his hand from mine, also touching my hand in the process. Within seconds they both lay dying upon my floor. Panic filled my heart.

"Soul-searing remorse soon joined my panic. I had unintentionally done what I had been designed to do. I had only just found my new life in this place and I feared that I would either be driven out or killed. How many times and ways can a man's life be ruined?

"I found the darkest place that I could find and hid their bodies there. I hoped, and even prayed, that no one would ever find them. I guess this just wasn't to be. Do with me as you see fit, but please do not send me back to Reks's humant hoards, I would rather die."

Looking at him I thought of my dead friend and felt my trigger-finger instinctively tighten. At one time I believed that the only good humant was a dead humant. I was not so sure, any longer. I knew someday I would have to face my feelings about humants. Gritting my teeth tightly and letting out a sigh of my own I slowly lowered my weapon.

"You *should* have shared your 'ability' with those around you. If you had, your new friend might not now be dead. For now, I am going to leave you in protective custody, for your own good." I left to contemplate the growing humant problem.

I reported what the humant had shared to the group. In Derik's absence all decisions were made by vote and I was given the assignment of deciding what to do with the humants. It was hard for me to imagine why I had been given the responsibility since I probably liked humants least of all. In fact, it is safe to say that my dislike of humants approached utter hatred, with the single exception of Alan.

I sensed the importance of the decision that was mine. I did not want to be remembered as a man that lacked foresight. I tried not to let my personal experiences with humants alter my decision. Memories of the fight on my first night in the World Outside and the cause of the death of my friend Derik filled my mind and threatened to dominate all others. The only thing that found its way past the confusion within my head were Bill's words. Were humants really the victims that he believed them to be? If so, how could I punish them more than they had already been punished? Few decisions presented the dilemma that

I then faced.

Humants by their altered nature frequently presented unusual and often unseen dangers to those around them. No longer would the people of Duluth allow them to share the same neighborhoods. It was thus determined that a small, walled-off section of the city would become the home of all humants that came to live within. I felt more than a twinge of guilt as Alan was also forced to move into the new area.

Anyone wishing to visit those within the humant area of the city were allowed to come and go as they pleased, but the same privilege was not afforded to those that lived within. I tried to visit Alan as often as time permitted. He assured me during one of those visits that life within the humant-city was still immeasurably better than the lives they would had led otherwise. I tried to believe him.

After Derik's death most of the people had accepted our small group as their leaders for a time. We had fed them, given them clean water to drink, and had provided a measure of protection to them. Many of the people mourned his loss.

Talk of a replacement leader eventually began. A handful of names were advanced for nomination. A date for a vote was set and I found myself the newly elected leader of Duluth by day's end. I admit that I expected to see Porthos become the new leader. A vocal contingent of his supporters expressed their dissatisfaction with the results.

If there were a time that the future of Duluth was in question, it was then. Threats, exchanged between the groups of supporters, lowered the atmosphere within the city close to that found elsewhere in the World Outside.

I contemplated refusing the vote results in favor of Mr. Higbee in order to maintain peace. But I realized that to do so would be to introduce more of an element of chaos than already existed. Doing so would be tantamount to giving up on the fledgling government we were trying to create.

However, tension and harsh words gave way to threats and violence. The only good thing about the contention was that the number of people in the opposition was small. So when they finally stated their intention to leave the city and start their own it did not have any appreciable impact.

My first experience as leader of the city had been negative and I only hoped that I could live up to the example that had been set by Derik. I genuinely wished them all God speed and did my best to impress upon Porthos that they were welcome any time. I would like to believe they left with few hard feelings.

Determined to make the changes in Duluth that I had envisioned on my trip back from Grand Forks, I began to draw up ambitious plans. I made certain to include Aurris in as many events as was feasible and took every available free moment to tell him about the greatness of his father.

Over the short period of time that I spent with Derik we had talked many times about past experiences, current beliefs, and future hopes and dreams. I struggled to remember them and did the best I could to pass them on to his son. He looked and sounded a lot like his father, but he certainly did not act like him.

He would listen with some interest to my stories, but I could see a hardness in his eyes that I had never before seen in the eyes of a child. I could only imagine what being a child and growing up in the World Outside must have been like. Whenever Aurris shared his experiences with me they were filled with ugliness and my heart ached for him.

Once I showed him a picture book that I had found in a public library and he looked at it with childlike enthusiasm, having never seen many of the wonders it contained. Watching him that day I determined that I would save the lives of as many children as I was able. It was something I had given considerable thought. The nightmares of the first child I had seen outside the walls of the Chicago still haunted me.

I presented a plan to the group to form two units of volunteers that would be trained to find and retrieve the doubtless many children that the World Outside hid within its darkness. Each unit would depart in an opposite direction and would dedicate two months at a time to the mission. During that time two more units would be trained and prepared to depart upon the return of the first two.

My plan was received with enthusiasm and the groups were formed. Bill and Keith were among the first volunteers and I was especially glad to see it. Training was planned, carried out, and then the groups were dispatched into the world to see what they could find.

As time passed each of the groups would return with a child here and a child there. Progress was slow but the Child-Angels, as they came to be known, grew famous. Parents seeking a better place to raise their children sought them out. Soon we had enough children to warrant having a school. So, with books rummaged from various libraries, and with the help of former teachers, we set up the first and so far only, school for the children of the World Outside.

Among the many accomplishments that were made at Duluth during that period, this was the one of which I am most proud. I took the opportunity as often as time permitted to visit the school and share with the children and the teachers how happy I was to see them there.

The Duluth that I had envisioned was beginning to take shape. It took lots of hard work and planning, but I had about thirty-thousand like-minded individuals to help me make it a reality; and that number grew almost daily.

People came from far and wide, some even from other nations. The efforts made by many to reach the new world that Duluth represented impressed us all.

Many of the groups and families faced grave dangers to get there. Many had lost friends and loved-ones along the way. My heart wept for them all, but particularly for those that had to bury their children before reaching us.

At last the plans were laid and the work had begun. Everyone that came to us, as long as they shared the goal of a new opportunity, found that they were gladly accepted. All were put to work in the building of our new city. And so arose what came to be known among the citizens as New Duluth. It truly was the dawning of a new day.

Chapter 13

"… you can't please all of the people all of the time."
Abraham Lincoln

The period that followed the death of Derik was a period of growth like no other. Thankfully I had little time to dwell on his passing. As the new leader of New Duluth I was busy every day. What little time I did find for rest and relaxation I spent with Ashleigh and Aurris.

The project of transformation that lay ahead of me seemed daunting. I knew that I would have to learn to delegate many of the duties that would be required. My first official act was to appoint Clay my personal assistant.

I had worked with him by then for a number of months and knew what kind of man he was. He never lost the edge that always reminded me of a young punk, but I knew that I could trust him to get whatever job that he was given, done. Whatever kind of person he was, I suspect that his resemblance to my little brother had quite a lot to do with my decision. I thought that if I could keep him close I could also keep him out of trouble.

There were many long days, some arduous, some tedious. Often I would finish my work and simply throw myself upon my bed without undressing. So involved did I become in the efforts around me that sometimes I even forgot to eat. Only after being reminded did I realize that I really didn't have the time to spare.

I discovered early on that rebuilding a city without the aid of electricity, as well as many of the other resources typically available to city builders, was difficult at best. I spent countless hours looking for solutions to the myriad of problems that arose.

Most of the time I was swept up in the effort and felt great satisfaction with even the small successes. At other times, I felt so low and ineffective that I could barely drag myself to my bed at night. These were the times that Ashleigh would really help me.

She always had encouraging words for me, but it was at my lowest that she helped the most. She would take me by the hand to show me the progress that was being made rebuilding the city. At times she would introduce me to the families whose lives had been changed for the better. Other times she would simply hug me close and hold me silently until I felt better. Whatever she did, it always seemed to be just what I needed. If it weren't for Ashleigh's constant vigilance and help, I doubt that I would have made it through that period of planning and problems.

One day in the midst of my busyness Bill showed up in my office. He wore a solemn look and concern quickly filled my heart. He didn't leave me wondering what troubled him long as he chided me gently.

"Stephen, some time ago you asked me to do something for you that went against my better judgment. I tried in earnest to impress upon you the commitment that would be required. Only after you nearly drowned did I believe the promise that you made to complete what you started."

He was right. I had failed to keep my end of the agreement that we had made. He had only promised to train me if I promised to be a true student. I had started my training with diligence, but as my time had become more and more difficult to find, I had let it slip to an unacceptable degree. Through the lessons that I had already had I knew what it meant to be a true student and I had ceased being one.

"I realize that you are a very busy man," Bill continued, "and that your time is at a premium, but you must decide what is most important in life and make time for those things. Helping other people is a noble pursuit, and if you did nothing more for the rest of your life, I would die respecting you. But what good is helping others when you cannot even help yourself?

"You cannot learn what you desire to know without the requisite time and focus. It cannot be done. I question if you have learned anything from me at all, for my pupil would understand that commitment to self is the beginning of commitment to others. If you let yourself down, eventually you will let other people down. You have let yourself down and now you have let me down, how long will it be until you broaden your scope of disappointment?"

His words stung me like a swarm of bees. Characteristically, he did not remain for my reaction. Like all great teachers, he knew a gentle nudge can send a boat a long way into the sea. I could not sleep for the next few days.

Seeking him out, I found him and offered my sincerest apologies that I had lost my focus and asked him for his forgiveness. Smiling knowingly he simply responded, "This too is a lesson if you take it as such."

As surprising as it may sound, the renewed focus that I gave to my training with Bill gave me renewed focus on everything else that I did. I found that my days passed with a good deal less stress.

I had not moved much past the meditation and basic skills that had been my first lessons. Moving on to the next steps of my training I realized why Bill had insisted on such dedication. Simply put, it was the hardest thing I had ever done – physically and mentally.

We spent countless hours training and I was always in physical pain when we concluded. Often we would train in the wilderness. Only complete removal from the distractions of the city allowed truly effective training to occur. I left a lot of projects in the capable hands of Clay. Whenever I moved the bar higher, he would always increase his stride to keep up. I was immeasurably pleased to see his progress.

This new phase of my training began with balance and ended with Bill finally placing a wooden sword, known as a Bokken, in my hands. It is hard to explain to one who has not experienced it for themselves the inseparability of balance and the movements required in using a sword, but without one you cannot have the other.

Bill devised creative ways to train my balance, some of those methods were downright dangerous. He had me on the ledge of a high building once, walking its perimeter. He told me that before he would consider that I had graduated from balance training I would have to walk a tightrope. Needless to say we had a long way to go.

When at last he placed the Bokken into my hands, I was filled with elation. For the first time since beginning I finally felt like I was making real progress towards my goals. At least until we started actually training with it. If I thought that I had been in pain before I was in for a surprise. Bruises became companions to my constant tiredness.

He taught me circular movement by exhorting me to "do as little as possible to lose the momentum of the sword," and "never let your sword rest until the battle is over."

I began to understand why each time I had seen Bill wield his sword in battles he was always little more than a blur."

During quiet times in our training Bill said "When you complete your training with your Bokken you will move onto training with a Katana and a Wakizashi – weapons of metal."

As time passed I did move from the Bokken to the weapons of metal. I was quite nervous the first time I wielded each as I was not anxious to lose any parts of my body. But the seemingly pointless training that I had been forced to endure for such a long period of time at last showed its fruits as I was able to move onto the metal swords with minimal effort.

Making time for training had reminded me of other areas of life that had become deficient. I had spent nearly a year fulfilling my duties. From the first meeting in Bloomington through the move to New Duluth, through constant work on the water plant, through food exploration, and the trip to Grand Forks I had never made the time for the woman that always had time for me. How had I let such a thing happen?

She made us who we were. We never grew apart during my tenure as the leader of New Duluth, she saw to that. But I did not feel that my treatment was worthy of her love. Seeking a suitable way to express the deep feelings that I had for her, I could think of nothing other than marriage. At last, knowing where my priorities had to be, I asked her if she would become my wife.

From the moment I learned that Derik had managed to marry, even in the craziness that surrounded him, I knew that I too would someday marry Ashleigh. Progress in New Duluth continued steadily and, despite the tiredness that I constantly felt, I knew the time had come.

Finding a religious man to marry us was not as hard as it had been for Derik. People from just about every conceivable walk of life had come to number themselves with us. This was particularly true of those who were religious. So, on a sunny afternoon, surrounded by what had to be every citizen not otherwise occupied, we were married.

Clean cloth is a hard commodity to come by in the World Outside and white, clean cloth is just about impossible. Nearly every piece of existing white cloth in New Duluth was used in the dress that Ashleigh wore that day. If I had taken her for granted, the people of New Duluth certainly hadn't for they had come to love her and had expended considerable time and effort in making that dress.

Speechlessly I watched her as she walked down the aisle. The radiance that she had that day is beyond the ability of words to describe.

The cares that had become weights on my shoulders were gone for a brief period that day. Our honeymoon was a simple one. We simply disappeared into our new home and did not reappear for a week. Well-wishers filled our doorway with gifts and all of our meals were anonymously provided. When the week was over, I emerged with renewed vigor. Rolling up my sleeves, I dived right in and got back to work.

As the number of citizens within the city continued to swell, so too did the level of crime that seems to come with large numbers. Inviting the residents of a penal colony to join you does have its drawbacks; some who accept the invention actually deserve a penalty.

They came for the food, water, comfort, and the opportunity to take advantage of their neighbors. Inclusion in the city meant vigilance and keeping an eye on your neighbor. Although most were law-abiding and grateful to have found a haven from the World Outside, it became necessary to establish a basic Code of Conduct for all citizens. To enforce the code a small police force was established.

I resisted the establishment of the police force for as long as was feasible. Everyone in the World Outside had stories to tell about their experiences with the police. Everyone, it seemed, had already suffered the indignities of the ultimate sentence.

Along with the police came laws and the penalties for breaking them. Only a unified people, one that shared common morals and values would long survive and those that would not voluntarily do so had to be excluded.

Necessity dictated expulsion of the more troublesome elements from our new society. The irony of this was not lost on me. The World Outside had its own World Outside and we were the authors of it. We did our best to give those that we expelled the dignity that was absent from the 'civilized' world's version of being banished.

Our police force consisted of residents that served on a part-time basis. I felt that it was important that the police stay connected with the common person that lived within the city. I appointed Miguel as the first Chief of Police. The population accepted the new force as a necessary element of civilized living, but I think we all felt a certain unease about it. Crime virtually stopped then. It was easier to leave the city, where no law existed, rather than stay and possibly be arrested, or worse.

Crews of laborers were sent to clean the rubbish from the streets and to tear down and remove the buildings that had been completely destroyed. Other groups were sent to rebuild homes and larger buildings in old downtown using recycled materials. One large group was assigned to build a wall to surround the city. One small group was even assigned to plant trees and other greenery within the city wherever possible.

Everyone seemed to fulfil their jobs cheerfully. It was easy to forget that our growing city existed within the World Outside.

Still the people came. As the work continued at a surprisingly quick pace, it became apparent that the work crews would run out of materials without some sort of replenishment. In short order all available materials within the city itself had been found and put to use, something more would be needed.

Looking at a map of the old United States, one could see abandoned cities literally dotting the landscape. So quick had been the exodus that entire households had, at times, been left to fate. Forming large groups and providing them with some of the bigger vehicles we then had, I sent these groups into the surrounding cities, and in time into the surrounding states, to gather supplies.

Fuel was a constant balancing act. Would the fuel expended on a particular material run be regained during that run? Would we retain enough fuel to continue to operate our fishing vessel without oars?

Material runs became a regular occurrence then. At first the groups returned regularly, filled with unclaimed treasures. The inventory of supplies quickly grew – building materials, medical supplies, fuel, and food to name just a few. But as the nearest cities and then states were plundered of their offerings, the returns grew less and less frequent. I knew that I had a future problem on my hands, but for the time being there was plenty to continue our building.

One especially enterprising individual, the one that had provided the first horses to New Duluth, started breeding them. Everyone knew that the fuel supply would ultimately run dry and an alternate method of transportation would have to be found. Locating a farm, and equipping it with all necessary supplies, including security, we started raising horses in earnest. As time allowed, we began using more and more of them on our trips scouting for materials. Only when large items and caches were located would a vehicle requiring fuel be dispatched.

The houses that we built were simple, particularly by the standards of the cities. None had more than a few rooms and yet the demand for them far outstretched our abilities to keep up. But they were our homes and they provided for those who lived within them a sense that life could once again be 'normal.' I, myself, spent as much free time as I could spare building a home. Few pleasures compare to the feeling of accomplishment I had when I walked through the front door for the first time. It was a feeling shared by many.

We were not free from problems during this period. Quarrels between neighbors increased in proportion to the number of homes being built and attacks from humant or cannibal hoards would occur from time to time during the warmer months of the summer. But thankfully, during this period, the aliens never appeared even once.

By the time the attacks by the humants and cannibals re-commenced the first summer in New Duluth, a number of citizens had moved beyond the walls of the city to begin farming. Many of the residents had grown tired of the fish-only diet and wanted to produce alternatives. Many had come to believe that neither the humants nor the cannibals would venture so far north.

I tried to discourage them. I knew that it was just a matter of time 'til we would have to face them. Thankfully, only a few of these souls were lost before I set out to form a standing army to deal with the threats. People literally flocked to the call to join our little army.

Young and old, male and female, they came. Some had military skills, most had none. As I stood before the group that had formed, I could not help but be impressed that so many were willing to risk their lives to fight for the freedom and liberty of another.

With the help of ex-military residents, a training program was established to help those that would serve in the army. I did not have to think long about the man that should become the commanding general of the new army. Bill became General Owens at my request. The first order for the army was to protect the farms and the farmers. We did not again lose another farmer to the hoards.

News of the happenings in New Duluth traveled far and wide, people from as far away as Europe, Asia, and Africa began to appear. I was baffled at the high number of them. Some had ridden leaky, rusty ships to get to us, others had no idea how they had come to awaken in a foreign land. No matter, we took them in as best we could.

The appeal of what we had accomplished created greed and envy in some hearts. More than once our army repelled attacks from jealous groups intent on taking over what we had built. Not everyone agreed with the way we ran things in New Duluth, but they all liked what they perceived that we had. It became apparent that our small army was all that stood between our town and its destruction.

Numbers within the army never had to be supplemented beyond the volunteers it received, there were plenty willing to fight to preserve our way of life. Before long General Owens was able to establish a rotation schedule and soldiers were allowed to return to their homes on a regular basis.

As citizens of New Duluth became ever more comfortable with their lives, realizing that the influence of the World Outside stopped at the front gate, confidence grew that businesses could survive in such a place. Soon they were springing up as people sold their wares and expertise. The only permanent marketplace anywhere outside of the cities was developed.

On a personal note, I proceeded to spend every moment that I could spare with Bill and Ashleigh. Ironically, he had become a very busy man and found it difficult to find the time for our training.

Right from the start Aurris had been keenly interested in the training I received from Bill. In my desperation to fashion any sort of relationship with him, I dragged him to one of our sessions. He sat raptly watching all that we did. Unfortunately, our association never became what I had hoped it would be.

Derik and Aurris had not had enough time to develop a relationship; the brief time that the trip back to New Duluth had afforded them had not allowed it. But, whatever Aurris thought or felt about his father, he never had the kind of respect for him that I felt he deserved.

Although I had committed to watch over him and raise him, many times while speaking to him he would shout something akin to, "You are not my father!" and "He abandoned my mother and me!" Then he would stomp away to sulk somewhere.

His apparent interest in the training provided what I hoped would be an opportunity for friendship, if nothing more. Excitedly I approached Bill to ask his opinion. He did not share my enthusiasm for the idea.

"Stephen, I understand why you want me to train the boy but I'm not sure that it is the best idea."

Taken aback I asked him why. He hesitated in answering; it was obvious he was afraid of offending me. I encouraged him to answer.

"How do I say this? I know how much respect you have for Derik and that somehow, in your mind, doing this for Aurris shows that respect. But I'm telling you, Stephen, he is not a good boy and training him would be a mistake."

He was right, I was offended. Not only did I see Aurris as the innocent victim of his surroundings, a harmless child, but he was also the son of a man to whom I owed my life. The least I could do was try to provide a better life for his son.

Taking a more serious tone I said, "I would *really* appreciate it if you would do this for *me*." Shaking his head he capitulated to my pseudo-demand. It was a moment I am not proud of. So training continued and Aurris became an avid student.

He learned quickly, he had had some training before and it showed. But, whenever he sparred he seemed to enjoy being as rough on his opponent as possible. It was not the only place that he took advantage of his skills. He would pick fights with the other kids in town and sometime later sent one of them to the hospital.

Bill lectured him on the Warrior's Code after that but listening and learning are two different things. Belief in

'...the defense of myself and others' and 'attack only when compelled by the system of defense' had rang true to my heart from the beginning, Aurris saw things a bit differently.

He was not well liked in the community. People had grown tired of his juvenile rants and his abusiveness. But when he took to sharing his opinions about his father, he found few ears willing to hear them. I defended him on more than one occasion. But my claims of adolescent ignorance and a troubled childhood grew tiresome to most.

He disappeared one day shortly after turning seventeen. I didn't regularly see him so it took some time before I even noticed he was gone. I checked and double-checked among his few friends and those that knew him, but sure enough he was gone.

After satisfying myself that he was not hiding in one of the many spots he had found within the city, I approached Bill and explained my dilemma. A small group of soldiers was gathered and dispatched to track him down. Three long days later they returned, Aurris in tow. He looked extremely unhappy.

My patience had finally worn thin and I decided it would be prudent to allow us both time to calm down before we talked. I never asked him where he went or why he had left, I simply told him that if he did not wish to live with me in the city I would not stop him from leaving. I had nothing more to tell him. Respect is earned or given, not assigned; and he had none for me, his father, or our beliefs. With a look of exasperation, I left him with his thoughts.

Among the many people that arrived in the city some few did leave. Of those that left, most where the children of those that came. It pained my heart each and every time to watch them go. Blindness to what the World Outside was really like combined with youthful rebellion sent them on their way. Precious few ever found their way home.

After a time Aurris emerged from his room and gave me a perfunctory apology. Realizing the concern and effort put forth for his return he promised never to disappear again. Things improved somewhat after that. We saw each other from time to time while meeting with Bill for our training, but as time passed we had only obligatory communications and we never became close.

As my physical abilities improved I joined with the growing army in taking turns in the rotations. I insisted on the same training as all the others. Being the Commander-In-Chief of the army presented some interesting challenges to serving. Some of the soldiers with which I served felt I should not have been endangering myself while others seemed uncomfortable in my presence. In the end Bill advised me that I could better serve by focusing on maintaining the city for which the others fought.

About ten months after my marriage to Ashleigh, we had our first child, a son. We named him Derik Paul Blake. I practically burst my buttons with pride. Nearly the entire city joined with us to celebrate. The tenuous relationship that I had with Aurris, for all intents and purposes, ended that day.

I was working on some plan a few days later when Aurris stormed into my office. He loudly demanded that we talk. Sending the others on break, I responded with my own rudeness. I was embarrassed and I wanted him to know it.

He spoke distantly to me, "I will no longer spend any more time here in your personal empire. I was happy in my old home. I had true friends there; they cared about me and wanted me to be truly happy. I liked the weather there better too. After living here for the past few months I no longer wonder if hell is hot or cold. Man was not meant to live in such harshness.

"I was living my life happily there when one day this guy shows up claiming to be my father. Failing to be of any help during a battle with the humants, he convinces the whole group to follow him into the great unknown and I am dragged to this horrid place.

"I've tried to fit in here, but you people think differently than I do. People here just don't know how to live life. The World Outside is how all life should be forever. I don't have to fit into anyone's mold there, I can be anything or do anything that I feel like there, good...or bad."

My skin crawled as Aurris put great emphasis on the word 'bad,' but still he wasn't finished.

"People go to such lengths to tell me what a wonderful man Derik was, well I didn't know him. The only thing that I am absolutely certain about is that this 'great' man left me and my mother before I was even born. My mother died from a broken heart!

"My spirit needs freedom and neither you, nor the memory of a dead man, will keep me here any longer. You told me once that if I ever decided to leave that you would not stop me. Well, here I am to tell you that I am leaving and I expect you to honor your word. I am going to shake the dust from this place off my feet and I will never look back. Set me free, Blake."

My heart sunk, but I was not surprised. Somehow I had always known that day was coming. Acknowledging my agreement with him with a silent nod, I could do little as I stood and watched him go. I couldn't help but feel that I had let my best friend down. I did not expect to see Aurris alive again.

Frantic parents paid me a visit after his departure. A number of the other teen-aged children of those within the city had decided to go with him. His impact on the community had been more extensive than I had allowed myself to believe. I could do little but offer my apologies. They sounded hollow to me and I can only imagine that's how they sounded to them.

Bill appeared then, shaking his head sadly. I was sure he had come to gloat, come to remind me that he had told me so. Instead he whispered through clenched teeth, "He took my sword. Heaven knows what havoc he can wreck with that." Then he disappeared into the surrounding crowd of concerned parents. Despite it all, I still wanted to believe that Aurris was the victim of a life that had offered him fear and hate.

I replayed our conversation in my mind; did I have a 'personal empire?' I wondered if anyone else felt that they were living in a de facto dictatorship. I became so consumed by the question that I started having dreams in which I was the king of my own kingdom; dreams that would almost invariably end violently with me overthrown and executed by the unhappy masses. When I could take my dreams no longer, I knew what had to be done.

Looking through the books at the library for particular information could be a time-consuming task. Most of the books had been either destroyed, looted, or just strewn about the floor. So early one morning, before Ashleigh awoke, I headed out. Making my way to the library I searched for it. I had anticipated days of searching, perhaps fate wanted me to find it. A short time later I had in my hands a copy of the Constitution of the former United States of America.

All nations had merged into one great whole with the creation of the Federaal Commonwealth of Nations. I had never seen a constitution written for that world-nation, so I had to look elsewhere for my inspiration. I remembered seeing a small copy of the U. S. Constitution on the pages of an old history textbook. My recent exposure to the quote from Thomas Jefferson had brought it to mind.

The government of New Duluth had been hastily formed. Growth had necessitated its creation. Before it, each group had made its own rules and important decisions. Those that had far-reaching implications were generally voted on by those groups. The new government had included a single elected office: City Minister. All other positions were appointed by the Minister, a dangerous arrangement for any man. I had not created what the city had become alone and I was determined that I would not lead it alone either.

Carrying my treasure to my office. I began to pen the words to a new constitution. I borrowed liberally from the words that I found in it, changing only those things necessary to recognize a different set of circumstances. Still the heart of it remained, that all men were entitled to the blessings of liberty, domestic tranquility, and a common defense.

I wondered if such a small group could be served by a document that had been written for a much larger nation. Ultimately, I felt that the government defined within it could be made to serve any size population. Only the number of representatives to be found therein would need to be different.

Eagerly I carried the constitution to the people. Public discourse followed. It was evident that the concept of self-determination and representative government appealed to the people. The vote of acceptance was almost unanimous.

I have never known how the news of what happened in New Duluth spread throughout the World Outside, but we continued to grow unabated. Our members had moved beyond the gates of the city and could be found in neighboring towns and inhabiting the countryside.

I became the first President of the fledgling government of New Duluth and within weeks elections for the Representatives and Senators were held. Shortly thereafter judges were appointed. As corny as it may sound, the realization that we had created our own sovereign nation occurred to us. A new pride and national identity began to sweep through the population.

Six years passed quickly as the numbers within New Duluth swelled past a hundred-thousand. Experts in nearly every subject eventually passed through the front gate. A hydro-electric plant was brought on line during that period of time, followed closely by food-processing factories and even a fuel refinery. Finding raw materials for the refinery was a difficult proposition. Lights, old appliances, heat, and even cars appeared among the residents. A new reality, beyond even my wildest dreams, was taking shape.

We realized early on that if we wanted to have food during the winter we had to store it during the summer. Often the lake would freeze near the shore and we were unable to move our boat to catch fish, and the ground became as hard as rock and planting was impossible.

Winters in our part of the World Outside were difficult at best. I had never had to experience a true winter without the resources of New Duluth. I knew from the horror stories I heard all-too-often that many people died during the winter months, some from exposure, many more from starvation. Living in the North only complicated things. Of all the reasons people gave for coming to New Duluth, the ability to survive the winter exceeded all others. No source of food production existed beyond our influence.

During the first year of my tenure I had appointed Keith Olson Agricultural Minster. I remembered from our trip to Grand Forks his desire to make a difference without having to fight. I wanted to provide him with the opportunity to do so. His was the job of securing satisfactory food resources by looking for new methods of production and regularly inspecting existing facilities. Time had seen our mutual respect for each other grow.

I made a habit of joining him, on occasion, on his inspections of the farms that dotted the countryside around our city. I wanted to show my support for the courage of the farmers and it always helped the morale of the soldiers that I met.

Clay had always accompanied me on those joint inspections as my personal assistant. He had matured considerably during our time together, but try as I might, I still saw him as a replacement for my little brother. We had just finished our visit with one of the farmers and were exiting the house when I saw them descending upon us.

Humants, what must have been hundreds of them, rushed towards us. I had never seen humants travel in such numbers, but when I saw the humant that led them, my blood ran cold.

That horrible humant that had ripped the hole in the hide-out of my first home, the one with the giant axe, the one that had nearly killed Derik and gotten away, led them.

At that moment it didn't matter how far I'd come or all the things I had accomplished since first seeing that monster, my knees grew weak and I felt the same sick sensation in the pit of my stomach I had felt then.

Rushing forward the humant army mercilessly fell upon the handful of soldiers that surrounded the farm. Many of the humants fell, but their sheer numbers finally overpowered the soldiers. Watching the unfolding defeat I could see the monster was heading directly for me.

As he charged I could hear him shouting orders to his humant troops and pointing them the directions that they were to go. Closing on my position he grasped his gigantic axe with both hands and smiled evilly.

While pulling my weapon from my belt, pictures of him escaping my last barrage as he scurried up the rope, filled my head. Quickly these pictures were replaced by visions of my life as it too began to flash through my head. I figured then I was about to die.

Both the monster and I were surprised when Keith, flying through the air and screaming at the top of his lungs, lunged for it. He knocked the monster slightly off center, but it simply swept its arm to the side, throwing Keith to the ground, motioning for one of his humant minions to finish him off.

I watched with horror as the appointed humant approached him, picking him off the ground in a vicious bear hug before disappearing into the surrounding hoard.

Shouting my rage as loud as I was able, I aimed my weapon at the monster and began firing. One, two, three, and on they went until my clip was empty. I barely slowed his approach. With my ammunition spent I could do little as he closed on me. Looking briefly at Clay I could see that he fought valiantly by my side. When the monster reached us he did not raise his axe, instead he raised one large fist and then knocked me unconscious.

I awoke a few moments later, bouncing along, hanging over the monster's shoulder. My head ached and I could tell without touching it that many parts of my face had swelled. I realized that I could only see out of one of my eyes. I was too shaken to put up a fight.

I could hear the faint sound of what must have been an engine. As we moved the sound increased to the point of deafening but I did not recognize what it belonged to.

Only after the monster removed me from his shoulder and tossed me into a small opening did I see that the sound belonged to an airplane engine. I landed with a thud. My vision blurred when my head struck the metal floor. Hearing a familiar voice, I turned towards it.

A few feet from me was Clay. He was tied securely. Relief flooded through me to see him alive. He shouted my name and begged me not to pass out while I looked at him. But as the engine sound increased enormously and the plane began to move forward, darkness closed in. I passed out with Clay's voice echoing loudly in my head.

Chapter 14

"He descended into Hell."
The Apostles Creed

When at last I woke from my unconsciousness and could hear the sound of the engines, I knew immediately we were still on the airplane. Turning my head ever so slightly and waiting for my vision to clear I looked for Clay. I found him laying close by, staring blankly into space. I spoke as quietly as I could.

"Clay? Are you okay Clay?"

Blinking a few times he looked at me. "I think I have a couple of broken ribs and my right arm has gone numb, but I'll be okay. You're the one that I've been real worried about Stephen. You didn't look good when they dumped you into the plane at first and when you passed out I thought you were a goner. It took me a while to see if you were even still breathing. How are you feeling now?"

My head still pounded so I didn't move much but I assured him that I would be alright. We were both in pretty bad shape and securely bound. All we could really do was lay quietly for a few minutes before we could hear sound coming from the front of the plane.

Craning my neck slowly, I could see that the humant monster that had carried me to the plane had entered our area through a small bulkhead door that he barely fit through. Closing it behind him, he knelt on one knee just above me. Although one of my eyes was nearly swollen closed, I turned my head and glared up at him through my one good eye. I was more than a little surprised to hear it speak.

Its voice was deep and gravelly and it spoke slowly. "You great Blake warrior. I see you before, you not look so great to me. Just fearful puny man."

I really did not know how to respond to it, speech was not an ability I had ever imagined it might have. I just continued looking at it as it continued speaking.

"Master Kriton want you now. I tell him you not worth trouble. He get very angry and have me beaten. I think you must have some purpose I know not. I am not happy that you, puny man, have caused me such big trouble."

As it spoke its face twisted into a snarl and it grabbed me by my neck in its massive clawed hand. Lifting me from the floor it went on. "I make Blake pay now."

The pressure on my neck increased and I quickly found myself unable to breath. Struggling against its grip I did not begin to have the strength needed to free myself.

Clay protested but was straightaway silenced by the monster kicking him solidly in the stomach. Grimacing in pain, he curled into a ball and was silent. I fought to breath as the monster maintained his grip on my neck, snarling at me wickedly.

While holding me off the floor the monster grasped my left fingers within its large free hand. Gritting its teeth and looking at me with obvious hatred, it began to bend them backwards. The pain then began to build as the bones of my fingers struggled against the massive pressure being exerted upon them. One by one I heard them crack, sending excruciating pain up my arm.

He dumped me unceremoniously onto the cabin floor once he had finished with my fingers. I landed on my shoulder and the side of my head. A low groan escaped my lips as I tried to endure the new pain that had been inflicted upon me.

Thankfully the monster left then and Clay and I spoke not a word during the remainder of our flight. We simply looked into each other's pain-filled eyes and hoped that the other would ultimately be alright. At long last, I could tell that we were descending by the noises coming from the engines and the popping in my ears. I was certain that the pain had only just begun.

Before then, I had never been to Long Island. I knew that Reks Kriton based his operations there and I suspected that that was where we were. It was dark as we were taken from the plane. The same monster that had tortured me on the way appeared once more to throw me over his shoulder. Other guards appeared and grabbed Clay roughly. Placing a gun to his head, one of them looked at me and said, "As long as you behave your little friend here will not be harmed." We were taken in different directions.

I did not move as it carried me, I was simply in too much pain. I felt beaten and defeated. We were in a large complex of buildings I assumed had been a college campus at one time. I was taken into one of the smaller buildings and to a room that was lit by electric lights.

Electricity did not exist in the World Outside beyond New Duluth. Only through extraordinary efforts had we been able to provide it there. I wondered what kind of man this Reks Kriton really was. I was set upon a chair at the end of a long table to wait. The pain in my left hand threatened to overwhelm me; I simply laid it on the arm of the chair and tried to ignore it. My wait was not long.

Hearing some commotion, I looked up from my chair to see what was going on. A small group of people were entering the room. Some of the people were obvious humants, some I could not tell, but they all seemed to be swirling around one older looking man in their midst. This, I assumed, was Reks Kriton.

I had never given much thought to what Mr. Kriton looked like. But I have to admit, that I expected more than what met my eyes.

Wearing a white lab-coat he entered the room. In his hands he carried my rolled-up beret. He placed it on the table next to him as he sat in the chair opposite mine. I could see that his blonder hair was turning gray and he wore a very thin moustache and neatly-trimmed beard of the same color. He looked gaunt and old. Had I not known who it was that sat across from me I would have thought him to be perfectly harmless.

Before he had a chance to utter a single word I jumped to my feet and demanded the whereabouts of Clay. He listened to my demands as the corner of his lip curled slightly in amusement. Then, motioning me to sit, he answered with a disarmingly quiet tone.

"Please, Mr. Blake, be seated. You and your friend are my very special guests and he is being taken good care of as we speak. We are tending to his wounds and will see to it that he is given our finest guest quarters in which to rest and recoup."

Relaxing slightly then I sat back into the chair, gritting my teeth from the pain in my hand and waiting for him to continue. Motioning to one of his associates, who approached me with some sort of medicine applicator, he began to speak. While he spoke they wrapped my broken hand and gave me what I hoped was some sort of pain medication.

"I'm sure you're wondering why I brought you here Mr. Blake. I've been in the World Outside from the very first day it was created. In fact, unknown to most people, I was its very first *official* resident. They tried to pick the most heinous person that society had to offer to be the first to go. Brilliance is often feared and misunderstood, so

I was given the label and, after a kangaroo court, was promptly expelled. Few people comprehended what society was losing. C'est 'la vie, their loss.

"I've seen thousands of people come and go in my time here. I've seen just about every shape, color, and size of man, woman, and child imaginable. I've seen the smart ones, the dumb ones, the skilled, the not-so-skilled and the ones that I put on the front lines because that's about all they were good for. I've met the tacticians and the scientists, but I don't believe that I've ever come across anyone quite like you Mr. Blake."

Over the years I had spent in the World Outside I had created my own demonic image of the man who was now speaking to me. He was kind of like the boogie man of the World Outside. So I genuinely did not know what to think as I heard him say such things about me, so I silently continued to listen.

"You came into the World Outside under controversial circumstances, the suspect of a murder that you claim to have no knowledge of. A man that had spent his life as a lowly hydrological technician. You enter the World Outside and within a few short years rise to become one of the most ambitious and respected men – besides me, of course – to have ever lived here. Am I accurate?"

I sat in profoundly stunned silence. How could Reks Kriton, a man that had spent more of his life in the World Outside making humants then in the cities, know so much about me? Through my pain I pulled myself up to listen with interest as he continued.

He must have seen the puzzled look on my face then. "I have maintained various connections to the world within the cities over the years. This has proven to be very useful to me. But I won't bore you with minor details that right now."

Minor details?! Just who was he kidding?! Not once, not one time ever, had I met a person that had an ongoing connection to anyone in the cities. And yet here was a man, probably the most notorious resident of the World Outside, sharing this fact with me. I remained too stunned to respond appropriately.

"Anyway, back to you Mr. Blake. Take, for instance, that lowly burg Duluth. Although I can't imagine why anyone in their right mind would want to live in such a frigid place personally, no matter. You take this run-down destroyed hole of a city and transform it into a place where people flock to live – even in the dead of the winter. I understand people have come unimaginable distances just to live in your city.

"At first I only heard rumors of this place where people went to escape the World Outside, along with the stories of the man that created and lead it. But soon the rumors grew into longer and longer tales until some of the stories that I heard sounded more like fantastic legends than any real place. How could I help but take notice of these things and the man that had single-handedly accomplished them? You should be proud of yourself Stephen, men have been trying to accomplish what you have for years. So I decided that I just had to meet the man that I had heard so much about. And so here we are."

It seemed like an obvious question to me, but I asked it nonetheless. "So what do you want Mr. Kriton? Something tells me that this is not just a social visit."

He smiled with obvious satisfaction then and continued. "You are very perceptive Mr. Blake, I appreciate that trait in the men and women that I work with. I want you to work for me, you and your city in old Duluth."

"Work for you?" I croaked out in response, "Why would I ever want to work for you?"

The matter-of-fact way that he responded allowed me a brief look inside the man and gave me shivers.

"Because you see Mr. Blake, there are only two kinds of people in the World Outside: those that work for me, including those that will eventually, and those that do not.

"You see the World Outside belongs to me. I *am* the World Outside and I control everything in it and you, my friend, are part of that world. I believe that my organization could use a man like yourself. The choice you face is a simple one, either join me and benefit from our association or never leave my complex alive. I simply cannot have a man like you doing things that are not approved by me."

The arrogance that dripped from his words nauseated me. I had no doubt that an unwanted answer from me would bring dire consequences, so I played along. "What you say sounds like a reasonable offer Mr. Kriton. What exactly would you want of us?"

Looking somewhat surprised, but pleased, he continued. "You seem to be a wise man Mr. Blake, few of the people to whom I make these offers are ever able to see the big picture. I would like to use you and your army to help me rid myself of some particularly pesky groups. My humants have been unable to defeat them, due mainly to their defenses. They are all well-fortified within some structure, be it a cave or a valley or something similar and they always mow my armies down as they approach. I need a group that can get into their bases and destroy them from the inside. In short, I need a Trojan Horse. If you do this for me, I will make sure that you are *well* rewarded."

Just the mere suggestion of what he wanted me and the people of New Duluth to do to our fellow beings infuriated and sickened me, but I had to buy time to think. So I asked him if I could ponder it for a night. He readily agreed.

I was shown to a plush room. It was huge by most standards and contained an overstuffed bed with satin sheets. There was an attached bathroom that was almost as large as the living room of my home. I was offered any food that my heart could desire to snack on, but I turned it down. The bed was as comfortable as it had looked but I laid upon it unable to sleep for most of the night.

The next morning I was taken to a large dining room where I was served a huge breakfast. Reks appeared quietly and sat opposite me once again. I had never seen so much prepared food in one place since entering the World Outside. Not only was food scarce, but making so much food, ensuring a certain portion would go to waste, was unthinkable. I ate my fill quietly, avoiding the inevitable for as long as possible.

We did not speak as we finished our meals. Reks was done before I was since I was eating slowly, stalling for time. Watching me patiently, he finally spoke.

"Usually my guests are overwhelmed at the delights that I can offer them here; food that exists only in their memories along with warm and comfortable beds. You've probably seen your share of those reactions, haven't you Mr. Blake? I am still amazed at the things people will do for a full belly. But I digress.

"How would you like a tour of my humble facility here, Mr. Blake? I would be delighted to hear the opinions of the man that built a city virtually out of nothing."

I doubted his sincerity but I had spent a good portion of my night wondering what secrets he kept there, so I readily agreed. It allowed me the chance to further stall what I knew was coming.

Our tour commenced with the dining room where we had just eaten. I had been too absorbed in my thoughts to have taken notice of the works of art that hung from the walls. They were quite beautiful when Reks pointed them out to me. He shared that his complex had two such dining rooms and that we had been in the other the previous night.

He spoke of his fondness for beautiful works of art. At once I found myself pondering the paradox that was this man, creating such ugliness in the humants. Yet again, I wondered how he had come into possession of such things.

I was led from the dining room into a much larger room. This, I was told, was the grand ball room. It was even more ornately decorated than the dining rooms had been. Exquisite works of art hung from the walls, huge chandeliers hung from the ceiling, and plush-padded furniture scattered the room. I marveled at the thought of the balls that might be held there. Who would attend such an event?

We left that building and entered a large tower. Within the lobby was the largest group, besides the army that had taken me, of humants that I had ever seen in one place. I saw children, some as young as five or six among them. Like the child that I had seen so long ago, outside the walls of Chicago, I became sick at the sight of them. How could Reks commit such atrocities on children? I knew that asking would seal my fate so I held my tongue and continued the tour. In the past I might have been shocked, even stunned, at what I saw. But I had long since become hardened to many of the horrors that were so common in the World Outside.

As I looked at the humants I noticed that many of them looked at me with suspicion as we walked past. Seeing my concerned look, Reks assured me. "Don't worry about them Mr. Blake. This old college dormitory is where my children live when they are not off doing my bidding. They won't harm you as long as you are with me and I don't tell them to."

I'd had considerable exposure to humants by then, and had even grown to know a few, but they had not lost their ability to make me uneasy at their mere presence. I was happy when we left that building to continue our tour. On my way out I looked up at the tower and counted at least twenty floors. It must have housed hundreds, perhaps even thousands, of humants, and it was not the only tower on the campus.

At that point I asked Reks, "Mr. Kriton, how do you make them? There are so many different variations. I'm aware that there have been many marvelous advances in genetic engineering, but I can't believe that it alone can account for the vast differences that we saw in that last building alone."

Turning towards me and giving me a wink he said, "Well, let's just say that I had a little help from our alien friends." I tried to ask him what he meant but he stopped my further questions by simply placing his finger to his lips with a silent "Shhh". I took the hint.

We walked for a time towards the edge of the campus. I looked at the various buildings as we passed and wondered what nefarious things were going on within their walls. But I could not get his last comment out of my mind. What did he mean? I would soon get a front-row seat to some of the worst of it.

When at last we reached the edge of the campus we entered a large warehouse-like building. The front of the building had one large door that bent horizontally in the middle for raising and lowering. It had a normal-sized door in the bottom right corner through which we entered. Within the building, parked in random positions, were a number of airplanes.

It was quite a sight. The transportation system between the cities had made airplanes obsolete. Aside from my unfortunate ride to that place, my experience with them had been confined to history books and museum displays. Many times our material teams had happened upon them, but with no identifiable value, we had left them all. Could our appraisal of their value been incorrect?

Some of the older ones had propellers, some had rotor blades, a few had anti-grav engines. They all appeared to be in working order as humants scurried about them. Some of them had their heads under open hoods and some were cleaning them off.

"I'm quite certain that this is a collection like none that you've ever seen in the World Outside. Am I correct Mr. Blake?"

Nodding I mumbled, "Nope, not in the World Outside or in the cities. I've never seen this many aircraft in one place."

Reks smiled with evident satisfaction. "They do come in handy when I need to get things done; like inviting you here, for instance." Without looking at him my eyebrows raised with the thought, 'some invitation'.

We walked past each craft in the hanger heading towards a door at the back of the large room. Once there we entered the room beyond. It was much darker, but as my eyes adjusted to the light I could see that it was a large utility room. Water boilers, chillers, and scores of electrical junction boxes lined the walls and floor. They all hummed with evident activity. Seeing nothing to lose at that point I had to ask.

"You know Mr. Kriton, I spent many months in my attempts to provide electricity for the residents of New Duluth. There have been good days and bad days. Weeks have passed since the plant came back on line and still we are plagued with regular black-outs. Even when it is working, lights flicker regularly as the supply is unsteady. Since arriving here I have not seen a single hint of fluctuation in your power. How do you do it?"

Smiling smugly, he answered, "Let's just say that it has to do with my connection to those within the cities."

Once again my eyebrows flew up and I asked incredulously, "Just what do you mean by that?"

"Well, I provide important services for a certain group of people within the city of New York. They happen to be a group of people that are well-connected. One of my fees for helping them is a direct connection into their power grid. After all, I decided a very long time ago that I was not going to live like the rest of the ilk that exists within the World Outside. I saw an opportunity and I took it. Not only do they provide me with all of the power that I could ever need, but they also provide me with food and fuel. See what you could become a part of?"

It was a compelling offer. But everything about the man felt wrong. What I really wanted to know was how he had made his connection to the group that he had mentioned and what he could possibly offer them for which he was being so handsomely rewarded.

I couldn't contain my thoughts any longer and I blurted out, "What could you possibly do for anyone in New York that is worth all this?" I finished as I motioned all around me.

Smiling even more smugly he said, "Every great civilization needs a mad man on their payroll, someone that isn't afraid to function outside the law. However, despite how useful such an 'employee' is to the government, they could never acknowledge that they exist. That is not a problem that exists for someone like me since I am the law here. You might say I am the Minister of Dirty Works for the Commonwealth." As he finished he chucked slightly before continuing, "We really need to finish our tour Stephen, we have so much to do."

I could feel the tension building within me as I followed him out of the utility room and into a large multi-stall garage. There I found a brief respite from my concerns as I stood to take in the many vehicles that surrounded us. I had seen antique vehicles before then, had even worked on and driven a few of them. But never had I seen so many perfectly-preserved cars in my life.

They ranged from small and swift to large and powerful. I recognized the make of most but some I had never heard of. My breathless awe gave me away and Reks said knowingly, "Ah, a fellow aficionado. Most people are not interested in such relics, preferring the cold and emotionless skimmers that are so prevalent today. But not me. These represent a bygone day when craftsmanship and the beauty of a creation meant something. These were built by people that understood such things.

"Whenever I lack inspiration or motivation for a project upon which I am laboring, I simply come in here and look at them for a few moments. After that I am able to return to my work and create truly glorious things. Maybe someday, after you have proven yourself to me, I will allow you to drive them."

I took a mental note of the location of that building as we exited. I kept looking back towards it as we walked to another part of campus. We spent a short time then in a large impressively well-stocked library before moving on. What I saw no longer impressed me. He had not built what we toured from the scratch of burnt-out rubble; he was borrowing his extravagance from the city of New York. He saved the worst part of our tour for last.

The next building we entered through a large security door. It and the next door required a security code to get through. Between the two doors I felt and heard the air exchange as we proceeded through an airlock. Beyond the second door we entered a long hallway, bordered on both sides by large windows. A single door could be found in the middle of each window, mostly window themselves.

Beyond each long window was a single room. Each room was outfitted as a surgical suite. I feared what I would see there, and as we continued down the hall I could see that some of the rooms were occupied. Most of the occupants were sedated, some were not. Mercifully none appeared to be aware of what was happening.

I knew immediately, from the many terrible stories about that place, where I was. It was the stuff my darkest nightmares were made of. I knew the terrible things that happened there and I tried my best to look straight forward as we walked down the hall, but my eyes wandered for brief moments a few times.

Words would fail to communicate the horrible things that I saw as I walked down that hall, Mr. Ranston. My entire being filled with awful dread as we continued. The things that were being done to the people within each of those rooms were never meant to be. I actually found that I had tears welling up in my eyes and my heart went out to each of those poor souls. If I had had the means to do so, I would have stopped the atrocities that I was witnessing. As it was, all I could do was continue past them.

Passing the final set of windows in what felt like an endless hall I turned and met the gaze of a condemned soul as she lay upon the table. What was left was barely human. Covering my mouth in gut-wrenching horror I realized that she was conscious. Her eyes betrayed her awareness as they pleaded with me. They seemed to say, 'Kill me. Please.' I turned away quickly and stifled the vomit as it rose into my throat.

Reks looked at me then and could see me turning a few shades of green. He actually chuckled heartily, slapped me on my back and said, "Oh, don't worry about this place Stephen. You'll get used to this eventually. It is, after all, what we do here." He then opened the door at the end of the hall and motioned for me to enter. I was more than happy to leave that place.

The room beyond was obviously an office. It contained various filing cabinets, and a large desk in the center of the room strewn with papers. It looked like any other office, but I knew that it belonged to Mr. Kriton when he took his seat behind the desk.

I sensed what was coming next. He asked me if I was impressed by what I saw; I answered honestly that I was. In fact, I was overwhelmed. At last he began to ask the question I had avoided, but before he could finish his sentence one of the individuals that had been working in one of the surgical suites opened the door and frantically motioned Reks to follow. Looking with irritation at the interruption he arose and asked me to excuse him for a moment.

The moment turned into minutes and the minutes dragged on. I stood and waited and wondered what my answer would be. I knew that if I answered incorrectly my chances of ending up in one of the rooms I had just passed were good. Just the thought made my heart sink.

I noticed then that some of the papers on his desk had photographs attached to them. Creeping forward to get a better look, I began to read the top-most paper. What I read there made by blood run cold.

In large letters at the top of the page was the letterhead of the City-State of New York. It was split into two sections. The first section of the page was a short memo with a request from the New York City-State Department of Health and Research for a very specific genetic experiment to be conducted on a 'volunteer'.

Following this was a completed section titled: RESULTS. I assumed that Reks had provided the results. Attached to the paper was a before and after set of photos. The after photo barely resembled a human and once again I had to work at not vomiting.

No wonder Reks was provided with all the comforts that he required. Experiments like the ones that he was conducting would have been absolutely illegal. But the corrupt politicians had found a way around that little problem. They had a dirty little secret and his name was Reks Kriton.

Afraid of what I might yet find on his desk, but afraid not to, I continued to riffle through the papers. There were literally dozens of 'experiment' papers on his desk alone. Looking at the far wall of his office I counted eight full-sized filing cabinets. Reks had been at this for a very long time. As I shuffled through the papers a picture caught my eye and I stopped short.

There, attached to a blank 'experiment' page was a picture of Clay. Looking at his 'before' photo, all of the nightmares I had had about my brother entering that awful place and being subjected to surgery flooded into my head. Anger surged within me then as I held the crumpled paper to my face. Then I heard the door close behind me.

Spinning quickly I tossed Clay's sheet towards Reks and shouted, "You are a sick man. You promised me that my friend would be taken care of and yet, I find that you have done these terrible things to him. I could NEVER EVER be your associate Mr. Kriton. You are an abomination of nature."

Pursing his lips and gritting his teeth he pondered a moment before picking the sheet off of the ground. "I am disappointed in you Mr. Blake. I guess you are not the leader that I thought you were. You are a small-minded individual obsessed with trifles. Great leaders do not allow themselves to become emotionally attached to the people that serve them. Doing so is a weakness, a weakness that can be exploited by your enemies. This was a test that you have failed.

"It's a shame really. We two cannot exist in the same world, Stephen. One of us would eventually have to die. I assure you that it will not be me. But just to show you what a gracious person I really am, instead of killing you, I'm going to give you the opportunity to play the Grid.

"Every player that has ever played the Grid has had the benefit of surgical improvement before they played. It is highly doubtful that anyone not so improved could live through the experience. You are very full of yourself Mr. Blake and so I am going to give you the first ever chance to play the Grid just like you are now. I have heard that you fear humants, so it seems fitting that you will live your last moments with them. In the end you won't make it, but it'll be fun to watch."

I lunged at him then, but he simply raised his hand and I was thrown backwards into the desk by an unseen force. I found that I was unable to move my limbs and so I could do nothing but lie there and wait. Summoning two guards to retrieve me, Reks stood above me and simply shook his head in disgust.

Unable to walk, I was dragged from the office. We headed to the basement as I was hauled down a flight of stairs. I noticed a foul stench as we continued, one which grew steadily worse. Both guards grumbled as we entered that room, plugging their noses with their free hand.

In the middle of the room was a large pit, some thirty foot square. It was filled with a foul greenish-yellow substance. The ceiling was covered with holes and tubes that led to who-knows-where. Peering over the side of the pit, I could see what looked like feces and liquid spill from a number of holes and fall into the mire below.

The stench in the room was overpowering. As I stood contemplating what I was seeing, one of the guards pressed a button on a small plate just inside the door and put plastic gloves onto his hands.

A low grating noise followed the button and soon a small concrete pylon rose from the center of the muck in the pit. It resembled a miniature obelisk, with a metal ring set into the point at its top.

At that moment the guard to my right grasped my arms firmly and placed handcuffs on my wrists. Threading a small chain through the handcuffs, he handed one end to the other guard. Reaching forward he grasped the filth-covered metal ring on the concrete pylon and started threading the other end through it. I knew then why he had put on gloves.

It began to dawn on me what their plan was. At first my body did not respond to my attempts at resistance. But as they hooked both ends together, completing the length of chain thereby connecting me to the pylon, I found that I was able to move my arms and legs ever-so-slightly.

To my dismay I was lifted from the floor and simply dumped into the pool of detestable matter. The weight of the chain along with my restricted movement caused me to sink to the bottom. I struggled with all my strength while I held my breath, but the unknown force that held my body was unrelenting.

This was a lesson I'd already had, at the edge of a pond years earlier. Calming myself I thought of the meditation training I had received. How grateful I was then, as the strength returned to my arms and legs and I stood, for the quiet insistence of Bill. Breaking the surface of the pool I could not believe where I found myself. I tried to clear my face by rubbing it on the sleeve of my shirt.

No sooner had I gained my footing but I heard a soft gurgle as the metal-ring on the tip of the pylon slid under the surface. I could feel it as it descended and pressure began to build on the short chain that held me fast. My hands and arms were forced back into the muck and I was actually forced to kneel on the floor of the pit. At that level only my head, just above my chin, cleared the surface of the pool. I looked incredulously at the guards as they laughed heartily and left the room.

I really have no idea how long I remained there. I had no sense of time. My back and neck ached as I struggled to keep my face above the surface. Constantly, the sounds of liquid and solid matter falling into the pool surrounded me. I was forced to close my eyes to keep them from being splattered.

I became exhausted and had to fight the urge to sit a number of times. I wondered how much longer I could make it when I was startled to hear a familiar voice call me from somewhere above. Cracking my eyes through the muck that then covered my face I looked towards the door to see who was speaking.

There, standing defiantly with arms crossed, stood Aurris, the son of my mentor and friend Derik. He had a wicked grin on his face as he began to speak.

"I'm glad to see that the information I gave Mr. Kriton paid off and that he was able to find you. I told him that you would never join him. You have the same silly devotion to 'honor' and 'duty' that fool, my father, or Bill, have."

Stunned to see him there, I interrupted. "Why are you here, Aurris? You must know what this place is. Please tell

223

me you're not working for Reks. Did I teach you nothing?"

He continued with obvious disdain. "No! I learned what I needed to know from Bill, and that did not include any of that bleeding-heart drivel that you and he liked to spew. He gave me the tools to defeat fools like you. I know how you tick.

"Leaving you was the best thing that ever happened to me. You were holding me down with all of your rules.
I wandered for a short time after leaving you, traveling east. I found some people that thought like I do, but I also found a lot of people that were traveling to Duluth. Idiots!"

"I tried to tell them what they were in for, but none of them ever listened to reason."

I couldn't help but smile just a bit upon hearing that. Still, he continued.

"I finally found myself at the coast and heard about this game called the Grid. It sounded exciting and I could hardly wait to see it. I accompanied the group that I had more or less joined up with to the game, and it was better than I had imagined it could be.

"After witnessing its absolute brilliance, I knew that I had to meet its creator. So, after a few well-placed inquiries, I found myself in front of Mr. Kriton, a man whose genius you obviously do not understand or appreciate. No matter, when he learned who I was he offered me a position within his organization. I, unlike you, can see an opportunity when it is placed before me and I accepted."

"You keep referring only to yourself, what happened to the others that followed you here?" I retorted.

Looking thoughtful and then amused he responded, "Oh yes, the morons. Well, my offering of Duluth's youth to Mr. Kriton earned for me something of far greater value than any of the pathetic recycled junk that you ever offered me: his gratitude. He made me a General in his Army and put me in charge of procuring volunteers. Your buddy Clay was real eager to participate."

He laughed shamelessly as I strained against the chain that held me tight, groaning in anguish.

"Watch it Steve, mind the Warrior's Code. Incidentally, that twisted Code prevents true progress. Only in the World Outside can one achieve genuine greatness, only here can one actually experience what training can only attempt to teach. Death, real death in all its forms, is the best teacher of all."

I croaked my response around the lump in my throat "Bill was right, you are evil and your heart is black Aurris. What has made you so?"

"Black? Well that really depends on your point-of-view, doesn't it? I prefer to see myself as ambitious. But you never did understand me and I don't expect you to start now. Well, I've got to go now Stephen, but I understand that I'll be seeing you again real soon in the Grid. You're gonna love it. Ta ta."

Once again I felt as if I had failed Derik as I watched him go. I had been unable to see him for who he really was, he was Derik to me. Only the memory of my friend, and the knowledge that he would mercifully never see what his son had become, kept me from sinking into oblivion.

Chapter 15

"It is a place you send people to die — creatively."
Reks Kriton

My time in that disgusting pool went on for what felt like an eternity. I was thoroughly defeated. I had been taken away from all that I had grown to know and love with little effort and the son of my friend had become my enemy. I wondered if I would ever see my wife or my son again.

I was finally removed from the pool and taken to a small holding cell. There I was roughly cleaned and given medical attention for my broken hand. It seemed that Reks wanted me in the best possible shape before going to the Grid, at least without the 'benefit' of being 'improved'.

A few days passed and by the time they came to get me for transport to the Grid, I had regained most of the strength and flexibility of my hand.

Leading me from my cell, I was loaded onto an old helicopter. Wind whipped my face as we approached its side. Taking a seat, two large humant guards sat on either side of me. It was a silent, but mercifully short, ride to our destination.

I was in an area of the country I had never seen before and I tried to see out the windows of the craft. The ground sped quickly past. Recalling my geography lessons from school, I wanted to keep track of our progress, but as the cities, buildings and all, rushed by in a blur, I found my head hurting instead. Closing my eyes, I decided to spend the remainder of the trip relaxing in preparation.

When progress slowed a bit, I opened my eyes to see that we were approaching a significantly-sized city. It was as large as some of the shielded ones I had seen and I wondered where we were. Landing in a clearing in what used to be a large parking lot, I was forcefully removed from the aircraft and escorted towards a large stadium. I recognized it as an old football stadium and I wondered where we were. My guards continuing moving me through the ramps that would lead me to the interior of the stadium. Eventually, I reached a place where I was instructed to sit.

Surveying my surroundings, I could see that considerable changes had been made to the stadium. Extensive renovations had been made to the stadium and it barely resembled what it had been built for. Huge metal beams rose from the floor to support the beams that held a roof since it had not had one in its original state. A large complex of metal walls filled the field before me, held aloft by a maze of metal beams and tubes. Only hints of the grass that had once filled the place poked through at the edges.

A few minutes passed before Reks Kriton entered the area. "Welcome to Baltimore, Mr. Blake, at least what's left of it. What do you think of the new use I have found for this old football stadium? I was always surprised that Baltimore wasn't one of the cities that made it through the massing. Oh well, it has provided me with the ideal setting upon which to build the Grid. Want a tour?"

Of course I knew that a tour would help me know what I was up against and so I simply nodded my head in response.

"Great! Right this way."

Motioning me to follow him, he led us onto a large stairway that made its way to a system of catwalks suspended above the complex of metal walls.

Some twenty feet below the walkway I could see that contained within the outer metal walls were numerous small rooms, without ceilings, each measuring exactly ten feet by ten. The rooms were nestled one against another, literally filling the field. It was a hypnotizing pattern. Beyond the field many of the seats of the stadium were filled with spectators, come to see what I did not yet know. With curiosity I looked at Reks.

Raising both hands while motioning to the grid below us and looking at me he spoke, "Welcome to the Grid. Since you're going to be playing very soon allow me to share the rules with you.

"As you can see, the Grid is a large series of connecting cubes through which the players must pass. It is split into four separate quadrants and there are four entrances and a corresponding number of players. Contestants are pitted against randomly selected opponents and obstacles that they will find in each of the cubes; but they are also playing against each other. The objective is to be the first player to reach the center of the Grid.

"There are two types of cubes through which players must pass: fight cubes and obstacle cubes. In the fight cubes competitors must fight – to the death – randomly selected opponents from a pool of available humants. These fights are scored for ability, creativity, and time. When the fight is complete, depending upon the score received, one of the walls of the cube will open. The higher the score the more direct the route that the opening will provide to the center of the Grid. If a player manages to fight a perfect fight each and every time that they face an opponent, it is theoretically possible to reach the center of the Grid in as few as five moves. But no one has ever done that before.

"Every other cube is an obstacle cube, therefore in a direct path obstacles will follow every fight. Fights will follow obstacles which will be followed by fights, and so on and so on and so forth. Only a contestant that garners enough fight points can enter the center obstacle cube. Many games have ended in stalemate, all players eliminated.

"If, once they have reached the center cube, the player is then able to overcome the final obstacle, they will win the game. Remaining players will be instantly eliminated by poison gas and the game will be complete."

Although I was pretty sure what the answer would be, I had to ask, "So, what happens to the player that actually wins the game?"

Looking at me with a sneer he said, "No one has ever won the Grid, Mr. Blake, it wasn't designed for that. It was designed to be the meat-grinder that has become its nickname. It is a place you send people to die – creatively. We play tomorrow. Good luck, Mr. Blake. I will be watching this game."

He motioned to the guards, who grabbed me roughly by each arm and hauled me away to spend the night in yet another jail cell. Anxiety assured I got no rest that night.

The next morning I was given what amounted to a last meal. It reminded me a great deal of the final meal I had been given in the city prior to my expulsion. I had until the middle of the morning to finish it.

About ten-thirty, I was escorted to a room that looked very much like one of the cubes I had seen the previous day. The room itself was a ten foot cube, only it had a ceiling. There was a single door on the far wall. Looking at their watches the guards waited until the precise time to prod me through the door.

I resisted their attempts to force me to enter the first game cube. The electric shocks from their prods brought a quick change of mind. I assumed as I passed beyond the door that the game of the Grid had begun. I heard the door slam shut behind me while I looked about nervously, waiting to see what would happen next.

After a few brief moments a small door on the opposite wall opened and a large man, one that could barely fit through the opening, entered the cube with me. I looked up to see the walkways above filled to capacity with spectators.

If I hadn't known better I would have believed that I was attending a major sporting event with the intensity that accompanied the shouts. They were savage and filled with a lust for blood. Without warning the large humant lunged for me, swinging at the same time.

His body absolutely bulged with muscles but his bulkiness disguised his agility. Not only was he incredibly strong, but he moved with speed that took me by surprise.

The phrase 'to the death' echoed through my mind as I laid upon the ground attempting to fend off the blows that he threw at me. I knew that if I did not do something very soon, the fight would be completed and I would be the loser.

There had been times in the past I had been forced to take the life of another in self-defense, in the heat of battle. But somehow, fighting with an opponent in the cube felt different. My reluctance to defend myself was quickly taking its toll.

Images of Ashleigh and our son, Derik, filled my vision. Who would take care of them? What would become of my home and New Duluth? Would these things that I had come to love so much cease to exist without me ever seeing them again? Gathering strength from my thoughts and with grim determination I realized what had to be done. It was going to be him or me, whether I liked it or not. Releasing myself from the reluctance that held me captive, I began to fight back.

Drawing upon my training I rose to my feet and began to drive him backwards. I kicked and I punched, but they were pretty ineffective against his massive bulk, all I could do was knock him off balance momentarily. I was growing weary and would not be able to maintain my defense for long; I knew that I needed something more.

Taking stock of the situation an idea came to me. Landing a kick with all of the force that I could muster, I knocked him off balance once again and quickly undid the buckle on the belt that I wore and yanked it with a loud crack from my pants.

My opponent was growing impatient with the fight and the crack of my belt infuriated him further. Screeching at the top of his lungs, he ran towards me. Crouching, I waited until he was almost upon me and then a split-second before he reached me jumped into the air and landed on his shoulders. Stunned and filled with rage, he reached up and back to try to remove me. But before he had the chance to do so I whipped the belt around his neck and grasped each end, pulling it tight.

Realizing his situation the humant started flailing about violently, trying to dislodge me. He dug his fingers into my sides and scratched me viciously. Speeding towards the nearest wall he slammed me between himself and the wall in an attempt to dislodge me from his shoulders. Wincing in pain I held on with all my strength, although he knocked the wind from me.

Slowly his movements decreased but I knew that I could not let up even as he crouched to his hands and knees. Gritting my teeth and trying to remember that I was defending myself, I held on until he slumped to the floor.

I stood beside his unconscious form, unsure what to do next. As I watched him breath shallowly, cries of 'kill him' and 'finish it' descended from the walkways overhead. I looked up at the frenzied crowd and was met with shaking fists and demands that I finish the fight. Many of them looked at me with disgust. I shouted back at them that I would not satisfy their lusts for blood.

As if by cue the shouts from the crowd grew quieter. The next moment the shock began to run through my body. I found myself fixed to the spot where I stood as pure energy streamed through me. Intense pain filled every part of my being, but I was unable to scream; the muscles in my jaw clenched tightly. I fell to my knees the instant the energy released me.

I was still on my knees when I was struck from behind in my back. Turning to see the large man rising from the floor, instinct took over then as I leaned towards him and, with my open hand, struck him as hard as I could in the center of his nose.

It was a defense that I had learned from Bill. A brief groan escaped his lips as his eyes rolled slowly back into his head while a small trickle of blood ran from one nostril. He fell back again, permanently.

I stood then and looked down at his motionless form realizing what I had done. Looking at my hands I felt that terrible feeling that killing inevitably brought. Self-defense does little to temper those feelings. If the crowds above could see the regret in my eyes they didn't show it. A loud cheer, louder than any before, descended to me. My stomach filled with bile.

I looked about unsure what was next. A moment later one of the walls slid open to reveal the cube beyond. Stepping over the form below me to get to the next cube, I looked down silently and whispered, "I'm sorry". As I entered the adjoining cube the wall slid shut behind me.

Right away I noticed the multi-colored checkerboard on the floor in front of me. I stood on a drab-gray section of floor that measured two foot by ten. Directly in front of that were three rows of differently colored squares. The second, or middle, row spanned the width of the cube, containing four squares. The first and third row contained only three squares each and these squares were staggered on the middle row. The colors, from left to right, of the row closest to me were: blue, red, and yellow. The colors of the middle row, from left to right, were: yellow, blue, orange, and red. The farthest row, from left to right, were: blue, violet, and green. On the other end of the checkerboard was another drab-gray section of floor.

Blue		Violet		Green	
Yellow	Blue		Orange		Red
Blue		Red		Yellow	

Looking at the checkerboard, I laughed to myself since I had absolutely no idea how to proceed. Were there three other doors or just one? What did all of the different colors mean? I imagined that I could hear a clock ticking as I considered the obstacle. I couldn't afford to spend too much time thinking so, taking a chance, I closed my eyes tightly and took a step forward. Nothing happened. Cracking one eye and looking about I let out a sigh of relief. I had stepped onto the red square.

Emboldened, and without any further thought, I stepped forward onto the blue square ahead and just to the left of the red one. As my toe touched the square, an awful pain ran up my leg and through my body. Lurching backwards from the pain, I fell over, landing on the gray squares. The same moment my foot left the square the pain ended.

Dazed, I decided a more prudent approach to the problem would be needed. My fingers and toes continued to tingle and my head ached slightly while I pondered my next move.

Try as I might, I did not see any order to the squares before me. Frustration mounted as I grew ever-more desperate for a solution; and still the clock ticked away. I noticed that a path of blue squares went from one side of the room to the other. It seemed too obvious but I had no other ideas. So, once again squeezing my eyes closed and gritting my teeth, I gingerly placed the toe of my right foot on the blue square that bordered the gray ones. Once again, the pain greeted me and I quickly pulled my foot back.

My frustration intensified, I knew that my step onto the red square had come with no pain so I once again stepped onto it. The choices I had from this square included blue and orange. I tried to find a pattern in the squares.

A lot of things went through my head then but I eventually found myself thinking back to an art course that I had taken in school. I remembered studying the color wheel and the combining of colors. The first row contained all of the primary colors: red, blue, and yellow. But only one color in the middle row could have been a result of the combination of the two primary colors it touched in the first row: orange. So, closing my eyes tightly and gritting my teeth I took another step forward onto the orange square. Nothing. Was I on to something?

Art had never been a strong subject for me and I was lucky to remember the primary colors from the color wheel. Hitting my head lightly with my fist, I tried in vain to remember the wheel. Looking at the board I wondered if I would get green from red and orange or violet from blue and orange. The first combination seemed unlikely so I decided to try the latter.

Hoping that I had solved the riddle of the checkerboard, I took a tentative step onto the violet square after steeling myself for the possible pain that might come. Nothing happened. Pleased with myself, I stepped onto the gray strip on the other side of the board. Immediately the wall slid back to reveal another cube. Knowing that I must continue, I wasted no time congratulating myself before stepping through the opening. The wall slid back into place behind me.

The fight cubes all looked the same, they were completely featureless. Another humant entered through an opening opposite me. He was a bit smaller than myself and had what looked like a light coating of sweat covering his entire body.

Unlike my previous opponent he did not rush towards me, in fact he looked at me with a measure of fear in his eyes. Thinking of the humants that lived in New Duluth, those that did not wish to fight for the tyrant Kriton, I knew right away that this was going to be a difficult fight.

For the first few moments we circled each other slowly, neither willing to make the first move. It was apparent that we did not wish to fight and I wondered what happened to unwilling combatants. I was certain that Kriton would have planned for such a contingency; I was right.

After about a minute of circling two of the walls of the cube began to close in on us, forcing us ever closer to one another. As the room took on the shape of a hallway, we each took positions on opposite ends. It wasn't until the walls threatened to rub our shoulders that the humant let out the scream of a man that had nothing to lose and he ran headlong towards me.

Stepping to the side and hugging the wall behind me, I was able to position myself to place him into a headlock in order to control him. But as we came together, I was only able to grab one of his arms with my left hand. When my hand made contact with his skin it instantly slid off of his arm and was lightly coated by whatever it was that covered his skin. Within seconds my hand began to tingle and then go numb. Shortly thereafter, I found that I was unable to move it or even feel my fingers. Whatever substance coated his skin had paralyzed my hand. Suddenly, the fight had become much more difficult.

Without the ability to touch my opponent I would be unable to defeat him. I stepped away to ponder what I would do next. It was difficult to avoid his touch as he continued to rush blindly towards me in our confined space.

An idea came to me and I grasped the bottom of my shirt tightly, ripping it off. Holding the end in the palm of my right hand, I wound it around my fist until it was nearly covered. Pushing the end under the upper band of the strip using one of my paralyzed fingers I then used my teeth to pull it tight. With renewed confidence I stepped towards him.

I had never particularly enjoyed the times that Bill had insisted I train using only one arm or leg, I was not graceful and I fell a lot. I would often try to talk him out of those training sessions, usually to no avail but I was certainly grateful for them then.

Only through that training was I able to effectively struggle against my opponent with only my right arm and my feet. Aside from running at me, my opponent made no attempts to defend himself. Either he was incapable of fighting, didn't know how, or was simply too afraid to do so.

Initially many of my blows slid off of his slick skin. But as we continued each attack scraped a bit more of the covering from his skin and it became progressively less slick. His ability to function was somehow tied to his skin covering and within a couple of minutes he was lying prone upon the floor.

He looked up at me with evident fear in his eyes. Wondering if I could fool the crowd I leaned forward and knocked him out with one solid punch. I tried to make it look as much like the open-hand strike that had dispatched my previous opponent as I could in hopes that the crowd would believe that I had killed him.

Looking up I waited to see if any walls opened, they did not. The volume of the crowd above me increased. I knew that my hoax had failed but I was loath to do what was required of me if I wished to continue the game.

"Kill him! Kill him! Kill him!" filled the air. Looking at the crowds above me, I shouted, "No!"

I knew what to expect next and I tried to prepare for it. I fell to one knee as the pain slammed into me and, looking at my opponent, I could see that he too was being hit by the shock as his unconscious body convulsed.

Standing and looking defiantly at the crowd once again, I shouted as loudly as I could through my firmly clenched lips, "No!"

Again the pain hit, but with more intensity than before. I fell all the way to the floor and curled-up as I tried to deal with it. Still I refused to comply.

It was during the third round of shock retribution that I noticed that my opponent had stopped breathing. Crawling over to him, I could see that he did indeed look bad. Apparently the shock had been more than he could take. I knew he was dead but I also knew that I had not killed him. Nevertheless, moments after a new doorway slid open. Apparently, *cause* of death did not stop the game from progressing. I dared not wonder what effect that it would have on my score however. So, wasting no time, I stepped through to discover what was on the other side.

Looking about the new cube I could see a row of levers that spanned the width of the wall to my left. They were all in the 'up' position. Moving towards the wall I heard a grinding sound coming from opposite the levers. Turning to the sound I could see spikes extruding from the wall. They covered the entire wall from floor to ceiling and were evenly-spaced, about six-inches from each other. When they reached about four-inches they stopped extending. I watched them suspiciously for a minute, before I was fairly sure that they were done moving. Even then I would steal glances over my shoulder to watch them.

Looking at the levers, I could see that each had a number written on the wall directly above it. There were eighteen levers in all, numbered two to nineteen respectively. All I could do was look at them blankly. As with the previous obstacle, I had no idea what to make of it.

Feeling the rush for time I decided to do a little experimenting and so I pulled the first lever, numbered two, down. Nothing happened. I hoped that, like the previous obstacle, nothing happening was a good sign, so I continued.

Pulling down lever three, I closed my eyes and waited. Still, nothing happened. I became concerned then, nothing in the Grid should be this easy and I was certain that I would find the trouble soon. It came with the next lever.

Pulling down lever number four, I could hear the grinding sound behind me once again. Spinning about I could do little else but watch as the spikes extended out of the wall a whole extra foot. Now sticking out sixteen inches, I knew that I needed to figure this obstacle out quick.

Pain was one thing I could deal with, death by impalement was quite another. Despite the passing of valuable time this was an obstacle I could not afford to get wrong. I really have no idea how long I stood and looked at that series of numbers and still I was no closer to a solution than when I had begun.

Seeing no other method to continue I pulled lever five down. Again, nothing happened. So levers two, three and five had not made the spikes advance but four had. What did the first three numbers have in common?

I had never particularly enjoyed math classes. Unfortunately, they had been part of my engineering curriculum in college. But one lesson, way back at the beginning, came to mind then: prime numbers. Was that it?

Skipping over lever number six, I pulled down lever seven. Once again, nothing happened. Taking confidence in my theory I pulled lever eleven down; again, nothing. So, one after another, I pulled levers thirteen, seventeen, and nineteen down.

Once again I could hear the grinding sound behind me. But as I looked at the spikes with fear I could see that they were retreating back into the wall. Following the spikes another opening appeared in the wall opposite the one through which I had entered. Hasty to leave the spikes, I entered the cube beyond.

I had completed two fights and two obstacles. Knowing that Reks had said that a perfectly played game would take the player to the central obstacle within five moves, I wondered how close I was. I really had no time to contemplate the fact that I was not supposed to actually leave the game alive. Rather, I found that I was filling with anxiety to finish the game and so I was prepared when the little door opened to allow my new opponent entrance into the cube.

This humant was quite tall and had four arms, two on either side. It reminded me of one of the humants that I had fought on my first night in the World Outside. Since it held a large sword very much like the one my friend Bill used, I was grateful that this humant did not have the ability to spin its arms quickly like the one I had met so long before. Assuming that having the sword meant that it knew how to use it, I frantically tried to remember every unarmed sword defense that I had ever practiced.

None of my other opponents had possessed any external weapons and I was dismayed to find myself facing one. It certainly tilted the odds in its favor, bare hands against a sword was a poor position to be in.

After a brief, single circle around the cube, we rushed towards one another. It attacked me with all four arms simultaneously. I had become adept at fending off attacks from two, even ones with weapons, but found that I was woefully unprepared for attacks from twice that number. Within moments I had sustained a number of cuts on my arms and chest and even my face. I was naked from the waist up by then and blood ran down my chest and back. I knew from experience how sharp a samurai weapon was and knew that a single well-placed strike would certainly end our conflict.

It did not take long for me to see that it did not know how to use the sword that it wielded. Swinging wildly, it actually caused some damage to itself. Seeing this, I wondered how it had come into possession of it. Though its swings lacked precision, they contained great force and I knew that fighting this opponent head to head would ultimately prove unsuccessful. I fell back and circled the cube trying my best to stay away from it as I considered my next move. Not only did it have twice as many arms as I had but had a very dangerous weapon as well.

Moving towards it, I positioned myself as if I were going to attack its upper body with my fists, but as soon as I was close enough I crouched to the ground and swept its legs with mine. Falling backwards it hit hard with a loud thud and lay stunned upon the ground. With its hands momentarily motionless I was able to wrest the sword away from it.

It remained stunned only for a brief moment and I was startled when it began to move. Quickly, it pulled itself up on its double elbows. By then I had grasped the sword with both my hands and the blade pointed towards it. Enraged that I had taken it from him, it lunged for me impaling before I had a chance to do anything. Howls of approval met my ears and I looked up at the spectators with deep disgust.

Rising to my feet, I casually slid the sword into my belt as one of the walls slid open. No one appeared to take the sword from me, no one seemed to care. I was armed then and knew that the remainder of the Grid would be different.

Within the new cube a column of water, held in place by an energy field, filled the majority of it. There were small particles in the water and I could see that it flowed from a hole in the floor of the cube quickly upwards and disappeared into a large tube overhead. The tube was higher than the walkways above so that it would not impede their view of the game.

A leather belt floated in the midst of the column of water. Attached to each side of the belt was a chain that exited the field and was anchored securely to one of the cube walls. Also in the water, a small piece of metal extended from the edge of the hole in the floor and on it was what appeared to be a rotary dial. The dial had a digital readout above it that displayed up to three numbers. Right above that was a larger display. Once again I was puzzled by what I saw.

Leaning close to the field in order to get a better look I could see a message in the large display. The water and the energy field made it difficult to read, but I was able to make it out, "Place the belt securely about your waist and enter the water column. Further instructions will follow."

Enter the water column? I absolutely did not want to do that, I have never been a particularly good or strong swimmer. But what choice did I have? Pulling on the chain closest to me I was able to pull the belt down and out of the column. Once out, I reluctantly fastened it around my waist and gasping as large a breath as I was able, stepped through the field and into the rushing water.

Immediately I was swept from my feet and flipped over into a head down position. The water flowed past me with considerable force and I had to squint in order to see. The belt strained to hold me against the current, and I knew that without some change I would not be able to leave the column on my own power.

The instant I entered the water the large display changed. It read, "RIGHT: How many hydrogen atoms are there in a water molecule?"

It was exceedingly difficult to concentrate on the task at hand since I began to feel the lack of air in my lungs right away. It is in the nature of man to panic under such circumstances but I had to fight the urge to do so, while at the same time attempt to solve a riddle. Thinking back to my meditation training, I tried to empty my mind and calm down.

Looking anew at the display I assumed that RIGHT meant I was to turn the dial to the right. So reaching out I began to turn it. I could feel clicks as it turned and so I turned it twice until the small display above it read "2". Looking up at the larger display, I watched as it changed to read, "LEFT: What is the temperature, in Kelvin, at which water freezes?"

A difficult question to be sure, had I not studied water in school I knew that this obstacle would have been over then and there. Grasping the dial again I turned it to the left until the smaller display read "273". I had to turn it numerous times to reach that number and I turned as quickly as I could. Again the larger display changed. It read, "RIGHT: What is the rounded molecular weight of water?"

This question presented me with a bit more of a challenge. I had to think back to my chemistry class and the periodical chart. Would I be able to remember the numbers that I had so often read there? Hydrogen, if memory served, was one point something and oxygen was fifteen point nine. Adding two hydrogen and one oxygen together in my head I arrived at eighteen.

Once again grasping the dial, and feeling the pressure building in my lungs, I hoped that this combination only required whole numbers. Turning the dial I stopped when the small display read, "18".

The flow of the water eased quickly and then stopped. Pulling myself from the column by using one of the chains, I gasped for breath. I sat on the floor for a minute just breathing even after one of the walls slid open. Finally, when I felt less light-headed I walked through the opening to see what was on the other side.

Catching my breath had given my next opponent an opportunity to enter the adjoining cube before me. Like so many other humans before, this one was unlike any I had seen before. It had arms that were nearly twice the normal length of human arms and each ended with a fearful set of razor-sharp claws. Its feet had opposable thumbs like those of a monkey and its mouth was filled with inch-long jagged teeth.

The instant I entered the cube it attacked. Swinging its super long arms it was able to reach me while keeping me too far away to make an effective counter. After the first swipe cut my chest and shoulder I began to bounce about the cube in an attempt to avoid its reach. At the same time I pulled the sword from my belt and used it to strike at the nearest arm.

Screeching inhumanly it pulled back its injured arm, only to renew its attack with increased ferocity. The monster simply swung its huge arms wildly in hopes that it would connect and cause damage. Its arms were so large that each time it swing them it took the creature a few moments to regain its balance. Each attack had predictable results: the humant would swing, be thrown off balance, screech with frustration, and then face me for yet another attack.

Gauging its attack pattern I was able to avoid its attacks with ever-increasing effectiveness. Only when the arms came within striking range did I counter, but with each swing the strength of its attacks grew steadily weaker. After multiple injuries, it was unable to use its arms at all.

Dragging its arms on the ground it screeched again and ran at me. As it did it started to spin its whole body quickly The centrifugal force lifted the arms from the ground and they became flailing weapons.

Moving my blade into their path I was able to dispatch the creature's arms. Incredibly, this only further infuriated the creature and it continued towards me. I had hoped that, freed of its arms, it would have stopped. Reluctantly, I swung again and with one quick strike to its neck, ended the fight. Its head fell to the floor with a long crack and its body fell backwards with a thud. This was extra-gratifying to the bloodthirsty crowd gathered above me and they rewarded my efforts with loud cheers and screams. Disgust doesn't truly explain what I felt for them.

The wall to the next obstacle slid open and I quickly entered. A large hole nearly filled the floor of that cube. It was eight feet across, three feet deep, and spanned the width of the cube. Peering over the side of the pit I could see that it was empty. Hanging from beams spanning the cube above the pit, spaced equally and forming a square, were four bars suspended by chains. Each bar had a chemical symbol carved into its surface. Running my hand down my face and sighing, I again had no clue how to proceed.

Reaching out for the nearest bar I grasped it tightly. Assuming that it was for swinging across the pit, I lifted my feet from the floor and transferred my weight to it. No sooner had I done this and I could hear a metal grinding sound as a door in the side of the pit opened to reveal bars. To make things worse the bar that I swung from gave way and me and it fell into the pit below. I fell approximately eight feet to the bottom and landed solidly.

Until that moment I had not known that in addition to creating humants from humans, Reks Kriton was also the creator of mutant versions of animals. With a guttural growl a large dog-like creature with what appeared to be scales as skin moved to attack me, emerging from a tunnel behind the bars in the side of the pit.

I used the heavy-metal bar that I still had in my hands to swing at it but it possessed immense strength. I was barely able to hang onto it when it grabbed the bar roughly in its teeth. With all of the strength that I could muster I threw the bar and the mutant-dog to the side of the pit so that I could pull the sword from my belt.

Rising and shaking its head the mutant-dog looked at me and growled again. It leaped into the air with incredible strength as I leveled the sword in front of me. It fell on my blade, howling in pain. But before it died it was still able to grab me in its vice-like jaws.

Fire ripped through my shoulder, into my chest, and down my arm. Visions of the various effects of humant bites raced through my head. But I did not have time to think about them then. The beast further squealed in pain as I turned the sword back and forth in an attempt to dislodge its grip. Finally, it grew limp and it released my shoulder.

Removing the beast from on top of me I looked at the blood-stained sword in my hand. How grateful I was to have had it, an unarmed player could not have defeated the mutant-dog.

Crouching down and looking into the small tunnel that disappeared into the darkness, and I could faintly make out the outline of bars on the far end. Barely able to fit, I quickly shimmied through the tunnel. Sounds of outrage from the crowds followed me into the tunnel. I was not playing the game right.

Emerging out the other end I found myself in the cage wherein the mutant-dog had been kept. The gate of the cage was closed with a simple latch that I easily opened. I stepped through the door with anticipation, certain that guards would be arriving soon.

Instead, a single man, protesting that I had killed his pet, ran towards me angrily. Looking around to see if he was alone I simply knocked him out with a single punch. Still no one arrived to stop me so, stepping over his body, I began to sprint in the direction from which he had come.

I ran past mazes and masses of wires and computer terminals as well as pipes, gears, and other mechanical items. I assumed these all constituted the obstacle cubes and made them function. Looking up I could see the bottom pattern of the numberless cubes that constituted the Grid.

I dared not slow to examine anything closely. My final cube had been poorly made and I was the lucky recipient of its inadequate design.

As I ran, I passed-by numerous cages containing a dizzying assortment of humants. Some called out to me while others grew excited and screeched or growled. Although I suspect that there are those few who volunteer to play in the Grid willingly, I knew that most of the participants were just as much casualties of Kriton as I had been designed to be. It was a game as evil as its designer. But I did not have the time to save even one of them.

I had absolutely no idea where I was running. The underbelly of the Grid was a tangled mass of winding hallways and dead-ends. I was beginning to entertain ideas of possible and inevitable surrender when I caught what appeared to be sunlight out of the corner of my eye. Turning towards the source I could see an opening to the outside. Running for all I was worth, I ran towards it.

A large rusting hole provided the exit into the outside world. Emerging into the sunlight I turned and looked up to see the massive outside wall of one of the stadium that housed the Grid. I was surprised to hear the shout of a solitary guard.

I heard his weapon fire as I rolled towards him quickly. Knocking him out, I bound and gagged him. I had seen enough killing that day to last a lifetime. Looking about in an effort to establish my bearings I headed off towards what I hoped was Long Island. I had left a comrade there and I meant to rescue him

Chapter 16

"Greater love hath no man than this,
that a man lay down his life for his friends."
John 15:13

I moved as quickly as stealth would allow. My many injuries, particularly the one in my shoulder, hindered me. Moving at night I followed the coast on my way to Long Island. I passed numerous cities along the way, ranging in size. Many of them appeared to be inhabited, but since I worked at keeping myself hidden, it took me a while to determine by whom. I spent my days resting and spying on the surrounding towns.

At length I was able to determine that nearly all of the groups occupying the towns I passed were affected to some degree by Reks Kriton and his humant armies. I had never suspected that his power extended to such lengths. But I lived in an area that was over a thousand miles away from him. I could only imagine what living in his front yard would be like.

I eavesdropped on their conversations and learned that he taxed all of the cities within an established radius of his stronghold. Apparently, in addition to receiving assistance from the city of New York, Reks also supported his operations on the backs of those surrounding him. But, for whatever reason, none of the people I listened to ever mentioned losing people to become humants themselves. Evidently, living close to the madman did have its advantages.

The closer I got to Reks' compound I began to notice that many of the cities actually had electrical power and many of the creature comforts conspicuously missing from the rest of the World Outside. Reks not only had power within his personal campus, but he had established a small-scale, but still quite large, power grid for the people that lived within his area. I could not help but be impressed at the influence that he possessed. How a man like him ever got such power has continued to mystify me.

Because I was traveling so slowly it took me a number of days to reach Long Island. The wounds in my shoulder became infected and it grew increasingly difficult to move my arm at all. By the morning of the seventh day I could see the familiar glow of the field that surrounded New York, and Long Island beyond that. My pace slowed somewhat as I took extra precautions not to get caught.

Since my entrance and exit from Long Island had been by air, I had not considered the problems that I found myself facing. The city of New York covered the entire entrance onto the island and the only way to get to it was by air or by water. Both methods seemed impossible.

Looking about for a method of transport I spied a narrow dock to which a number of small boats were moored. Two guards walked in opposite directions along the entire length of the dock. I tried to figure out what I could do as I sat looking at the dock for a time.

After considerable forethought I decided my best approach was to pretend to be a lost local so I approached the dock as innocently as I could. Motioning to the nearest guard he turned and walked towards me while demanding to know what I wanted. Seeing the commotion, the other guard approached as well. I was pleased that my plan appeared to be working.

When the first guard had reached me I tried to fill my 'lost' role by acting confused and asking him for assistance. Waiting for the second guard to be within range I continued my act. Both guards were not overly helpful but did manage to explain, in general terms, where we were.

In the middle of a sentence I struck out at the nearest guard and the very next instant I took out the other. I had no idea how long I had before the missing guards would be discovered so I quickly picked the quickest looking boat that I could find, climbed on board, released the moorings, and pushed the throttle to full open. The engine roared loudly and I turned towards the island beyond New York.

As with most of what I had discovered from my time of wandering through what I had come to call 'Kriton Country', many powered forms of transportation existed among the locals. The fact that a powerboat, full of fuel, was available at a small dock just outside of New York and very close to Long Island did not surprise me at all.

When I had departed in the helicopter for Baltimore the portion of the trip that took us over the land of Long Island had been very short so I hoped that what I sought was not far inland. But I really had no idea what part of the island I was looking for. Spotting an empty beach I turned the boat towards it. Pulling it onto the shore I headed for the nearest cover.

It was total blind luck. I started a search pattern, weaving back and forth as I headed eastward and before the end of day the familiar buildings of Reks' campus compound loomed in the distance. I waited until dark to approach any closer.

I did not know what building I would find Clay in. I knew from the paper I had seen on Reks' desk that he had been scheduled for an experimental operation. But whether or not he had yet been subjected to it, I had no way of knowing. Thinking back to the few papers I had quickly skimmed I remembered mention that those who underwent surgery required considerable recovery time. Reks had not shown me a recovery room during my tour, but I assumed that, like hospitals, recovery rooms would be very close to the operating rooms.

After nightfall I began to search for the building where I had seen the surgery victims. Thinking I had found it, I quietly entered one of the adjacent buildings. A cold breeze met me as I opened the door. I could see row upon row of the kind of body-drawers that are found in morgues; wrong choice. Exiting quickly I moved onto the next one that connected to the surgery building.

I had found the building that I sought. Countless people lay upon beds that were crammed into the rooms and even the halls of the building. Some of them slept, some moaned. There was little room within which to walk.

The people took little notice of me as I walked through the beds looking for Clay. Those that were awake were experiencing their own hell and had little concern for me. From time to time one would reach out weakly for me and ask me to help them. All I could do was turn away and continue moving.

The variations that I saw of the human body within that place could fill a book. Not even in my wildest nightmares would I have imagined some of the things that I witnessed there. After touring that building it was rare to see a humant variation I had not seen before. But, try as I might, I did not find Clay among them.

I knew where I had to look next, but every fiber of my being screamed not to. Approaching the door that I suspected connected the recovery area with the surgical building I grasped the handle tightly and tried to prepare myself for what I was sure to see beyond.

Opening the door I peeked inside to ensure that there were no people. A short hall beyond led to and connected with the infamous hallway through which I had passed more than a week earlier. Closing the door quietly I proceeded.

The first time I walked that hall I had the luxury of being able to turn away from what I saw. Unfortunately, this time, I had to look into each and every surgical room. Mercifully, the majority of them were empty, only a few contained occupants, and these were unconscious and attached to various life-support equipment.

Approaching the end of the hall I peered through the next-to-last glass and my heart sunk. There, upon a bed, with tubes extruding from under his blanket lay Clay. Opening the door to the room I entered with my emotions threatening to overtake me. In my mind's eye I saw my brother lying upon that bed.

I looked for changes in his appearance as I approached him. I saw none on the surface, but like all other humants I was certain that they existed somewhere. I had not arrived in time to save him. But I would not leave him in the hands of a lunatic.

Pulling the tubes and wires from the machines to which he was connected, and hoisting him onto my shoulder, I quickly exited the building. Before reaching the door I could hear voices behind me and knew that the machines that had monitored Clay had set off an alarm. I quickened my pace.

I knew exactly where I was headed. Running as quickly as my battered body would allow I headed across the campus to the building where I had seen Reks' car collection. I was surprised to find the door unlocked. Mr. Kriton evidently felt secure enough on his campus compound, surrounded by his humant army, to be rather slack in security.

I had just loaded Clay into the back seat of the nearest vehicle when I heard a familiar growl from behind me. I turned to find myself face to face with the monster mutant that had become some terrible shadow to me.

From the time I had seen him on my first night in the World Outside, this particular humant had dogged my steps and now stood before me. How many friends and

251

acquaintances he had killed during humant attacks I would never know. But I did know one thing: the fear and terror that I had once had for this creature had been replaced by anger.

Although in the back of my mind I knew that it was useless, I lunged at the monster. I accomplished exactly nothing with my attack, but instead found myself dangling by my throat. The room filled with sound as every garage door in the building opened in unison as I struggled for breath. I could see Reks, backed by his humants, looking in on us and I knew I was in big trouble.

Stepping into the garage Reks looked at me with disgust and spoke. "Mr. Blake, your weakness for people has proven, beyond doubt, to be your worst downfall. No one has ever escaped from me, and certainly never from the Grid. I was utterly humiliated when people realized that you had somehow found your way out. When I decree death for a resident of the World Outside, it is carried out. It makes no difference to me whether you die in the Grid or on the operating table but I have imagined the terrible price that I intend to exact from you. You cannot begin to fathom the horrors that await.

"I was sure you would be half-way back to that pathetic hovel you call home by now. But I guess even I underestimated the level of weakness you have for those that you call 'friend'. And now you will die for one of them, I wonder if they would do the same for you. Poetic don't you think?

"I am going to make you suffer Mr. Blake. It will be long and torturous and it will be like nothing you have ever experienced before. You have seen my handiwork and you know that I *can* do to you exactly what I say. Don't you Mr. Blake?"

A cold chill ran down my spine. I knew that I would rather die than allow myself to fall into his hands. I struggled against the huge, hairy hand that held me. Evidently he had anticipated this as he motioned to one of his humants that stepped forward with what appeared to be a dart gun. He intended to tranquilize me.

Fear seized my being and with strength I did not know I could summon I kicked the monster that held me in the knee. Howling loudly he actually dropped me and I was able to dive behind the car containing Clay as a dart flew closely overhead.

Reaching into the car quickly I retrieved one of the weapons I had taken from the guards. Grasping it in my hand and running my finger along its surface thoughtfully. I had no intention of allowing Reks the control that he sought, I would shoot Clay and then myself before that happened. I looked into the car at Clay and hoped I could summon the strength to do what I had to do. But, at that moment, I could hear a loud commotion from outside the building.

Cautiously peeking out of my hiding place I could see the small humant army fighting someone outside the building. Peering closely into the fray, I saw people I recognized, people from New Duluth; a lot of people. My heart, which had reached the lowest point it had ever reached, leapt for joy.

Combatants on either side fell, but the humants were in complete disarray, overtaken in their territory by complete surprise. In the center of the battle, I saw Keith. The last time I saw him he was being carried away by the humant army that had taken me. I had assumed he was dead. Yet there he was, leading the army that was fighting for our lives.

Our eyes met and he fought his way towards me. Reinvigorated, I entered the fray. Soon Keith had reached me and through the thick of the battle screamed, "Are you alright?"

I nodded blankly in reply.

"And Clay?"

My grave look was all he needed to know that things had not gone well. Concern furrowed his brow. I briefly explained that he had been subjected to Reks' surgery and that he was in the back seat of one of the cars. I then asked him how he had gotten there.

Before responding to me he handed me an item that resembled a gun, but it was completely white, had no opening for a barrel, and looked like it was made of plastic. Studying it closer I could see that it looked very much like the new energy weapons that had appeared in the hands of the police just before I had been expelled from the city. Just then I remembered a brief look that I had gotten of the alien artifact I had brought back from Grand Forks, and it was then in my hand. I had spent so much time in building and improving New Duluth that I had actually forgotten that it was in our possession. I had never seen it function.

I looked up at Keith then, "We found an old abandoned tunnel that goes from the mainland under the city of New York to Long Island." Reaching into his pocket he gave me a hand-drawn map. On the map I could see the compound where we were currently, the city of New York, and the location of the ends of the tunnel.

Closing the map into my hand he continued, "Take Clay and get out of here, Stephen." When my look told him that I had no intention of doing that, he continued fervently.

When you disappeared the whole city went into shock, no one could believe that you had been stolen from under our very noses. We dispatched a unit of the army to come and get you almost immediately. No one doubts that you would fight to the death for your friends Stephen, but the city needs you, and Ashleigh needs you, so get going!"

Never had I left a battle. I agonized over the decision for a few brief moments as his words echoed in my head. It was against my nature but, at last, visions of Clay being returned to the custody of Reks helped me make up my mind.

Looking at Keith, and wishing him God Speed, I headed towards the car I had chosen. But before I could reach it I heard a familiar roar and looked up just in time to avoid the head of a gigantic axe as it struck the floor just inches from me. The monster that had met me on my first night in the World Outside, the same monster that had carried me to the plane and proceeded to break all of the fingers of my hand, the monster from whom I had narrowly escaped, now stood before me.

Thinking of the alien weapon I held in my hand I raised it and aimed at him. Unsure how to make it fire I depressed the area were a trigger should have been, but nothing happened. A surprised look covered my face to which the monster laughed wickedly, striking my hand forcefully. The weapon fell to the ground where it slid noisily across the floor and under one of the cars.

I was in serious trouble. Two times I had seen the monster sustain numerous bullet hits and get away. The sword was in the car and my hands and feet presented no danger to him. With my remaining energy I tried to avoid the monster as he swung his axe and fists at me.

I was able to avoid him for a few minutes, but my energy was quickly waning. He had just finished striking the floor near me. Small pieces of stone flew in all directions and the floor all about us was riddled with the impact scars. Until then I had managed to move away from the axe while he lifted it for yet another attack, but this time I moved a bit too slowly. Rather than lifting it above his head and repositioning for a new attack, he swung the axe broadside and struck me forcefully.

I was thrown into the nearest wall, where I fell onto the trunk of the car next to it before sliding onto the ground. I knew from the pain that I had broken a few bones and I lay on the ground, unable to move.

Growling fiercely the monster approached the car looking for me. Unable to fit between the two vehicles he pulled the one forward until it had cleared the other. The sound of screeching rubber filled the room as the tires tried to halt the forward movement. When the monster spotted me he smiled with a toothy grin and the sound stopped as he moved towards me.

"I have chance to kill little Blake. No one ever escape like little Blake. Killing friends not as pleasing as killing little Blake. I kill you now!"

Blood streamed into my eyes and it felt as if I was moving in slow motion. Through my blurred vision I could see that the car he had pulled forward was the same one that the alien weapon had skidded under.

I knew I had only one chance and so gathering all of the strength that I had left I pulled myself forward. My movements were agonizingly slow as I watched the monster continue towards me. Within two pulls I reached the weapon. Grabbing it in my hand I turned it over trying to determine how it fired. I could see a small, barely visible, finger-sized indentation on its side, close to my thumb.

Squinting as if I were looking through fog I once again raised the weapon and took aim at the monster. "You have taken the lives of the last of my friends. Never again will I have to see you!" I screamed. Then, hopefully, I inserted my thumb into the shallow indentation. Brilliant light filled the room and a beam of unimaginable energy flowed from the tip of the weapon straight at the monster.

It howled in pain as it was struck by the beam. It lasted for only a fraction of a second and was gone. Standing motionless with its axe above its head and a huge black indentation that took up most of its chest, the monster's face seemed frozen in a look of surprise and confusion.

It stood for a few seconds longer before the axe fell from its grip with a loud clang. The whole battle froze for the lingering moments before the monster fell backwards. It was hard to believe what I had just witnessed. The monster that had so often haunted my dreams and had terrorized so many, at last lay upon the ground, dead.

Looking at the small weapon in my hand, I smiled. I knew that I had the means of effecting great changes and I had to return home quickly to plan them. So, once again approaching the car that contained Clay I opened the door, sat in the driver's seat, and started the engine. Putting the car into gear I pulled through the open garage door. I passed many people I knew along the way, all of them locked in heated battle with the hordes of humants that surrounded us.

It pulled my heart from me as I watched some fall to the humants. But I knew I couldn't stop as I continued to drive away from the battle and the campus. When I had cleared the group and knew that I would not hit anyone I floored the accelerator and quickly left.

It was difficult to drive as the various pains wracked my body, but the anticipation of seeing my believed wife and child gave me the strength to press on. Driving down the roads of Long Island, heading for the island-side entrance to the tunnel, I was surprised at how clean the roads were; every time I had driven any vehicle on the roads that surrounded New Duluth I had been forced to deal with numerous obstacles blocking the way. I guess when a man as powerful as Reks wants to joyride in one of his cars on the roads surrounding his stronghold, and when that man has an army of humants at his beck and call to do his bidding, the roads are going to be cleared.

The map led me right to the opening of the tunnel and I entered cautiously. It was empty and within minutes I emerged out the other side. I could see the city of New York in my rear-view mirror as I sped away. I drove until my tank was dry.

Throughout the night I heard baleful moans emanating from the backseat. I didn't know how much longer I could continue but my concern for my friend drove me on. When I stopped to check on Clay I could tell that things were deteriorating, even with my limited medical training.

Desperate to get home and turn Clay over to Dr. Taylor I rummaged through the trunk to see if there was fuel stored there. Sure enough the trunk contained two extra full cans of fuel. Filling the tank of the car I sped off again.

I borrowed energy from a higher power that night, and it was that power that kept me from hitting anything, delirious though I was. Throughout the long night I would look into the back seat to see that he was still breathing every few seconds. About nine o'clock the next morning I noticed that he had stopped.

Screeching to a stop I threw the doors open and anxiously pulled him from the back seat. Tears filled my eyes as I laid him upon the ground. I started CPR on him immediately, but after a few minutes I knew that he was gone. I wept then, laying my head on his chest. At last, all of the horrors of the previous two weeks were coming out and my soul wept with wretched anguish for a time.

*　　　*　　　*

Stephen stopped then for a few minutes, and I could see that tears once again filled his eyes; the emotion that I felt as he talked filled even mine. I offered him a tissue which he accepted and we both sat silently for a time. I could only imagine the horrors that had filled his life. No man should ever have to see the things that he had. Sometime later he continued.

*　　　*　　　*

Although I was near complete exhaustion I loaded my friend into the backseat of the car with what little strength I had left and departed. Fever from the infection in my arm raged within me and I stared blankly at the road ahead of me as I sped along.

Sweat poured down my face causing my vision to become blurry. I was completely delirious by then but I did not know it. It is a miracle that I did not hit anything. All I wanted to do was get home to my wife and son and give my friend the burial he deserved. Eventually the road, along with everything else on the horizon, blurred into one gray mass. My breathing became labored and my eyes rolled back into my head. It was then that I blacked out.

Chapter 17

Who knows why they do what they do?
Resident of the World Outside

How long I lay asleep I had no idea. My delirium provided me with endless hours of strange and often frightening dreams. Once previously I had been the prisoner of my own nightmares, but with the fresh new images of horror that had so recently been introduced into my mind, my nightmares reached new lows.

All too real visions of the contorted faces of everyone that I loved, strapped to one of the surgery tables in Reks Kriton's compound, filled my head; each of them reaching out for me, begging me to save them from their torture. I could hear each and every one of their voices as they moaned and wept out in terror for what was happening to them. And I could save none of them.

But that was not all, these same friends and loved ones became immersed in their own games of the Grid. Of course none of them won. Some died at the hands of some particularly terrible opponent, while others were shredded, impaled, drowned, or crushed by the obstacles that my fevered mind created for them. Still others, after running out of time, were simply poisoned to death.

Once in a while I would get a brief reprieve from my nightmares and I dreamed about my family and my home in New Duluth. But these were always fleeting and far too brief. Expecting, and even hoping, to die, I was surprised when at long last I awakened.

My eyes protested as light flooded into them. For the first few minutes I couldn't focus on anything, but as things became more and more clear I was uncertain what to make of the things I saw.

I was in a room of what looked like white plastic walls, looking up at a ceiling made of similar material. Numerous tubes and wires hung from the ceiling. They extended in all directions and some extended to the bed upon which I lay.

I became aware that my mouth was covered by some kind of mask attached to one of the many tubes suspended above me. Moving as if in slow motion I brought my hands up to my face and removed the mask while trying to sit up. I could see that my clothes had been removed and replaced by a skintight suit of a strange material that covered me from my neck to my wrists and ankles. Many of the small tubes attached to the suit in various places.

A single band held me in place. Squinting at the latch through the steadily-clearing haze I was able to release myself from the restraint and sat up slowly.

The wall across from me contained a large display, nearly as large as the wall itself. One of the items on the display pulsed rhythmically in harmony with my heart. All of the read-outs were labeled with symbols written in a language foreign to me. It did not look like any writing I had seen before.

Sitting up and looking about the room I realized that the pain that had wracked my head, shoulder, and most of my body, was gone. Looking over to my shoulder I could see that the mutant-dog bite that had threatened to kill me was nowhere to be found. I touched it just to be certain I was not still dreaming.

As my energy began to return, I felt better than I had in many days. I wondered who would, or could, have done this for me.

My bed was bordered on each side by a nearly translucent electrical field. I could make out outlines of shapes from the other side that looked like more beds, and at least one had a figure laid upon them.

Lowering my legs over the side of the table I tentatively extended my fingers towards the field surrounding me. I felt the slightest sensation of an electrical current as I made contact with it and the hairs of my arm stood on end. Standing, I removed the many small tubes that connected to my suit and pushed my hand through the field. Satisfied that I would not be significantly shocked I ventured beyond the field to investigate. Cautiously peering around the fields of the bed next to mine I was astonished at what I found. There, breathing slowly but alive, lay Clay. I rubbed my eyes in disbelief, still uncertain that I had actually awakened from my dreams, but when I opened them again he was still there.

Pushing my way through his field and approaching slowly I tentatively reached out to touch him, half expecting him to disappear in a puff before I was able. But when my fingers made contact with his side he stirred slightly and let out a low moan.

How, I wondered. I had held his lifeless body in my arms and driven with him for a period of time before I passed out. How could this be? Had he actually been dead or just so close to it that I could no longer tell the difference?

I actually wondered then if I had died too but as I stood contemplating my surroundings his eyes fluttered as he began to awaken. Like me, it took a few minutes for him to come to. I spoke softly to him to let him know I was there. He smiled weakly as our eyes met and he spoke through the mask on his face.

"Stephen, is that you? I've had some of the worst nightmares ever." Then, spotting the white plastic ceiling, he continued. "Where are we? Those were nightmares, weren't they?"

I did not know where to begin. "No Clay, they weren't. But, for whatever reason, you're okay now. We don't have time to talk about it though, we have to figure out where we are and get home." He nodded his agreement as he removed his mask and stood.

Together we finished investigating the room and found that we were the only two occupants. The room was large enough to accommodate ten people like ourselves. Pulling the small tubes from the suits he wore I noticed a small monitor display beside his bed change and a number of large bright lights began blinking rapidly. Looking at Clay I said, "Clay, I think we need to go. Now."

The large metal door of the room slid open automatically as we approached it. Beyond the door a large hexagonal hallway extended in both directions. Twenty feet in either direction, the hallway turned away at a forty-five degree angle. Like so many of the decisions that I had made in the recent past, I was forced to decide randomly. We went left.

The first door we encountered in the hall was on our right. Since we had no plan at that point we looked at each other for suggestions. Shrugging our shoulders we entered the room beyond the sliding door.

It was not a large room but as the door opened a foul stench met us. Aside from a few objects that resembled art hanging from the walls, the room was mostly barren.

There was a large display encompassing most of one of the walls, right next to a small panel of flat buttons and in the middle of the room sat what resembled a large metal tub, with two cut-outs on either side. The cuts extended all the way to the floor. The tub had what appeared to be a large drain and the smell found within the room seemed to emanate from it as we cautiously approached it. A thin layer of clear liquid, resembling mucous, coated the entire inner surface.

Obviously we had no idea what the purpose of the room was and decided to move on. The next few doors we entered were nearly identical to the first, although many of the items hanging from the walls were different. Also, the level of stench that came from each varied from barely discernable to overpowering. Opening every door did not appear to be a profitable venture.

Continuing through the halls we discussed what method we should use in entering doors we saw. But when the sound of oozing fluid came from around the corner in the hall ahead of us we looked at each other with alarm. We had to find a place to get out of the hall. Doubling-back on our path we both spotted the grate of an air duct.

The covering was not securely attached and was easily removed. An identical duct and grate could be found on the opposite side of the hall. Taking opposite ducts, Clay and I climbed into the tubes as quickly and quietly as we could manage, placing the grates back over the openings. We waited nervously for whatever it was to pass.

My mind had difficulty processing what I saw then. We saw its shadow before we saw it. It moved slowly as it rounded the corner and I held my breath as it passed, praying it would not discover either of us.

From the time that I had awakened and found Clay alive, I had suspected. When I saw the architecture that surrounded us, I suspected. As we entered room after room containing the strange metal tubs and even stranger artwork, I suspected even more. But when the alien passed in front of my grate I knew beyond all doubt that we were on an alien ship.

Remembering the abductions I had witnessed a long time ago, I imagined myself and Clay being taken, along with all of our belongings, on board the ship. The only thing I couldn't figure was why they had gone to so much trouble to heal us. But I was unable to think of any of that as long as I watched incredulously while it moved past my position.

It was large, about ten feet from front to back. It resembled a gigantic slug with eyes perched on eight-inch long stalks that moved independent of the other. It held its head about three feet off the floor as its body scooted along the floor.

Its skin was gray with huge blue veins that could be seen running this way and that, entirely covering it. At the front of its grotesque body, close to the floor, were two arms. Unlike yours and mine however, there was obviously no bones within them. Although it appeared to be able to move without them, it used its 'arms' to pull its mass quicker. Throwing each one forward with a wet thud, it pulled itself by bending its appendage in the middle.

It left a slime trail as it moved past, a trail that slowly dried and disappeared. The purpose of the metal tubs that we had seen in so many of the rooms became apparent then. I surmised that they must have been some kind of quarters and what looked like tubs must have served them as beds. I grimaced when I realized that the drain must have been the equivalent of a toilet; a bed and toilet all in one, how pleasant.

Neither one of us was quick to emerge from our hiding place after it was gone. Minutes passed before I came out and then only after I was certain it had gone. Once Clay saw me he exited his hiding place as well.

Words really couldn't effectively cover what we had just seen, so with a telling look we didn't say anything about it. Instead, I simply asked if he was ready to continue to which he nodded silently. His answer wasn't very convincing. The realization that we were aboard an alien ship and could be heading just about anywhere in the galaxy, certainly made life more complicated.

Having seen the alien, we were a tad less eager to enter doors as we happened upon them. But, wandering aimlessly about the ship would get us nowhere so, after summoning some courage, we again picked a door at random and entered.

We both let out loud sighs of relief when we saw what looked like a storage room beyond. Piles of metal boxes, crates, and barrels filled the room, some all the way to the ceiling. We entered the room in order to search it but didn't need a reason other than to be out of the hall.

In amongst the piles we found a car that looked like the one we had taken from Kriton. I gave Clay a look of suspicion that he returned. Unsure what to do, we approached the car slowly and cautiously, peering through the windows.

Inside the car we could see our packs and weapons. It was the car we had driven and whoever had taken us had only bothered to remove us from the vehicle before storing it. As surprised as I was that our belongings had been ignored by our captors, I was shocked when I found the alien weapon and my sword beneath my pack on the seat.

Counting our lucky stars, we changed from the skin-tight suits into our own clothing. It was some time before we decided that we needed to continue. The comfort provided by the items we were familiar with was reassuring. Eventually we knew we could stay there only so long. So, reluctantly, we returned to the hall.

Each and every door on that ship looked exactly like all the others. It made determining which doors to enter and which ones to skip a matter of gambling. Security did not seem to be an issue on the ship, so it surprised us when the next door we approached did not instantly slide open. It did not open even when we stopped and actually reached out to touch its surface.

A locked door on an open ship certainly made us curious. What was on the other side? No apparent method of opening the door could be found and we were about to give up and move on when we heard the sound of another alien approaching.

Hiding ourselves once again in the nearest convenient air duct, we waited. Approaching the door and stopping, the alien ran a small object over the door frame and the door opened. This door was thicker than the others we had seen and opened very slowly. We could not see into the room beyond, since it was poorly lit. The door remained open for almost a minute after the alien had passed through.

Waiting again to ensure no inadvertent encounters we had not yet emerged when the door opened again to an exiting alien. It remained open as it moved down the hall and before it closed we both made a dash to enter.

A short hallway led away from the door into a massive room. It was a large open space and we found ourselves on a ten-foot wide walkway that we assumed circled the entire diameter of the room.

Approaching the guard rails of the walkway we looked up and down. Similar walkways on each level of the ship could be seen. We counted eight below us and three above. We were unable to see either the ceiling or the floor since darkness enveloped much of the room.

The air within was noticeably cooler then in the hallways or the other rooms and we could see our breath. In the center of the room, some thirty feet distant from the edge of the walkway extending as far as the eye could see, were row upon row upon row of small glass capsules. These capsules were stacked one upon another, reaching into the darkness above and below us.

Each capsule was illuminated by a single internal light and we could see that each had a small display located on the top.

Many of the capsules were empty, as was the case with the majority near us. But, as we strained to be certain what we were seeing, it became apparent that the ones just within normal visual range contained bodies, human bodies. Hundreds on them were occupied. "So this is what happens to all of the people that are abducted", I thought to myself.

All of the capsule occupants remained utterly still; it was obvious that they had been placed in some sort of stasis. There had to have been tens-of-thousands of them in that room. I could only speculate why they were there, but my imagination ran wild.

We moved about the walkway for some time, trying to arrive at an estimate of the number of people contained within the capsules. Both of us wondered silently why we were not two of the newest occupants. It was a disturbing thought indeed.

Circling further we noticed that there was no apparent method of reaching the tubes from the walkways. We lost track of the time we spent in the room and did not speak much during that time. It was oppressive to just be in that room and we both knew that we needed to move on. We had to figure out some way to get off the ship.

Neither of us remembered the door through which we had entered but it didn't really matter since all of the halls looked the same to us. Luckily, the lock that had prevented our entrance seemed to work only one way. But, exiting the storage room into an adjoining room, made us instantly wish we hadn't.

The room we entered was furnished with a number of metal tables. We could see the back of an alien in the midst of eating as the door slid open and we moved quickly to the side of the doorway where we crouched behind a table.

Moving to a position that would afford us a better view of the alien, we tried to stay hidden from its view. However, revulsion threatened to overtake us. There, upon the table, the object upon which the alien feasted was a human body.

Not bothering to see who had entered what must have been some kind of dining facility, the alien continued to dine. Leaning forward it opened its large mouth slowly. There were no teeth within its maw, but rather a mass of wriggling snake-like appendages, each with a small mouth of its own.

The appendages actually hissed somewhat at the sight of the 'food' lying upon the table before it. Then, leaning forward and placing its open mouth directly on the body, we could here wet ripping sounds as it ate.

I had seen my share of horrors but I could still feel the bile as it rose into my throat. Clay was turning a deep shade of green and threatened to retch. Staying low we both hurried to leave the room and moved quietly towards the nearest door. It was not the door through which we had entered.

A cloud of cold air flowed out of the new door as it slid open. Within, hanging from hooks, were human bodies. They were in various stages of wholeness, and some of the hooks contained only parts. We had discovered at least one terrible reason that the aliens abducted people: food. Our desire to get off of that ship was increasing exponentially by the minute. So, moving under the cover of the nearest tables, we moved to yet another door through which we hastily exited.

With new found desperation we moved through the halls hoping that the next room we entered would provide a means of escape. I for one hoped that we would stumble into lifeboats, but it was not to be.

We entered a handful of bedrooms in our frenzied search; one even had a sleeping alien within. Only after a string of these did we enter what could only be described as a computer room.

Displays literally covered the walls of the room and a number of button pads were affixed beneath each one. But what interested us most was the large pedestal that rose from the floor in the middle of the room. Just above it, spinning slowly, was a holographic diagram of the ship. A small red dot indicated the location of the room we were in.

That ship, like so many of the other alien ships I had seen over my lifetime, was a large round disk. The huge central room of the ship, the one that contained all of the capsules, occupied more than half the space the ship actually had.

We stayed in that room for a time pondering what to do. Clay, being the ever-interested computer hacker, paced around the room studying everything that he could. Throughout my time of working with him I had come to realize that, despite his appearance and demeanor, he was one of the most intelligent people I had ever known. Still, it surprised me when he stated confidently that he believed he could make out some of the words that were flashing on the displays around us and that he had located the bridge of the ship. With those words my desire to escape from the ship changed into a plan.

I instructed Clay to find the most direct route to the bridge. While he did that I took inventory of the weapons we had. Along with the two weapons I had taken from the guards on my way to Long Island was the sword that I had won in the Grid. We also had the weapon that came from the aliens themselves, the same weapon that had finally put an end to the demon humant who had tormented so many for so long.

The aliens we had seen to that point did not look overly dangerous. They moved excruciatingly slow and had no obvious defenses. I realized however that these *were* the same creatures that had built and brought the ships to Earth. Still, I was confident that with three types of weapons: energy, projectile, and an ancient sword, that we could find some method to defeat them. At least we were going to go to the bridge and find out.

When I shared my plan with Clay a single eyebrow shot up as if to say, 'We're going to do what?' But whatever he was thinking, he said nothing, simply nodding his agreement.

Keeping our trip to the bridge as brief as possible, we made our way through the halls, prepared to disappear into one of the many doors or air ducts that lined them if the need arose. We met no one on the way and at last reached the large metal door that led to the bridge. Looking at each other one last time before entering, I could see that Clay looked extremely nervous as sweat had begun to bead on his forehead.

When the door slide open we realized that we had found what had to have been the majority of the occupants of the ship. And for the first time since waking and entering the halls of the ship, the aliens showed their awareness of us.

The nearest alien to the door was the first to see us and let out an ear-piercing screech. Clay turned his human weapon towards the alien and, pulling the trigger, put an end to its screech.

Chaos, or at least what appeared to be to me and Clay, ensued. Aliens, all screeching then, moved about the room, only they were moving quickly this time. They were able to move just like earth snakes move, by undulating the muscles in their bellies. Coupled with their front appendages they were surprisingly fast.

As they moved not one made a move towards us or acted as if they were going to attack. A number of the aliens crowded around a central computer pedestal while the rest scurried off to the right of us.

Proceeding past the doorway and into the room we could see that the aliens that had moved to our right were crowding to get onto some kind of metallic mesh set into the floor. We watched in stunned amazement as each one disappeared a few seconds after moving over the mesh. Where they went I do not know.

I had never encountered an enemy that did not fight back and was unsure what to do. Without warning, large characters appeared in the holographic display above the central pedestal. The characters began to change at regular intervals. Even I didn't need Clay to tell me that it was a countdown.

Pointing to the display I shouted to Clay that we needed to stop it if at all possible and that he needed to get right on it. With the majority of the aliens rushing to the metal mesh, I moved towards the pedestal myself to remove the aliens that remained there, blocking Clay's approach.

I did nothing but approach when the aliens screeched and even hissed a little before backing away from the pedestal. The sounds of electricity emanating from the mesh filled the air. Just then I remembered some of the articles that I had read years before. It seemed that the human race had had some difficulty understanding the motivations of the aliens since none had ever been caught alive. This was my chance; I moved to stop the last few aliens from getting onto the mesh.

At last I had discovered something that made the aliens aggressive. Pointing my weapon from alien to alien I attempted to stop their approach. Opening their large mouths and extending the snake-like appendages within, they approached me quickly. I stopped the closest two with two well-placed shots. Seeing their comrades fall did nothing to dissuade them and I knew that I would have to shoot them all in order to stop them thus defeating my goal.

Looking for an alternate method I turned and looked down at the mesh on the floor. A number of small metal tubes ran the width of the mesh and entered through a small opening on its side. Removing my sword from the sheath on my back, I angled the blade into the opening between the edge of the mesh and the floor and with one sweep cut them all.

Only one alien remained then. Enraged, it let out a low rumble as it moved towards me. Visions of the unfortunate victim upon the dinner table entered my head as it opened its large mouth. The snakes within danced wildly as it approached. Although the disgust within me cried out to kill it, logic dictated otherwise.

With a simple uppercut to its large mouth, which slammed shut roughly, the alien passed out. I was surprised that such an attack had worked and hoped it wasn't dead. Clay continued to work on the self-destruct as I tried to figure out some way to tie the creature up. After some thought I removed the rope from my pack and wrapped it round the creature until I had used it all and then I tied the end snuggly. I could only hope that it would keep it contained if it ever did wake up.

I don't know how he did it, frankly I don't care, but Clay was able to stop the self-destruct from destroying the ship. And if that weren't impressive enough, after some study and examination, Clay was able to operate the central pedestal in a rudimentary fashion.

I watched as he brought up a holographic diagram of the Earth with a small red dot that hovered above its surface. This, we hoped, was us. In the time we had been on board that ship we had flown to the other side of the world. If, by some miracle we found a way off the ship we would be about as far away from home as we could possibly be and still remain on the same planet.

It hadn't occurred to me before then that keeping the ship was a feasible plan and so when Clay informed me that he believed he could pilot the ship back home it took a moment to sink in. Filled with new excitement over the prospect that this presented I encouraged him to try.

With a few presses of buttons, the little red dot actually began to move over the surface of the holographic Earth. We moved at an astounding rate and within only a few minutes were back over home soil.

Unfortunately, even Clay had his limitations so when we approached New Duluth and passed quickly overhead I looked at him. He wore a perplexed expression as he manipulated the buttons when, all of a sudden, we made a sharp turn and began to descend, without slowing, towards the ground.

I watched the small red dot and said, with evident distress, "Clay? Are you aware of what's going on?"

Responding briskly he said, "Yeah, yeah. I know, I know. I don't know what…" But before he could finish his sentence we felt the ship lurch as we came to a sudden, and complete, stop.

The impact of the crash should have thrown us across the room and into the wall. Neither of us should have survived it. Yet, the most we felt from the crash was a slight sensation that we had stopped.

Looking at Clay with a broad grin I said, "Well, we're here." We both had a brief laugh.

"Why don't you find an exterior hatch for us." I knew that one of us was going to have to stay with the ship so once he had located an exit so I instructed him to leave and return with help. A few protests later he left.

It took three days before a team from New Duluth arrived. In that time our alien guest awoke. My bindings held it fast while it screeched in protest for a time. I tried numerous ways of communicating with it, but after its initial protests was silent the entire time.

I ate the remaining rations in my pack while I waited. But, knowing what that alien preferred to eat, did not offer it any food. It was a long silent three days. I dared not sleep. I began to wonder what I would do with the alien if the time arrived that I would no longer be able to stay awake. I was glad I never had to make that decision.

Before leaving, Clay had locked the door to the bridge. Expecting that I might have to contend with visitors while I waited for Clay's return, I was extremely surprised when one showed up. We never did find any more aliens on the ship when we searched it but we found plenty of those metal meshes in the floor.

When the team from New Duluth finally arrived they found me on the bridge. By then exhaustion was beginning to take its toll. When Bill entered the bridge and saw the alien he could barely contain his excitement. With a team of people we were able to physically remove the alien from the ship. We fed it fish and other meat. It didn't seem to like them but ate them nonetheless.

I had to shade my eyes against the brightness of the sun as I emerged from the hatch. Turning and looking up at the ship I was overcome at the sheer size of it. Although I knew it was a large ship from the diagram that we had seen in the computer room, I was not prepared for the sheer physical enormity of it from the outside. Yet there it was, and it was in our possession.

While waiting for the team from New Duluth I had been upset about the crash. But upon emerging I could see that the ship had burrowed into the ground upon impact and had actually created its own cave. The edges of the crevasse that it had created on impact were plainly obvious from my vantage point, but when we exited the hole, the ship disappeared completely from view.

A large holographic image covered the entire chasm, projected by the ship itself. Dirt, plants, and even trees dotted the surface of the image and it blended into the real surroundings flawlessly. I could not tell where one ended and the other began. The aliens had certainly planned for all contingencies. I had to wonder if any other ships had been planted in the earth and had simply never been discovered.

Departing for home I practically salivated at the technological treasures that the ship represented. Not only did we have something invaluable to the people that lived in New Duluth, but we had something that would have been invaluable to the people in the cities. I knew things were going to be different in the future.

Turning away from the ship and towards my home my thoughts turned to Ashleigh and Derik. At that moment, seeing them and sharing my love and concern for them became more important to me than anything else I could do.

Chapter 18

Brief reunions and introductions…
Stephen Blake

Our journey back to the city took an exceeding long time. My mind was a jumble of thoughts from my family, friends, and loved ones I had left in New Duluth, to the recent events that I had been a part of on the eastern coast. I was restless to arrive. I had so much to share.

At long last I could see the skyline of my beloved home in the distance. Anticipation filled my heart as we neared the front gate. Although I had only been gone for a short period of time I was ready; my heart ached to be home again.

Pulling into the center of town, I saw many faces that I knew, but the two I sought most were nowhere in sight. Jumping anxiously from the vehicle I tried to be polite to the many people that welcomed me home. I had no idea how much the city had missed my presence until that moment as each person I met shared their happiness that I had been found alive and well.

Pushing through the crowd as quickly as politeness would allow, I continued to search. Among the many well-wishers one face did stop me. Keith, the leader of the group that had come to my rescue, the man that I had given-up for dead more than once, stood before me.

Grabbing each other in a firm embrace, we expressed our pleasure to be re-united. Parting, I looked at him and said, "I feared that I would never again see you alive, my friend. Someone, somewhere likes you. Fighting Reks Kriton on his home territory would be suicide for most ordinary people. I'm certainly glad to see that you are not an ordinary person. What became of the battle that I left you waging?"

His demeanor changed and he looked down briefly before responding. "I lost way too many men that day, many my friends and neighbors. But they fought bravely and did not shy away from the humants that came at us in waves. Unfortunately, only a handful of us made it off the island. We knew we could never defeat the armies we would face there so once you were away I ordered a retreat. I was one of the lucky ones that got out of there. It is good to have you back at home, safe and sound. You are the reason we went."

Not daring to think about the significance of that statement, I asked, "What of Reks?"

"Being the coward he truly is he was the very first to leave the battle and he escaped. I saw him leave, but the intensity of the fighting around me prevented my pursuit. All I could do was watch him recede into the darkness, cursing my lack of fighting skill. Only after we knew that you were safely away did we start a fighting retreat."

As his words sunk deep, my heart grew heavy with the guilt I felt for the lives given in my name. It is hard for a man to live with the knowledge that so many others had given theirs. But he was not yet finished speaking. He tripped over his words; it was obvious he did not want to share what he had to next.

"There is one other thing you should know, Stephen. Your humant friend, Alan, was the one that told me how to get to Reks' compound. When he heard you had been taken, he knew the immediate danger that you were in and scaled the walls of the humant section of town to warn someone, anyone who would listen.

"He tried to find someone from our group, you know the ones from Bloomington, but instead ran into a number of others. They were not happy to see him and some of them attacked him. By the time he finally found me he was near death. I rushed him to the infirmary where he shared the information with me, but it was too late.

"He lived through the night, often calling out names of people that no one knew, but the one name he repeated over and over again was yours. By morning he had passed without ever waking. I'm sorry Stephen, but I knew you'd want to know."

I had often worried that my fateful decision to separate the humants from the remaining population of New Duluth would come to haunt me. I never would have imagined that it would cost the life of the only humant I ever called friend.

Feeling considerably less jubilant to be home I left him then to continue my search for my family. It felt like I met every citizen of New Duluth before I finally found them.

Running breathlessly we threw ourselves into each other's arms. Ashleigh covered my face with her kisses while we embraced. My son, clinging to his mother's leg tugged on my shirt. Grabbing him in my arms my family was complete once again, we were whole.

I spent the next few days with my family, unwilling for them to be out of my sight. Each night I slept I feared that I would wake only to find it had all been a dream. Of course my nightmares made their nightly visits. But each morning it was Ashleigh's face that I woke to, and each morning I would simply hug her close for as long as I could.

As time passed I knew that I would eventually have to resume my regular life. There were duties that demanded my attention. The alien ship required study and its location needed to be protected. It was difficult to determine who should be assigned to the job, since it was absolutely essential to keep it secret even from the general populace of New Duluth. A few of the citizens of New Duluth had served previously with some of the best special warfare teams of the army; these were sent to begin their work on the alien ship.

Before regular activity resumed, there was one important thing that needed to be done. Assembling what remained of the army, and those close to him, I called Keith to the main hall of the city. For years he had loyally served our group and the citizens of New Duluth. For years he had given his talents freely, and yet he had never done those things required to earn the Savior's Beret. However, in the previous two weeks he had endangered his life for the good of another. At last, he had earned the right to wear one.

Calling the room to attention and calling his name I read the list of achievements warranting the award of the beret. I don't believe I ever saw him happier as he approached the podium. Extending the rolled up beret to him, I could see tears welling in his eyes. We saluted and he returned to his seat. I was very pleased for my friend as it was an award years in coming.

Many other people earned awards that day, far too many of them posthumously. At the end of the ceremony I made the one award I knew could be controversial. After posthumously granting the humant Alan Foster membership, and an honorary commission, within New Duluth's army, I awarded him his own Savior's Beret. When a number of 'Boos' reached my ears, I knew that I had to say something in the defense of my friend.

"Everyone here today shares a common hatred of the World Outside. Most of us had lives in whatever city we were expelled from and many of us left families behind that we will never see again. That is, after all, why we are all here in New Duluth today. We seek to replace what we lost when we were thrown out of the only homes any of us ever knew.

"Our great city is literally filled with every imaginable kind of people and yet we have never separated into racial groups, or ethnic groups, or even formed into unions. We share the common bond of our beliefs and values. With this binding tie we have found strength in the diversity that surrounds us. Without the electricians to provide the power, without the farmers to grow the food, and without the soldiers to protect it all, none of this would be worth living.

"This brings me to my next point, a point I do not believe all of you are prepared to hear. As far as I know no one, not one person, has ever chosen to be a humant. They were all simple residents of the World Outside, just like you and me, before they were victimized further by that madman Reks Kriton. The only difference between them and us is they have made the journey of the damned, the journey to Kriton's hell. I have seen what he does to people and it would sicken you all if you could see what I have seen.

"Some of you know, many of you don't, that I have as many reasons as anyone to hate humants. They welcomed me into the World Outside my first night by threatening the very group that rescued me. One of them even took the life of my very best friend, a man many of you had the privilege to know before he was taken from us. But when I saw what happened to the people that entered Kriton's compound, my heart wept for them. It is hard to say why they fight for the likes of a man like Kriton. Too many have no choice if they want to live.

"Unfortunately, we fear what we do not understand. Without walking the path that they tread it is difficult to do so. But fear based upon the lack of understanding is irrational fear and must be avoided.

"I realize that the mere presence of some humants presents danger to those around them, but this is rare.

Regardless, this was the basis upon which I made the decision to separate the humants from the general population. Humants that declare their abilities and take appropriate precautions should present no danger to those around them. After being in the very heart of the humant factory, I submit to you now that that decision was erroneous."

A few grumbles could be heard from the audience as I continued. 'Separating the humants from ourselves is the same as the cities casting us away. Are we no better than they? Do we want to do to them what the people in the cities have done to all of us? We are better than that!

"A life lived in fear is no life at all and a life without risk is not worth living. We all know how paralyzing fear and the inability to take risks can be. We've all experienced that fear as we looked out the front windows of the pods that took us from the cities, leaving behind all that we knew for an uncertain destiny. We also know that we are the lucky few that actually made it past our landing. We should spend our time counting our blessings rather than condemning others.

"We should tear down the walls of humant-town. Sure we should remain vigilant and sure we should continue to be selective of those we allow to join us, but we must become one; for we are truly stronger together.

"Today we decide what kind of future we will provide for our children and our children's children. Will we rise to the occasion or shrink into the shadows, unwilling to accept the challenge of living with those that are different than ourselves? My friend Alan, a humant, died to save the life of a human. *I honor his memory this day!*"

Finished, I stepped away from the podium as a small number of people rose and left the ceremony. A few claps, followed by a few more, and eventually rising to a cacophony of sound filled the hall. I was pleased to see many in the audience rise to their feet to show their support. Alan would have been pleased too. We lost a few residents that day but we were closer as a people.

You see Paithar, the World Outside was unwittingly created to break a man's spirit and to steal his humanity. Some of us hang on to it with tenacity, some of us don't; but we all have to make that decision for ourselves ultimately, even those whose decision is unjustly influenced by others. Alan never gave up his humanity right to the bitter end. It is hard not to have respect for a person like that.

Many things have happened to me since entering the World Outside. I often wonder what kind of man I would have been had I become a member of a group of cannibals, or if Reks had decided to make me a humant after all. I question whether I would have been strong enough to maintain my humanity. I hope you will never have to find out Paithar."

*   *   *

Just the mere mention of what had happened to Stephen, and to so many others, made me thoughtful. I was all too keenly aware that it was not beyond the realm of possibility for anyone living within the cities, including me, to experience it. Thankfully, I did not have much time to ponder the comment as Stephen continued.

*   *   *

Life returned to normal then in New Duluth as people busied themselves tearing down the walls of humant-town. After returning to my job my wife shared the welcome news that she was, once again, pregnant. But things were happening in the 'real' world that would shortly change my life yet again.

After six grueling years my brother Paul had finally solved the riddle of what happened in my basement that fateful day. I really don't know how he did it; I only know that he did. At last he had proof that I was innocent of the crime for which I had been expelled from the city. Knowing that he would get no satisfaction from the main stream media outlets, and knowing that only the potential embarrassment of the Commonwealth would get the results he desired. He took the news to the underground news outlets and shared the information he had found with them.

I can only begin to imagine how unhappy the Commonwealth bureaucrats must have been to have had their hands forced. But, a few days later, two helicopters departed the city, one to the east and one to the west to find me. Landing at pre-selected spots along the way, residents of the World Outside were questioned and the search continued. It didn't take long for the questioning to lead towards New Duluth so the helicopters made their way there.

I was out in the countryside that day. Things would likely have been very different had they been forced to enter the city to retrieve me, but as it was my heart jumped a beat when I heard the blades chopping the air.

Right away I assumed the worst, only Reks Kriton had access to such things in the World Outside and I feared that he had come for me once again.

I was not far from the city, not far enough to have felt the need for security. Yet I was far enough that a sprint on foot would not have been sufficient to get back through the gates in time. Rising to my feet and unsheathing my sword, I prepared to fight whoever approached.

I could see the side-door of the helicopter opening as it grew closer. A man with a megaphone stuck his head out. The voice I heard speaking my name sounded familiar, but it simply could not be who it sounded like. I had not heard my brother's voice for such a long time I had almost forgotten what it sounded like. My heart skipped a beat and I feared to hope.

The helicopter circled once and began to land. Peering with interest into the cabin I could not believe what I saw. Smiling broadly and looking a bit older, my brother Paul stood, waiting patiently for them to land. He seemed to be exchanging words with one of the others in the cabin.

I ran towards the helicopter as fast as I could. At the same time Paul jumped from the door as the chopper was still a couple of feet off the ground. An amplified voice demanded we stop as we ran towards each other. Ignoring the repeated demand, we didn't even slow down.

Thoughts flooded my mind as I ran. I had so many things to share with him and so many questions to ask. A single solitary shot flew through the air as we were about to embrace. From the sound I knew that someone had fired a weapon. It wasn't until Paul's expression changed from elation to the blank look that men get when they are about to die, and he fell forward into my outstretched arms, did I realize what had happened. My brother had been shot by one of the guards just as I was about to embrace him after so many bitter years.

His blood ran through my fingers as I laid him upon the ground. Looking up at me he spoke, coughing up some blood.

"Oh Steve it hurts." Rubbing his checks, tears ran down mine. I tried to hold on to him. "Hang on Pauly, we'll get you help."

Screaming at the top of my lungs I tried to get some help, but no one could hear me over the sound of the helicopter. His face grew terribly pale and I knew that the end was near. Speaking laboriously he uttered, "I love you Steve. I came to save you." Then he was gone.

Something snapped in me then. Gritting my teeth and shouting my outrage to the heavens, I stood and turned towards the chopper. Gripping the sword firmly in my hands I bounded towards it, fueled by my rage. A few shots flew by me as I moved, but I made myself a difficult target.

It was the first time since entering the World Outside that I lost control. I had no plan beyond exacting revenge as I ran up to the craft. Swiftly the man that had shot my brother in the back lay bleeding, missing the arm that had held his weapon.

Terrible pain filled one of my wrists then as bursts of light filled my vision. I screamed then while I raised my sword above my head. Standing motionless, I watched my sword, with my left hand still clinging tightly to the hilt, fall from the helicopter door and onto the ground. One of the guards had fired a burst of energy directly through my wrist, virtually sheering my hand from my arm.

In my rage I had failed to maintain an awareness of my situation. It cost me dearly. Darkness quickly enveloped me then and I spent the remaining time unconscious. I assume the ride back to Chicago was brief. The guards left my brother's body where it had fallen.

I woke sometime later lying in a hospital bed, handcuffed to the bedrail. A metal monstrosity, attached to my arm, replaced my missing hand. Turning it over and over I looked at it with rising revulsion. Moaning with despair I realized that what I had just experienced was no dream. I cried for a time for the loss of my brother. The last connection I had with that infernal city had been taken from me; I cannot begin to explain my grief.

Ironically, not only had the city taken my only living relative, but in one sweeping event had removed me from the life and family that I had found and grown to love.

Nurses and doctors were my only visitors for days. Most of them were friendly enough, but I spoke to no one. Even the psychologists did not pry after I gave them a look that said, "leave me be". I simply couldn't eat and only after being threatened with a feeding tube did I finally relent.

The metal hand they had attached to my body was something right out of my many nightmares. Attempts to make it similar to a human hand had been made, but it left a lot to be desired. Each finger had a pad on its end to relay sensory information to my brain. But, as it turned out, I found that I had simply lost nearly all ability to feel anything with my new hand.

A technician visited me one day and, after opening a small access door in the top of my hand, instructed me on its functions, showing me how to care for it. I learned that, with the right tools, it was possible to increase the gripping power of the hand. I was sure to pay close attention to that feature.

And yet, this hand was not mine and it made me feel less than fully human to have it. Only then did I begin to understand how some of the humants must feel. Being stripped of a part of oneself against your will brings a feeling of violation. Oh how I could now relate to humants in an entirely new way. I've tried to hide the shame of my new hand behind gloves.

*   *   *

I had all but forgotten about the gloves that he wore; I watched with renewed interest as he removed them. His new hand looked as if it were made of chrome, the luster had been allowed to tarnish behind the cover of a glove. He turned his hand slowly so that I could see it in its entirety. Sitting back in his chair and leaving his gloves off, he continued.

*   *   *

I was beginning to wonder if that hospital was to be my new home when the same government employee that had spoken to my brother, came to visit me. Ordering my release he informed me that I was to appear on television. It seemed I was to be the centerpiece of a propaganda campaign, a campaign to prove that the government actually cared about the guilt or innocence of those that it expelled from the cities. I laughed to myself at the absurdity of the prospect.

It was then I was informed that the guard I had attacked had died from his wounds. He notified me that I had instigated a brutal and unprovoked attack for which I would be tried.

A trial? Since my 'crime' had been committed in the World Outside and since no police camera had recorded it they were forced to provide me with an actual trial. But, more importantly, too many people knew who I was since the press had extensively covered my return. They didn't dare return me without at least the illusion of a real trial.

Until that date I was free to go. Leaving my hospital bed I left the building, unsure where I would go. Although I had no relationship with any of the people within the city, I did have some ideas of places to go and people to see. I believed it important to visit the relatives of some of those I knew in the World Outside to let them know that all was well.

The first visit I made was to the wife of my friend and mentor, Bill Owens. She was not easy to locate and I had to travel some distance to be able to find her. When I did finally meet her, explaining who I was, she immediately broke down in tears and wept for a good while. Filled with gratitude for the news that I bore, we simply shared our silence for a while.

We shared stories about him with one another, stories from our own unique experiences. Bill had been something of a prankster, a fact he had never revealed to me in all the time that I had known him. I wondered if I would ever have the chance to ask him about it.

Eventually the time came for me to leave and we parted. It was a rewarding experience, and the opportunity to help fill the void that had so long plagued her heart is one I shall not soon forget.

Next, I endeavored to find Keith's parents. They were not as hard to locate as Bill's wife. When I met them I quickly learned that Keith was an only child. It had been the hardest moment of their lives when he had been sent away to the war, but it was harder still when he was exiled for his crimes into the World Outside.

Pictures of their son literally covered the walls of their small home and they were quite happy to receive the news. Giving their son up for dead, they were pleased to know that, not only did he still live, but he had made a difference to many of the residents of New Duluth.

They beamed with pride when I spoke of the lives their son had saved, particularly my own, and when I shared that he had just been awarded the Savior's Beret you would have thought he had been awarded the Medal of Honor. When we parted, I believe they were happy. Proceeding to my next stop the only regret I had was that I was only a representative of their loved-ones. How I longed to reunite them all.

Things were different when I tried to visit with Clay's parents. Their reaction to my arrival was disturbing. I had always known that Clay possessed a rebellious streak. I would never have guessed that his parents would be so relieved to be rid of him. When they realized what I was there for, I was not welcomed into their home. Indeed, I think his father was actually a little disappointed that he was still alive; mumbling something about it under his breath. I wasted little time moving on from them.

I saved the next two stops for last as they meant the most to me. From the very first mention of Ashleigh's child, and since she had become an important part of my life, I had always felt as though a part of us remained inside the cities. At last, I had the opportunity to see her child.

Finding the address of her ex-husband was more difficult than any of the others. Responsibility and self-reliance are not words I would use to explain him. The chain of addresses, and the attendant information that I found, spoke loudly about the character of the man.

I knew that visiting the child would require discretion, but I felt it was important for her to know something of her mother.

Deciding that the best chance for a brief meeting was between home and school, I waited for the end of the day. Neither Ashleigh nor I had ever known whether her child was born a boy or a girl. The name listed on the school roster told me she was a girl. She was a beautiful child and had her mother's eyes.

Approaching discretely, I simply handed her a picture of her mother and said, "You don't know me, but I know your mother – your real mother.

"I don't know what you've been told but you have a mother that you've never seen and she loves you and misses you very much.

"I know this is probably very confusing but it was important that you know the truth. Ask your father, but don't ever show him this picture cause if you do he'll take it away."

I knew I had very little time with her. As I left, I said. "I've got to go now. Hopefully, some day you'll get the chance to meet her. Oh, and by the way, you have a half-brother and he lives in the World Outside. Goodbye, sweetheart."

I left her there looking very confused and looking at the picture in her hand. Before she passed out of sight I could see her carefully put the picture in her backpack. I mused over the interesting conversations that were sure to occur.

At length I set off to find the woman whom my brother had engaged to marry. She was the last living connection I would ever have with him and I wanted to meet her. Meeting her turned out to be more providential than I would ever have imagined.

Chapter 19

"Home isn't the place where you came from; it isn't the place that's most comfortable or even the place where you know the most people. Home is the place where you go when you have a choice, wherever that happens to be, and regardless of what anyone else thinks about it."
Stephen Blake

I set out to find the woman that would have married my brother. My desire to meet his fiancé derived from my wish to keep his memory alive, I suppose. I believed that, in some small way, knowing her, and knowing that she too knew him, would allow me to do that.

As luck would have it she lived in the same city where I was and finding her was not difficult. I was unsure what I would say to her when I met her, after all, she had just lost someone very close as well.

Standing on her front step I tentatively rang the bell and waited nervously. When she opened the door I stammered my first few words before I made any sense.

"Hello, my name is Stephen and my brother was Paul Blake. I am the one that he saved from the World Outside and I wanted to meet the woman that he loved."

With a little hesitation she invited me in where we exchanged pleasantries. At first, we just sat across from each other silently. She wore a look of sadness, mixed with a little anger. Finally, she opened up and did share some things about her life with Paul. I wondered aloud why they never married. That was a mistake.

"You owned his heart, Stephen, in a way I never could. A day never passed that he wasn't obsessed with rescuing you. His passionate compassion was one of the reasons I loved him. But I have to admit, it made it difficult to like you."

I was taken aback by this revelation. But I understood. Eventually, she loosened somewhat and we began to share our memories of Paul. It was nice to hear stories from the time that we were separated. We visited for most of a day and into the evening before she mentioned the picture.

"When Paul left for the last time I would see him he left instructions to give this picture to you should anything happen to him. I am remiss to part with it, but after listening to you speak of him I can feel the love you have for him. We share a terrible emptiness in our hearts.

"Paul said that you would understand the significance of the picture and that it would tell you everything that you would need to know."

It was a simple picture, captured when Paul and I had taken our only vacation together during my spring break while I was still going to college. Paul had taken a few days so that we could make a crazy trip to one of the cities that contained a beach. I had great memories of the trip but didn't really remember that picture. Standing below a faux street sign reading '318 Lower Street' we both sat at a table, smiling happily to the camera.

The same frustration I had felt in the Grid during the obstacle cubes returned. How was I going to solve this riddle? At least I was not battling the clock and so I thanked her and left with the picture.

I went into Paul's apartment then to collect his personal belongings, being his only living relative. I hoped that I would find something there to clarify the mystery I had been presented. Among other things, I found journals and pictures. He had lots of pictures of us as boys on his walls, and his journal was filled with the thoughts of a man driven in a cause.

Before going to his apartment I filed a request at the government records office for recordings of Paul's life. Along with the stacks of records he already had covering a majority of my life, I spent countless hours viewing the records of his. Thankfully, most of it was unclassified.

The cares of life and new responsibilities at work dominated much of his spare time. I watched as relationships came and went. He spent hours watching his recordings and I can only imagine what the monotony of watching the same tapes over and over was like. As time passed he spent less and less time at it. After months and then years of little progress, I assume his belief that I was actually innocent must have begun to fade.

As he took notes, Paul was keenly aware of the cameras surrounding him. Instead of keeping notes on one of his numerous computers, he kept them all in a notebook while hunched over, blocking it from the sight of the cameras. It was impossible to know when he actually figured it all out.

Although I had spent considerable time trying to solve it, I was still no closer to the end of the puzzle. Sorting through his personal belonging, deciding which to save and which to donate or throw-away I stumbled across a letter from the company Paul worked for.

The heading caught my eye as it read:

Paul V. Blake
Technotronical
Electronics Division, Lower Level

The words 'Lower Level' nearly jumped off the page at me. Jumping up from my seat, I hastily searched for the picture his fiancé had given me, making a dreadful mess of the place in the process. Looking at the street sign above the table where we sat in the picture I read the words anew, 'Lower Street'. I hoped I was onto something.

I paid a visit to his work the very next day and met his boss. I learned that he was well liked. Bemoaning the loss of a 'talented, though obsessed employee' he offered to give me a tour of the place where he worked. I eagerly agreed.

Descending the steps into the basement of the building we were confronted with a large sign that read, 'Lower Level'. Behind a heavy door, row upon row upon row of computer boxes hummed in unison. Leading me into the room and down one of the aisles I noticed a small metal plaque affixed to each machine. Each of these had a number.

Hiding my building excitement I looked at the numbers as we passed each one. I almost shouted when we passed by unit number 318. I knew where I had to go next and what I had to see, but how?

Dropping to my knees I began to weep loudly, moaning and sobbing to add to the effect. Immediately, my tour guide stopped short and did his best to offer his condolences for my loss. Uncertain how to handle the situation, he left momentarily to get a tissue for my tears. It was just enough time for me to get a good look into the casing of the machine.

Sticking out from one of the air ducts was the corner of a small envelope, barely perceptible to the eye. Grasping it and pulling it from the case, I shoved it quickly into my coat and resumed my position on the floor.

Returning with another person and a box of tissues he offered me his hand. Standing, and making a show of wiping the tears from my eyes, I thanked him for his concern for my feelings. Turning to leave then it was all I could do to contain my real excitement.

Racing home I opened the envelope and dumped its contents onto the table, maintaining my awareness of the ever-present police cameras. A small stack of papers emerged. I was stunned by what I found."

*   *   *

Stephen paused then, retrieving more of the papers he had brought along with him. Handing them to me he said, "Read these, and you will know what happened to me."

I started…

My Dearest Stephen,

As I write this I sincerely hope that you will never read it. If ever you do it means that something has gone terribly wrong and this is the only communication I will likely have with you.

I have labored over the past few years to discover the reasons you were sent into that place. I have missed you so and it has not been easy to have a constant reminder that you are missing. I can only hope that you are actually still alive.

I have managed to locate a few pertinent papers to your case. I have included hard copies of each in this envelope. If you have opened it without me, stop immediately and make copies and hide them in a place that only you will know about.

After reading these things, it should all make sense to you.

I love you and I hope that I will get to see you again and have the opportunity to destroy this letter. If not, I will say 'hi' to mom, dad, and sis for you.

Love, your brother,
Paul

TOP SECRET

FEDERAL ENFORCEMENT AGENCY

M E M O R A N D U M

From: Federal Enforcement Agency, Population Management Division

To: Agency Group, Division, and Section Commanders

Re: Population Control

The City Overcrowding Study prepared by the Population Division indicates that population density within the available space of the city of Chicago has reached a threshold that is no longer sustainable. A Population Control Protocol is necessary.

Timing and availability of necessary resources indicate use of the Alien Poisoning Protocol.

All applicable level commanders within the city are authorized and required to implement this protocol immediately.

TOP SECRET

The next thing that he offered me was a paper entitled, 'Auto-sampling Water Test Results.' The paper also specified a testing facility and time of the test. It was a technical paper, listing all of the substances found within the water that was tested by chemical composition. None of it meant much to me, but to the bottom of the report was attached a small picture. Stephen explained.

"Every sampling is taken automatically. Each sample of water is first photographed and then run through a chemical analyzer. Sometimes the samples we got would include large items that were discarded. But before they were, photos were taken to see what things existed in the waters of the lake.

"Analyzing the results is monotonous and boring, I often took days to review results. This test result was no exception. Since the results weren't classified I had taken this particular one home with me to review at my leisure. I never did see the photo attached to this particular report. I was arrested and expelled before getting that chance."

Looking with interest at the referenced photo I noticed what appeared to be a small yellow metallic canister floating in the water.

"That canister is a container that once contained poison, a particularly lethal poison, known to be spread by the aliens. Only this one came with a government stamp."

Looking closer I was barely able to make out the small stamp of the Commonwealth on the canister casing.

"This is where my troubles began."

TOP SECRET

FEDERAL ENFORCEMENT AGENCY

MEMORANDUM

From: Federal Enforcement Agency, Special Projects Division

To: Chain-of-Command: Chicago, Section 45A Commander

Re: Incorrect Neutralization

The neutralization that occurred in Mr. Blake's premises was incorrect. A common thief had broken into the residence and he was the actual subject of the neutralization.

Once the neutralizer was free of the building, the actual subject of the neutralization discovered the body and the local police were alerted and summoned. The subject has been accused of the incorrect neutralization.

Due to the Double Policy, no artificial evidence will be required. The subject has been accorded responsibility for the crime, the subject does not have the means to pay the fine and will be expelled from the city.

The Group Commander requires no further action regarding this matter as expulsion is tantamount to death. A reprimand will be placed in the record of the errant Neutralizer.

TOP SECRET

TOP SECRET

FEDERAL ENFORCEMENT AGENCY

POLICY MEMORANDUM

From: Federal Enforcement Agency Directorate

To: All National Security Agency Group, Division, and Section Commanders

Re: 'Double' Policy

It is now standard policy to approach all neutralizations using the dress and appearance of the subject.

All surveillance cameras have an inherent flaw. At times, images of subjects appear to be in two places at one time. These 'ghost' images, as they are commonly referred to, are officially recorded as malfunctions within the system.

Using non-violent methods of neutralization allows all such neutralizations to be recorded as malfunctions.

This policy will, hereafter, be referred to as The Double Policy and is ordered for all neutralizations unless warranting reasons exist for non-use. All exceptions to this policy must be approved by a Group Commander or an officer within the Directorate.

TOP SECRET

Official Records Request Results

Requestor: Federal Enforcement Agency Directorate

Requested Records: All internal records, partial records, or references within records of, or held by, Technotronical referencing Stephen J. Blake and Paul M. Blake

Reason for Request: Classified by authority of the Director

Results:
No records, partial records, or references found for Stephen J. Blake.
Standard Employment File found for Paul M. Blake.

Looking at the last of the papers it became apparent that suspicion had fallen upon Stephen's brother. How he had managed to keep it out of the hands of the authorities, and away from the prying cameras, was an impressive feat. Stephen began again.

*   *   *

With the necessary evidence in hand, Paul finally approached the authorities. He was not well received. Had he not taken such pains to have hidden a copy of the same, we might not be speaking today.

At first the officials listened politely but did little else. He continued to call and eventually the responses became belligerent. It became apparent that a different approach would be required.

The next time that he spoke to the officials he made it clear that he would publicly expose the information that he had if they continued to refuse to take action. Even then, they only finally took action after he had released it to the underground news outlets. At last, he was taken before a sentence-giver who, listening with some interest became more and more annoyed the longer he laid the evidence before him. I couldn't believe it, it was the same sentence-giver that had sent me into the World Outside. He knew that Paul's discovery spelled considerable embarrassment for the government.

Giving him the run-around the sentence-giver stalled trying to decide what he should do. It would not be an easy decision, and certainly one of such a magnitude that it could not be made by someone at his level. Within hours it was on the desk of the nearest Group Commander, who consulted with, and I quote, 'those in a position to make such decisions'.

Only after many days, the period necessary to thoroughly search for the pesky evidence, did the government relent and actually agree to send out a search party to locate and return me. Seven years after my expulsion the order was written, the team was assembled, and the search was begun.

My association with Clay helped me to obtain copies of two important recordings. Unfortunately I do not have them with me now so I will have to explain what they contained.

That sentence-giver was angry with my brother. The threat of public humiliation was too much for his arrogance and he angrily charged the teams that were assigned my return to ,"Make sure he doesn't come back from the World Outside. I don't care how you do it, no one will see anything, just be sure I don't ever have to see his face again. And when you find his brother, bring him to me and we'll use him up for all he's worth."

It was the final irony. I had been cast from society and from all I had ever known. I was forcibly taken from the life I had built for myself and learned to love by that same society, and now my only relative had been taken from me by them. I was lost among strangers in a world I used to call home.

I have wandered from place to place since then. I know my time is limited. Whatever they decide to do to me will happen soon. So I decided to share our story with the rest of the world. I remembered your name from the first article I read on the military base in Grand Forks and that is why I came to see you Mr. Ranston.

*   *   *

I was honored he had felt I was capable of sharing his story. As he had said in the beginning of the interview, it was indeed a story that would have a lifetime of implications. Sensing that our interview was drawing to a close, we sat in silence for a few brief moments watching the sun as it began to rise above the nearest city wall. I wondered what it must look like without a force-field to block its splendor.

Our reverie was broken rudely as a group of policemen, followed by a man dressed in the unforgettable garb of a government employee, stormed into the room where we sat. Although I had never seen the man that had spoken to the Blake brothers, I assumed he was standing before us then. Speaking smugly he addressed us both.

"My congratulations, and my gratitude, for getting a confession from our friend here, Mr. Ranston. I doubt he would have said anything even remotely like it in court. I'm so glad that you broke your silence Mr. Blake, it will make returning you to the World Outside that much easier."

Rising to my feet I angrily protested the invasion of my office and demanded that they leave. I could not believe what I was hearing. I had been an unwitting pawn in the hands of that man.

With a look of defiance on his face Stephen rose from his seat and offered his hands to be cuffed. Having heard the details of the many battles he had fought I knew that defending himself from the small group assembled would not have been difficult. I watched, flustered, as they cuffed him and took him from my office.

The last to leave was the government employee who, looking back at me, said, "If you'd like to cover Mr. Blake's final minutes in the city, come to perimeter building three at ten a.m. sharp two days from now. I will see to it that you have the necessary clearances."

I followed the group as they left the building. Herding Stephen towards the nearest police vehicle I caught a glimpse as he turned to look at me. With a look of certainty that one does not see in the faces of many, he said, "I *will* see you again Mr. Ranston. Another time, another place." He was roughly shoved into the car then and was off.

I found my thoughts returning time and again to Stephen and his story. I was unable to concentrate at work and those thoughts kept me awake most of my nights. I wondered how to best share his story, I had to be sure to do it justice.

The clock became my worst enemy as I watched the hours click slowly by. I felt as if I knew Stephen. I had experienced some of the same feelings that his brother had when he was first thrown into the World Outside.

Finally, the day arrived. Fearing to be late I ate a small breakfast, dressed quickly, and made my way to the assigned perimeter building. I arrived with plenty of time to spare as I did not want anything to prevent me from seeing him off. True to the government employee's word I was given clearance, a visitor's pass, and shown into the building.

At approximately nine a.m. a group of morose looking souls was ushered into the building. Only Stephen did not wear a look of despair. The prisoners then heard a brief speech from the head guard, not unlike the one Stephen had shared with me.

Hearing about it did little to prepare me for the real thing. Just like the first experience that Stephen had shared, two prisoners took the option of execution. I jerked with each shot and was taken aback by the lack of concern displayed by those involved.

With the speech finished the prisoners were escorted to their assigned pods. Some of them resisted, but Stephen willingly walked to the entrance to his and, turning, simply waved and smiled. He then disappeared into his pod's hole. It was the last time I saw him.

Looking at the smug government official I could tell he had not expected Stephen's behavior. He looked angry, like a man who had lost an opportunity for revenge. Stifling a smile I turned and left the building. I had lost my new friend to the World Outside.

As I drove home I could see in my mind's eye his reunion with his wife, children, and other loved ones and knew that he had not been expelled against his will from the city, but rather had been returned to the home he had grown to love. I was happy for him, for if any man deserved happiness, it was certainly Stephen Blake.

Epilogue

...And No Justice For All
By Paithar Ranston

In everyone's life there comes an opportunity to learn and grow from the wisdom and experience of others. Some of us are fortunate enough to realize when we've met one of these individuals and that they can, and should, help shape our thoughts and form our opinions.

I have met such a man and his name is Stephen Blake. You probably don't know Mr. Blake the way that I have come to know him and that is a shame.

Over seven years ago he was ripped from his home, and all that he knew, to be thrown into the World Outside, to fend for himself, all on charges that were proven to be false. Yet no judge or jury heard his pleas of innocence and, in fact, none ever genuinely cared. Numbers, particularly those that begin with a dollar sign, matter more than facts in the system of Justice that is ours.

Even after Mr. Blake's innocence was proven beyond a shadow of a doubt, the government had to be prodded into action. Only weeks after his return from the World Outside, he is exiled once again.

Few of us can accurately imagine the conditions that prevail in the World Outside, fewer still would long survive the ordeals of expulsion. Thinking of these conditions one cannot help being impressed to learn that, not only did Mr. Blake manage to keep a solid grip on his humanity while enduring the indignities of the World Outside, but he helped as many as he was capable of helping, keep theirs. He helped them build better lives for themselves. One wonders what kind of man this is.

Your government has little regard for those it throws into the World Outside. Demographics and revenue are the overriding concerns. If you found yourself expelled from the city tomorrow, only your family would miss you. You would become just another entry in a book in the numberless files within the government.

This same government has used the World Outside as a place to put people that it cannot, or no longer will, deal with. The World Outside is the greatest social experiment to ever be foisted upon an unsuspecting public.

I fear for myself once this is published, but I fear more not to publish it. Hopefully I can limit my knowledge of the World Outside to the words and experience of Mr. Blake.

Whatever else happens remember that *you* decide what *you* will become *regardless* of your circumstances. Never let anyone tell you otherwise – so says my friend.

Chicago News in Brief

Local Chicago Tribune writer, Paithar Ranston, was arrested yesterday on the charges of Treason and Sedition. A search of Mr. Ranston's home turned up large numbers of brochures and pamphlets from groups known to be antagonistic towards the government. An anonymous party paid Mr. Ranston's massive fine and he was released. Mr. Ranston has been replaced at the Tribune.

ABOUT THE AUTHOR

For as long as I can remember I have been interested in Science Fiction and Fantasy. I wrote and illustrated my first story in fifth grade. If only I still had that story. I honed my skills as a storyteller by being the gamemaster of all the games I played with my friends. This was before the advent of video games. We would often deviate from the published materials, forcing me to fill in the gaps with the stories I would spin on the spot. I never got tired of telling stories, and sometimes I would even write them down.

Besides being a teller of tall tales, I am a pilot and an attorney. I live in the Midwest (where I have always lived) with my wife and six children. (Yes, they do provide a vast amount of inspirational materials – how lucky for me.)

www.ingramcontent.com/pod-product-compliance
Lightning Source LLC
Chambersburg PA
CBHW051408170626
46809CB00006B/2078